Ireland 1942. A poor, emerging

observer on the war that is ragin

In Madrid, British intelligence are at an impasse. They have lost two of their best agents in a bid to retrieve armaments plans which are being developed for the Axis powers. Britain now realises that something completely new and unexpected is needed to aid their desperate effort. They approach G2 (Irish Military Intelligence) with a daring proposal.

Anna Fingal is of Anglo-Irish descent and works as a linguist at the Department of Foreign Affairs in Dublin. Seamus Halpin works for Irish Intelligence. He has fought in both the Irish and Spanish Civil Wars. Finally, Captain Malcolm Mortimer, a British army officer, wounded in the field of battle, and whose remit now is to lead the mission, and get the information out of Madrid.

Three diverse individuals become bound together in a world of espionage and deceit where survival and success for the mission is the ultimate goal.

First printing 2015

Second edition 2016

ISBN-10: 1512357715

ISBN-13: 978-1512357714

For Peter, Helen and Hugh.

All bright stars.

Also for my Mum.

Many thanks to Brendan Foley (Under the Wire) for his advice and encouragement which has been amazingly generous.

This book, although fictional, has been inspired by the men and women of Ireland who fought so bravely in World War I and World War II.

In memory of Todd Finegan, Jack & Maggie O'Neill, Alex Uhl, David Katcher, and Gladys Uhl-Katcher.

About the Author – Angela Currie spent her formative years growing up near Navan, County Meath, Ireland. After leaving school she spent some time as an 'au pair' in Madrid. On her return to Ireland she decided to enrol for general nurse training in Dublin. In the early 1980's her career led her to Northern Ireland and the Accident and Emergency Department of the Royal Victoria Hospital, Belfast. In 1990 she left nursing behind and completed a full time degree at Queen's University Belfast. Following graduation she entered the world of clinical research. She retired from drug research in 2010. She is married with two children. This is her first novel.

The Training Ground

Angela Currie

14th Oct. 2017

To

Catherine at 'The Gathering' of
Wimbledon Tennis Club, Windsor Tennis
Club Belfast and Castleknock Tennis
Club Dublin.

Best Wishes

Anna Lennox

Chapter 1

Dublin, February 1942.

The Corpse, real name Patrick Herlihy, was a legend in Dublin from the mid 1930's right through to the 1960s. He worked within the environs of Dublin Castle and his reputation had as much to do with his bulk as it had to do with his success. He was a massive man in his frame, six foot four in height and regarded as an obstacle to be negotiated with caution and respect simultaneously. Despite his bulk he moved quite gracefully, and as many a civil servant subordinate would claim, quite silently.

His nickname had as much to do with his general colouring as anything else. He was incredibly pale of complexion, with fair wispy hair and very light blue eyes which were piercing in their quality and impossible to read. The Corpse was never knowingly witnessed by any member of staff at Dublin Castle to actually venture out and stand still in the sun, an object to which he appeared to have an extreme aversion.

Even with these characteristics, he had an incredibly benign and almost boyish face. This puzzling man was known to be very powerful within government, and rumour had it that he was in fact second in command of the Irish Secret Service, an organisation so unknown, unheard of even, that everyone thought it a joke.

Patrick Herlihy's official title at the castle was 'Director of Foreign Operations' with links to the Department of Trade. No other official at Dublin Castle was ever shown a budget for this directorate and they knew better than to ask. The Corpse did not use a secretary and the closest anyone got to him was the tea lady at the castle who on her daily rounds would knock on the extremely solid wooden door leading into his office. This lady knew better than to enter his room and always awaited the opening of the door which was heralded by the scraping sound of a bolt. The Corpse always smiled at the tea lady, and she for her part always returned the smile. She did not believe the rumours about him. But the truth was that Patrick Herlihy was second in command of the army section of the Irish Secret Service, and this was known as G2. The truth was that people had a right to feel a certain menace in his presence.

The Corpse was not happy. In early February 1942 he had received a summons to go to the Curragh in County Kildare. Based at this location was one of the main army camps in the Irish Republic, and it was also here that the head of G2 resided. The meeting was for the next day at 1pm sharp.

The following morning, as he waited for his car to be brought to the castle courtyard, the Corpse ruminated on the reason for the meeting. Most communication between the two men was delivered by despatch. They had four formal meetings a year, but this request was unprecedented because it was in fact the second within two months. This had never happened before within the seven years he had held his post. He was somewhat annoyed, partly because of the freezing day in question which did not agree with him, but he was mostly annoyed because he had no inkling as to the reason for the meeting.

Petrol rationing was a problem because of the war being waged in Europe, or 'The Emergency' as the Irish Government had come to term it. However, that very morning when he had phoned the Castle Secretary, John Halpin, there was no argument; everyone knew not to upset the Corpse. The plus side to the Corpse's journey was that he loved to see the Curragh. This lush, beautiful countryside appealed to his sense of solitude and to what he would ultimately regard as a perfect retirement location.

As he headed south out of Dublin the countryside was in the throes of heavy winter frosts. The roads were bumpy, full of pot holes and in dire need of resurfacing. For him the only aspect of the journey he truly enjoyed was when he reached equine country. He had always admired the suppleness and beauty of these powerful animals, and it was generally known that he greatly enjoyed attending the races at Leopardstown. He reached the army base in the Curragh in good time.

The Colonel was waiting. Colonel Anthony Shannagh was fifty-six years old and remarkably fit for his age. He was six feet tall, had an imposing presence, a very dark full head of hair, and dark but sparkling eyes. He was a classics scholar, an accomplished pianist, a noted marksman, and he spoke five languages fluently. He had a dead pan sense of humour which was not lost on his colleagues but which he knew irritated the hell out of the Corpse.

For most of his career he had served with Headquarters Staff specialising in Intelligence and he was now head of G2. Shannagh knew that the Corpse's main enjoyment from his invitations to the Curragh was the food, and a late lunch was planned. For officers at the Curragh, the Mess produced, despite rationing, quite a high standard of cuisine. With this in mind he arranged a placating dinner for the Corpse as a precursor to a most unusual request.

Whilst not actively liking the Corpse, he knew that Patrick Herlihy always got the job done, and to his recollection he had never botched, never even come close to having an operation scuppered, although this was to be on a completely different scale. For him, Patrick Herlihy was the ultimate perfectionist in any form of planning.

Ireland, or Eire as it was generally known remained neutral during the Second World War. The official name given to the raging war in Europe was 'The Emergency.' Because of Atlantic blockades and submarine warfare, commercial shipping traffic was, no matter what its cargo, extremely vulnerable to the perils of the warring seas. Rationing was therefore a necessity.

As a young emerging Republic, Eire chose the side of neutrality. It had an extremely poor economy based almost entirely on agriculture. Its military infrastructure, or more likely its lack of it could not have coped with the raging violent war that was happening in Europe. However, what it lacked in military might, it more than punched up to, and on many occasions above its weight with its obscure but relatively successful military intelligence. Whilst on the political surface this neutral stance appeared to irritate the hell out of the British, behind the scenes it was a very different story. The Irish Government knew full well that if Britain lost the war, Ireland's neutrality would be swept aside and a greater hell with unknown consequences would emerge for this young fledgling Republic. It was thus quietly decided that information would be supplied to British Intelligence that would help the Allied war effort.

The German Embassy in Dublin was watched and indeed several coded messages were intercepted and passed to the Allies. The Gardaí (the Irish Police) and G2 had success in the arrest of two German spies in Ireland; Dr Hermann Gortz (a former flying ace for Kaiser Wilhelm), and Gunther Schutz. The former, Gortz, had already been imprisoned in England for spying on RAF bases just prior to the Second World War, but he was later released after having served a prison sentence.

Also, on its own back door Ireland had the problem of the IRA collaborating with the Abwehr, the intelligence service of Nazi Germany for whom Gortz worked at the time of his landing in Ireland. The government also gave a nod and a wink to the air corridor used by the British to fly over neutral Eire via Donegal into the Atlantic. Catalina Sea Planes frequently took off from Lough Erne in County Fermanagh to the Atlantic Ocean. These planes played a vital role in the sinking of the Bismarck in 1941. Further collaboration was in the transmission to the British Representative's office in Dublin, of any reports of submarine activity from the Irish coast watching service.

Business and domestic lighting in coastal towns was extinguished as it was alleged to provide a useful landmark for German aircraft. The government continued to intern all German fighting personnel reaching Southern Ireland, but on the other hand after some negotiation, Allied service personnel were allowed to depart and full assistance was given in recovering any aircraft involved.

The man directly charged with the co-ordination and control of this information was Colonel Anthony Shannagh, Head of Irish Military Intelligence or G2 as it was known.

As the car containing Patrick Herlihy pulled up outside the Officer's Mess, the phone on Colonel Shannagh's desk rang with a short message confirming his arrival. The Corpse was duly escorted through the Mess to the dining hall, and courteously seated at the Colonel's table. He loved these surroundings, the old portraits on the walls, the old silver serving dishes, the wooden panelling; but most of all he derived great satisfaction from the formality of the occasion. Tony Shannagh had already taken his seat but rose and formally shook hands with Herlihy.

'Well Patrick, I don't believe that accommodation at Dublin Castle has improved or that the roads from Dublin have any fewer pot holes, however I can guarantee that lunch will please you,' said Shannagh.

'Indeed Colonel, all is as you have said apart from the fact that we are having a meeting which is not part of our normal yearly calendar. That means only one of two things; one, you want to sack me, or two, you have something very important in the pipeline,' stated the Corpse.

Tony Shannagh was surprised at the Corpse's number one thought and it showed him that perhaps even he had sensitivities which he would otherwise not have suspected. As their dinner arrived at that very moment, and as the meal was being plated, the Colonel collected his thoughts. He knew that the Corpse would be delighted with his roast beef dinner which would be served along with quite a robust red wine which had somehow made its way to the Curragh following a customs raid on Dublin port. Illegal trading had a life of its own particularly during a time of war.

'At ease Patrick, you know full well that it would take a hearing in front of the G2 Executive to bring about your sacking, and for that you have to be present. Your work is perfection itself and that's why you are here, and you're correct there is something urgent in the pipeline,' reassured Shannagh.

Although the Corpse did not show emotion or ever openly express delight, Shannagh knew he was pleased with the compliment. The Colonel signalled to the Mess staff that they were now to be left in peace to discuss their business.

What the Corpse was told at that meeting slightly stunned but also delighted him. He was being requested to put a female Irish agent into Madrid for the British. She had to be Irish for the practical reason that the British had already lost two agents on this particular sortie.

Franco's Spain is a hungry and desperate country embittered by years of civil war. That war had fractured Spain badly costing over a million lives, and it crippled the agricultural and industrial sectors of its economy. The current raging war in Africa with its successes for the Allies caused quite a few major gulps in Madrid. Spain knew it had no friends left. Previous to this on December 7th 1941, the Japanese bombed Pearl Harbour and only four days later Hitler declared war on the United States.

Franco's allies, Germany and Italy, had helped forge his victory in Spain. Although there were varied and numerous attempts by Hitler to entice Franco into the war, he constantly prevaricated. However, at the same time, he did continue to allow German agents to act with impunity in Spain. The Caudillo of Spain had very few tactics apart from his stealthy and agile dance around the Allies and Axis powers and he was an expert at dalliance with both. Somewhere along the line of this dance British and American negotiators were tapping their toes with the promise to Spain of much needed grain, petroleum and cotton. One vital element which the Allies were determined to freeze was the supply of tungsten ore, or wolfram as it was known, to the Germans for use in their ballistics industry. Although Franco had promised that no more tungsten would be exported to Germany, he turned a blind eye to its illegal smuggling.

The British also knew that Franco's fascist Spain was providing safe havens for German engineers who were safely developing industrial and ballistic warfare. They also now knew it was a waste of time sending in a British agent to retrieve copies of these plans.

The British now wanted to take a very different approach. Instead of just concentrating on how supplies of Tungsten were reaching Germany, they now wished to place someone in the German embassy in Madrid to pin-point where in this building the ballistics plans were being devised and hidden. Two of their best trained male agents had already disappeared, their bodies never found, and their betrayal never sourced. British Intelligence realised something completely new and unexpected was now needed.

It was in late January 1942 that the Irish Government was approached with the type of carrot only a madman would refuse. Shannagh was present at this meeting. His status as head of G2 was never mentioned, or discussed. The high ranking diplomat from the British Representative's office in Dublin, Sir Horace Harvey, normally the calmest and most polished of men, was not looking forward to the meeting. He expected that the Irish Officials would be more than a little outraged at the request he was about to make.

However, having spoken with very high ranking officials in both Whitehall and the War Office in London, he knew he had no choice. The meeting took place at a secret location in Adelaide Road, Dublin. Sir Harvey was under instructions to leave his car some distance from the meeting and make the remainder of the journey on foot.

Shannagh ensured he was discreetly followed. Sir Harvey's entry to the old but imposing house was not delayed, and Shannagh's agent signalled from the driveway entrance that the diplomat had not been tailed by anyone else.

Having passed along the oak lined hall and beautiful stained glass windows, Sir Harvey was led upstairs to a large room on the first floor. On entering, he immediately recognised the almost grey woollen headed and wiry figure of Aiden Powers from Irish Foreign Affairs, and he inwardly sighed knowing he was in for an extremely skilled but rough sparring match. To the left of Powers sat his Aide, Noel Halligan. Off to the side sat a third man whom he did not recognise and to whom he was not introduced. He knew not to ask. This was Shannagh. Negotiations commenced.

In return for a female Irish agent who would be placed in Madrid, and with the outcome of the war beginning to look more favourable for the Allies, Eire was being offered a reserve of gold bars which would more than placate any outrage the Irish officials might have been harbouring. They of course did not show this response, and indeed commenced a game of cat and mouse over further economic favours such as exports of cattle and other livestock to Britain for the duration of the war and once the war was over.

Shannagh was impressed by the level of negotiating skills on both sides. The Irish knew they were getting a great deal but were expert at making it seem little. After five hours of mean negotiations and with almost a reluctant sigh, they agreed to the terms. Both sides knew they had got exactly what they wanted, and Sir Harvey knew that he had survived a good belting session in the boxing ring.

After the formalities of shaking hands, Sir Harvey left the library, and was observed leaving the house by those inside. He had been advised that his car was not to pick him up within any close distance. Irish officials were as much concerned about the British diplomat being followed by German spies as anything else. Shannagh had again arranged for one of his men to shadow Sir Harvey in order to ensure that no one would tail him on his departure from the house. Aidan Powers, from the Department of Foreign Affairs, who had chaired the meeting along with only one other Irish official, now turned to Shannagh.

'That was one successful meeting. But where the hell are we going to get an Irish agent? I've just promised that man a female agent as if we have a stock pile of them! We don't have that level of sophistication. Do we have such a beast?'

Shannagh never made promises that he could not follow-up. He saw the predicament in which Powers had placed himself, but that was not his problem. He did however feel that the request from the British Ambassador was exactly what his team needed to spur it on to develop such roles within G2.

'Not as such, gentlemen. But we do have sources on whom we can call upon and they are on the lookout constantly for people that we feel may have something important to offer. I will make discreet inquiries and report within the appropriate time-frame.'

Aidan Powers could not hide the bemused look on his face. He knew Shannagh, but did not know him. He admitted to himself that although on the surface Shannagh presented a demeanour that was very amiable, and quite open in nature, he realised that this man made decisions at a level at which he never wanted to operate. Powers knew when someone commanded respect and for him Shannagh was that man. He also knew that Shannagh was now a major part in an economic deal that he had just made with the British Representative, and that the success of that deal was now mainly down to this man.

The cheek of the gamble that the Irish officials had taken in the negotiations was one thing, the promise that they had made another, but was it possible? That was the magician's trick that Shannagh had to pull off. Aidan Powers pondered for a moment on who might be the successful candidate and felt very uneasy with that thought.

Chapter 2

Anna was ten years old when the civil war broke out in Ireland. Both her parents, her older sister and younger brother had lived through, and survived, what was for an Anglo-Irish family, a very uneasy time - the Irish Civil War.

The most dangerous episode for the family was in late 1922 and early 1923. The Anti-Treaty guerrillas campaign had been reduced largely to acts of sabotage and destruction of public infrastructure such as roads and railways. It was also in this period that the Anti-Treaty IRA began burning the homes of Free State Senators and of many of the Anglo-Irish landed class.

Anna's father, Hugh Fingal, was regarded as a large landowner near Navan in County Meath, but fortunately for them all he was extremely well liked. He employed people for their skills, their diligence and no other reason. Hugh himself was a pragmatic man and he regarded the civil war as a time of new emergence for Ireland. The pro-treaty side won, and

Hugh's family was relieved to emerge unscathed and to embrace this new country.

Anna and her sister, Marion, were educated at St Columba's College, Dublin. Founded in 1843 the school enjoyed an enviable position amongst large acreage at the foothills of the mountains in south County Dublin in an atmosphere of which their mother approved. Both girls loved the old buildings, the Cloisters and the chapel and the wonderful views of Dublin Bay. The sisters differed in that Anna excelled at sport and languages, and Marion delighted in science subjects but enjoyed sports to a much lesser degree. Both girls loved the school which provided a broad and well-rounded education. Friends made here were friends for life and loyalties were forged which would not be broken.

Patrick, their brother, bellowed his way to boarding school in England. He made it quite clear that he did not want to go, and his father made it quite clear that this was the expected practice. Their father won.

On Patrick's arrival to his boarding school, and following completion of his registration, he was led to his dormitory where he noted several other boys who seemed to be very curious about his arrival. Having been pre-warned by his father, Patrick pulled back the bed-clothes, and he found as predicted the welcoming sods of bog turf, a traditional welcome for any new and what was regarded as Irish boarder. Patrick knew this was a small victory for him in discovering the turf before he jumped into bed, but he also knew there would be many more hoops for him to jump through. He was correct in all of this, but he survived and eventually entered the world of finance and banking in London.

Hugh's wife Imelda loved her children but her fascination and talent for art took up most of her time. Imelda frequently lectured in Dublin, London and Paris and was respected as an art critic writing for various domestic and international journals. Her travels, much to her annoyance, were hugely disrupted during the war.

Of any subject in school, for Anna it was always languages that danced off the pages of her books. From quite early on she was recognised as being extremely gifted. French, Spanish and German flowed quite easily for her, and on leaving school she studied languages at Trinity College Dublin and achieved a first class honours degree. During the time of her studies she shared a flat with her sister Marion in Rathmines.

They both loved Dublin. Marion was studying medicine at the Royal College of Surgeons on St. Stephen's Green. It was a rarity for a woman at that time to study medicine and a decision which her mother could not understand. By the outbreak of the Second World War, Marion had qualified and offered to work with the International Red Cross. After pounding the corridors of Mercer's Hospital in Dublin she felt she could cope with almost anything. Her mother was horrified but her father supported her for what he saw as a completely brave decision. Many Irish people, fifty thousand approximately, fought in this war from varied political, religious and socially diverse backgrounds. Anna and Patrick both realised that they had a very courageous sister.

Following Marion's departure from Ireland, Anna applied her language skills as a translator at the Department of Foreign Affairs in Dublin. It was here that her existence became known to the Corpse. As part of her remit Anna was required to offer language classes to departmental staff.

After the meeting with Shannagh, it was to one of these classes that the Corpse decided to send one of his operatives. Seamus Halpin was to assess what other attributes this woman may or may not have to offer. He also wanted a full profile of her entire family.

Halpin had pedigree. He also had the extra bonus of being fluent in Spanish and German. It was more than noteworthy that he had fought in the Spanish Civil War with the International Brigade. This group was comprised of individuals from the United States, Britain and France. Three hundred and twenty Irishmen joined up and a quarter of their number were killed in action. The reasons for which they joined up were varied. Some were opposed to fascism and believed they had had a taster of that with the Blueshirts and Greenshirts in Ireland. This group of disparate men fought for the Republican side against Franco and the Nationalists. The Corpse summoned Halpin.

'Sit down, sit down Halpin. It's encouraging to see you have fully recovered from that severe flu.'

Halpin was fuming. He looked dreadful, he sounded awful and he had by no means fully recovered. However, he knew better than to get on the wrong side of the only man he truly feared on this land mass which was saying something after his sojourn in Spain.

'Thank you, Mr Herlihy,' he replied. 'To what do I owe the pleasure of this invitation?'

'Well as you know we are trying to assess and recruit possible future agents both male and female. One I'm currently and particularly interested in is a woman by the name of Anna Fingal. She is a translator for Foreign Affairs and gives classes outside normal working hours on Mondays and Wednesday evenings. Next Wednesday it happens to be German on the agenda. Make sure you attend.

Apart from assessing her language skills, I want you to carry out an entire family background check. Parents are both alive, and she has a brother and sister. Get everything you can on them all, and I mean anything and everything.'

Throughout this instruction Halpin noted that the Corpse did not once look at him but out through the window. Not once, until he said get anything and everything. Then those eyes locked on him, and Halpin knew that what the Corpse really wanted was something, anything, that would if necessary ensnare this woman against her will. He replied.

'How long have I got?'

The Corpse unlocked his eyes from Halpin's for which he was silently relieved.

'I estimate less than a month. Here is her file. I want a more up to date photograph than this as it is outdated and blurred. Attend that language class. Get everything and don't let me down.' Again his eyes locked on Halpin's.

Halpin always inwardly remarked how chilled he felt from those eyes.

He took the file, thanked the Corpse and mentally kicked himself for feeling like an errant schoolboy up in front of a very scary headmaster. As he wandered down the corridor towards the stairs that would take him to the exit of the castle, he glanced at the file which contained only little information, and as stated by the Corpse a not very flattering and out of focus photograph of the intended, possible recruit. The photograph revealed little, but the most interesting aspect was her academic and family background. First class honours degree in languages, not easily done, and the notable fact that they were survivors through a particularly turbulent time in Irish history, and that was one of the few things Halpin respected and understood. He also noted that Anna was in her late twenties and not yet married.

He realised that he was already beginning to relish the job with which he had been presented. At thirty-eight years of age, dark-haired, physically strong and just under six feet in height, fluent in two languages, a noted marksman and extremely gifted in self-defence, Halpin felt a buzz in connection with this case. Having come home after the Spanish Civil War, Halpin was quite frankly bored as a civil servant. And yes, the Corpse, knowing Halpin's potential worth had snared him with the promise of trips away from his civil servant's desk job at the Department of Foreign Affairs. It was amazing how he now felt his flu was making a lightning recovery.

Wednesday evening rolled in quite quickly and as he walked by the Georgian houses with their elegant doorways and beautiful windows, Seamus had to admit that Merrion Square was one of the most, if not the most elegant in Dublin. It was on the first floor of one of these charming buildings that Halpin found himself in early March 1942. It was Wednesday and the German evening class was due to start in fifteen minutes at eight o' clock. Halpin was amazed at the number of people attending and although the room was by no means small it was quite crowded.

He registered with the clerk in attendance and showed his ID with the Department of Foreign Affairs so that his presence would not be remarked upon. He spotted George Grimes, whom he knew had struggled with learning German for years, and he nodded in his direction. Grimes honed in on him.

'Well Seamus what brings someone of your calibre of fluency to such a class? Don't tell me you're getting rusty in your old age?'

Seamus cursed his luck. Grimes was not tall and tended towards the rotund. He had a pale, almost waxy complexion, remarkable red hair, bulbous eyes and freckles galore. What he lacked in physical attributes he made up for in ego and was infamous for bull shitting his way to the top with what most regarded as his only talent.

'Well George, you know how it is, a little revision and update never did anyone any harm. And how are you getting on with the classes here?'

'Fantastic, this new girl is brilliant. She brings the entire subject alive and has an amazing capacity to explain it in very simple terms, not like those idiot teachers we had in school.'

Seamus inwardly smirked. It was the same idiot teachers that he had in school and it had not caused him to falter in languages. He thought perhaps

Grimes was exaggerating his new ability, as was his wont.

'That's excellent George, you must be extremely pleased with your progress. But now I feel we need to take our places as it seems our instructress has arrived.'

There was a flurry of movement in the room. George Grimes almost fell over himself to get to his already chosen seat in the second row from the front. Probably teacher's pet, Halpin uncharitably thought. He still could not see the woman in question as there was so much movement in the room and cigarette smoke was swirling in every direction, to which Halpin himself contributed. On further assessing the gender breakdown it looked to be ninety percent presence in favour of males with a sprinkling of females. There was also a very good age range within the room. Everyone now sat and Halpin got his first good look at their teacher.

Anna Fingal raised her head slowly and a very calm pair of eyes surveyed the room. Halpin saw a woman of average height whom he knew to be in her late twenties. As she moved across the room to her desk, he noted her shapely figure. Her natural blond hair was wavy in texture and tied back from her face in an unruly manner. She dressed well in a slightly bohemian style. Obviously not what would be worn to her office on a daily basis. Most noteworthy of all were her eyes. They were very large and light coloured and were the most striking feature of her face.

The Corpse was right about one thing, the photograph in her file gave no true indication of reality. She was not stunning, but she was very attractive and had a notable presence.

'Ladies and gentlemen, we will start this evening by breaking into groups of beginners, improvers and advanced. As usual I will work my way around the groups. You are all now being handed out some test work which you will now commence and I will assist with any problems as I rotate through each group. Please take your time, it is not a race. Beginners please to the front of the room, improvers next then advanced.'

Anna Fingal's accent was what Halpin termed polite or posh Irish. It was well modulated with wonderful delivery. It was a voice to which you would want to listen.

As the groups formed, Halpin went immediately to the advanced group and to his horror so did George Grimes. He wondered if this was a joke. As the test work was handed out, Halpin could see that the advanced group was at quite a high level. He watched as best he could as Anna made her way around the beginners and improvers. He noted the ease with which she worked, and more to the point, how everyone appeared to be enjoying the session. At last it was the turn of the advanced group which was composed of nine men and one woman.

On approaching the group Anna realised there were two newcomers, both men. The smaller of the two men was aged about thirty years, and he was dressed very well in a three piece suit. He rose immediately, spoke in German, not fluently but impressively good and introduced himself as John Gartland, explaining that he worked in the Department of Trade and was brushing up on French and German language skills. Halpin, not wishing to be outdone by this suave sophistication, also rose, albeit reluctantly, and introduced himself. Anna shook hands with both men and welcomed them to the group.

'Mr Gartland, you do seem to have a good grasp of German. I intend to carry out some group conversational sessions once everyone has completed the short test and we will then judge how we need to progress.'

Anna then turned her eyes on Halpin. He noted the direct steady gaze, an almost imperceptible smile and those large eyes which seemed to vary between a bluish-green colour. They were definitely her most arresting feature in an attractive face.

'Now, Mr Halpin, your accent and fluency I did not quite pick up on during our introduction, so if we could converse for a few minutes?'

Anna launched into a discussion on German writers and was surprised at the level of knowledge Halpin displayed on the subject. More surprising was his fluency and she increased the pace of the conversation with which Halpin more than coped. Anna inwardly puzzled as to why Halpin needed to brush up on anything when it was apparent that his spoken German was excellent.

She noted a well lived in but not unattractive face, and she sensed in him a disregard for formality which was highlighted by the way he sat with a knowing look in his expression. The other most noteworthy feature was a large ragged scar which ran from the base of his right thumb across the entire width of the back of his hand, and she noticed that he occasionally rubbed the scar as if it still troubled him. He looked like a man who had seen and experienced a lot from life, and perhaps not always to his advantage.

Halpin knew excellence when he heard it and there was no doubt in his mind that Anna Fingal was fluent with a perfect German accent. She could be a native German.

For Halpin the rest of the evening went smoothly. George Grimes had indeed improved greatly in his skills, but he was by no means anything as fluent as Halpin. His obsequious demeanour towards Anna was nauseating, but he gave her credit for never responding to it, except in the same manner in which she treated anyone else. She knew how to manage and control the group without being obvious, and was by no means put off by the presence of some very high ranking civil servants.

Now all he needed to do was to sit out the rest of the class and not leave before the cleverly arranged group photograph was taken. The photographer in question worked for G2 and he knew how to work a room. As if on cue, ten minutes before the two hour class was due to end, Bart Finegan arrived and stated that his mission was to take photographs for the notice boards covering social and extracurricular events hosted by the civil service. No one was suspicious.

Bart grouped various attendees and took numerous photographs. It was easy for him to suggest taking an individual photograph of Anna. For the first time Halpin noticed Anna hesitate and in fact thought she might refuse. She was that rare creature who did not appear to like her photograph being taken, but with Bart's cajoling, she eventually complied.

Finegan was happy with the amount of photographs he had taken, and thanked the group warmly for their patience. This simple event had given an added bonus to the evening and some of the advanced group suggested going upstairs to the club bar for a nightcap. Halpin thought this an excellent idea as he would see how Anna reacted on a more social platform, and he also knew, that the bar upstairs was heavily subsidised, which was always a perk in the economic conditions that reigned.

George Grimes fell into step with Halpin, an occurrence which suited him as he did not want to seem out of place. The old Georgian staircase was a beauty and Halpin noticed that Anna was speaking very eloquently in German on the architectural merits of the building with 'Mr Three Piece suit.' George Grimes hurried along to join in the conversation, and Halpin kept in pace.

'Miss Fingal, I also greatly admire these buildings and the heritage they represent to this city. The ceilings alone are a joy to behold. May I get you a drink?'

'That's kind of you Mr Grimes, but as I'm giving these classes free in my spare time, one of the perks has been that I'm allowed a free tab on the bar.'

She saw Grimes's beady eyes light up in anticipation, and then quickly added, 'But only for myself, not for the group.'

Halpin thought he would burst out laughing, he slapped George on the back and said, 'Mine's a whiskey George, thanks for offering.'

The next forty minutes were spent by this small group discussing prospects for the future, prospects for this emerging country on the short and long term, the restrictions on daily life and food provisions during the war. It was obvious that these people saw themselves as the trail blazers of the future. Halpin noted that Anna held herself slightly aloof from this conversation. However, she had a well-developed sense of humour which was interspersed with a hint of irony.

For her part, Anna noted how everyone intermingled well, but that Mr Halpin did not really engage with the rest of the party, and on more than one occasion she had caught him observing her quite closely. Anna wondered why he had bothered to come. It was obvious he did not need to brush up on his language skills. She doubted his return to any further classes.

Chapter 3

Two weeks later and very early on the Friday morning, Halpin returned to Patrick Herlihy's office with the dossier on Anna Fingal.

Bart Finegan had excelled himself with the turnaround time on getting the photographs developed, and had taken several good angles of his subject. There was absolutely no blurring in these photographs. This left Halpin with more than ample time to do a check on the rest of the Fingal family warts and all. For this he used another contact, Frank Tolin, as it was this agent that the Corpse had advised Halpin to use if he needed another pair of hands. He had heard of Tolin but had never encountered him.

The Corpse was a magician when it came to keeping some of his people apart. He had devised an ingenious way for contact to be made via the Civil Service postal boxes which had individual keys. That left identification difficult for anyone who might care to know. The box numbers were also habitually changed as an extra precaution along with the time you should collect from them. The corpse advised Halpin to return in the afternoon as he needed to read the information carefully and complete some phone calls.

Coffee was on Halpin's mind, and it was not a difficult decision to step it out to Grafton Street to his favourite coffee house, Bewley's. This particular emporium was opened in 1927 following on the previous tea and coffee houses in George's Street and Westmoreland Street.

This café was at the cultural heart of Dublin to which the city's writers, and other artistic clientele were frequently observed over the years. The aroma was breathtaking and the atmosphere buzzing with people who regarded Bewley's as a must visit on any trip up to Dublin.

By two-fifteen in the afternoon Halpin was back in situ. He sat at an angle to a very quiet Corpse who still seemed to be mulling over the dossier. He noted, that if it was possible, the Corpse was looking a paler shade of pale. His thick fingers were drumming gently on the massive desk as he started to speak.

'Quite pleasing photographs, Halpin. However, the personal and more detailed information on the family does not reveal anything which would give us some leverage with this woman. I see that her sister is a doctor with the Red Cross and is now overseas somewhere, destination undisclosed but then that's quite understandable. From this I have gleaned that her brother was in the Banking sector in London, apparently brilliant with numbers. I see that his whereabouts are currently unknown, now why is that Halpin? Why do you suppose this young man has disappeared? If he had signed up for the war you would have found out about it.'

This was uttered as a statement rather than as a question, and Halpin realised that the Corpse knew something which he did not.

Halpin inwardly muttered to himself over this realisation. He registered the fact that the Corpse was not requiring an answer, but he still thought that he would offer him an explanation. Besides he thought the comment unmerited.

'Despite my contact, I was unable to glean any other information, he just seems to have vanished.'

The Corpse enjoyed putting his agents on the back foot. Halpin was not noticeably uneasy but it was his wont to have a big ego which he felt had to be put down on occasion. For the Corpse, Halpin's strongest points were his bravery and loyalty. He was one of the most courageous men he had ever met. He decided it was time to confide some, but not all the information to Halpin.

Herlihy had already ascertained the exact whereabouts of Patrick Fingal. He had discovered what he needed to know following his phone call to British Military Intelligence, and it was information of which not even Anna's family was aware. It was a very recent event and the Corpse was now privy to that information.

It was revealed that Patrick Fingal was off the Richter Scale with regard to numeracy skills, and Military Intelligence had snapped him up to work in Bletchley Park, the code breaking think tank centre of excellence. Despite the Fingal family making several inquiries as to Patrick's whereabouts, they were always met with a wall of silence. However, now that British Intelligence wanted help from G2 the information was provided, but with the proviso that the family would not be told.

As Patrick was snapped up by British Intelligence he was informed that he could not have any formal contact with his family for the duration of the war. His family would be told quite a different story.

This suited the Corpse. He now felt that he had everything he needed to put his play into motion, albeit by a series of contrived lies and skilful deception.

Halpin who had served on the fields, the slaughter-house of the Spanish Civil War was not surprised by the story about Anna's family. What shocked him was the plan to have her placed in Madrid, in effect to work for British Intelligence. The Corpse remained tight lipped as to why this assistance was being provided by a neutral country but Halpin knew in his gut that something very lucrative would come of it. There was absolutely no other reason such assistance would be put forward.

'Mr Herlihy, for crying out loud have you read the dossier, she's posh Irish and she probably would not last two weeks in Madrid. What's the point in sending her? She has no field experience, what about Mary Cahill?'

'Cahill, is that a joke Halpin? Cahill would turn on a spoon to the highest bidder. She's brilliant with guns and her languages are good but she does not have what this woman has. Also her loyalty is more than questionable. Cahill needs kept closer to home where I can oversee her on a tight rein. Anna Fingal is an unknown – I like that. Her family have more than demonstrated that they are courageous. Their loyalty to each other is noteworthy and they have an inbuilt resourcefulness which shows that over quite a long period of time, that they are survivors, both politically and economically. From what I've read in this dossier this woman might well be up to the challenge.'

'Oh yes,' said Halpin. 'And how are we going to persuade her to do that? How will we train her, and under what pretext could you possibly place her in Madrid?'

Halpin suddenly realised that his questions were irrelevant. He knew that the man behind this old oak desk had already worked everything out, and to the very finest detail.

Since he had started to work for the Corpse, he realised that this was a man you would never understand, but he was also a man who never sent anyone down a blind alley. The Corpse was like a master chess player, he knew the moves before anyone else made them, and he always got the outcome he expected. Patrick Herlihy protected his people in the field, but even Halpin doubted how wide a web of protection he could weave in Madrid. The Corpse fixed his glassy piercing eyes on Halpin.

'This is exactly how we are going to do it Mr Halpin, and as a bonus to you and your current boredom with your office position, you will handle this agent. You have more than proved your ability to survive, and apart from that your language skills are equal to this woman's.'

He paused, and stared at his shoes before continuing.

'You have two months for her to undergo survival training at Beaulieu in England with the SOE, and we all know how harsh that can be. If there is any softie left in her that mad Scots instructor will soon sort that out. She'll toughen up quickly, and as I more than suspect she is just as equal to such a task as some of the other die-hards I've known. Oh, and by the way Halpin, when I said you will manage this agent, what I really meant was in the field, in Madrid, and not from your cosy office here in Dublin. You *will* go to Madrid. That should open up some memories for you.'

Halpin decided that the Corpse was an absolute bastard. It was unlikely that anyone would recognise him in Madrid, but the memories that he felt were never quite quashed and they were now beginning to flutter in his stomach with the added bonus of some nausea.

He had come to love that country, to understand it and to embrace it, and he had even married in it. Herlihy had him over a barrel because he knew that Halpin's Spanish wife had gone missing and that the very worst was feared. He had tried unsuccessfully to discover her whereabouts through many contacts in Spain, but to no avail. He still clung on to the image of her existence, and the carrot that Herlihy dangled was too great to resist. No, resistance didn't even come into it. It was now an imperative with two missions attached. Firstly, his quest to discover more about Sonsoles, and then, Anna's mission, whatever that might be.

Chapter 4

Although in many respects it remained a shattered city following the Spanish Civil War, with derelict buildings, broken minds, scorched souls and the hatred of brother against brother, Madrid remained a beautiful city. For Anna Fingal, now working at the Language School in Madrid, it was beautiful. It was now late October 1942 and the soul of this city was more than palpable, a   cautious beat was returning to its heart despite the economic climate, despite the war in Europe, and in particular despite Generalissimo Franco.

On a daily basis as Anna cycled or walked to work she saw the hardships etched on peoples' brows, their anxieties, their fears. There were still rumours that thousands who had fought against Franco, remained imprisoned, and even worse, the rumours that executions were still taking place. She understood these fears that reverberated around this city. The state of the war raging in Europe was on a more positive note for the Allies, and the Caudillo of Spain was beginning to feel isolated.

Anna reflected over the previous few months and the process by which she had arrived in this place.

Towards the end of March 1942 she was summoned to Dublin Castle in a most innocuous manner and by way of the fact that she had highly valued language skills. The meeting was set for 12.45pm on Friday 27th March 1942, not in Herlihy's office but in a similar one on the floor below. Already present in an adjoining room at the back of this larger one were Herlihy and Halpin. Waiting in the main room was a Spanish woman. Her name was Tory Bartlett, and she occasionally did translation work for the Department of Trade.

It was Tory Bartlett who answered the door to Anna's knock. She greeted Anna in Spanish, apologised for the haste with which the interview was arranged, made casual talk about the weather, fashion in Dublin and how difficult it was to get any accommodation decent enough to rent.

Anna responded in beautiful Spanish. She noted that Mrs Bartlett certainly had a Spanish look to her appearance. A dark beauty, small in height, and a tiny frame.

They sat on either side of a large old oak desk that had obviously seen better days and on which rested a radio and telephone. After twenty minutes of testing Anna's fluency, Tory Bartlett picked up the phone and buzzed three times into the back room. Herlihy and Halpin entered the room. They knew three buzzes meant Anna's Spanish had passed the test, an extra buzz would have meant her language fluency was not up to the task and therefore don't enter the room.

Halpin's first thought was that although Anna looked surprised to see him, there was no element of astonishment on her face, and he put this down to a remarkable composure that he had noted on their previous meeting. The Corpse now swung into action, expertly taking over the meeting. Tory Bartlett was dismissed.

'Miss Fingal, I have to apologise for our sudden emergence but you will understand soon in greater depth the reason for all this connivance. Mr Halpin, whom you have already met is believe it or not an agent for the Irish Government with regards to Intelligence matters, or in other words security of a very high ranking level. The reason you are here is because of your language skills and we would like your assistance in, how should I put it, ensuring that your brother is not tried for treason in England.'

What could she do – she had no option after the revelation about her brother. That man Herlihy – what a chilling presence, an extremely foreboding one. She knew there was no negotiation, no way out. She didn't want one. Her overriding concern was her brother's safety.

That revelation, that her brother was a German spy who had links through banking chains in Germany even prior to the war. That Patrick was accused of passing on classified information and was now incarcerated at His Majesty's pleasure for the duration of the war. She could not comprehend it, but it must be true. Why else had all communication with Patrick ceased?

She thought about this, and the training regime that ensued. Then there was her parents disbelief and the subsequent devastation by the news that

Patrick was an Axis spy. They felt that a gross misjudgement had been made – they knew their son. They were told the news by Anna who thought that her father aged before her very eyes. Her mother, normally vociferous, for once remained silent, now being more aware of her husband's needs and unusually putting them above her own, which Anna recognised as quite a feat. The family home, which was situated a few miles from Navan, remained subdued. That Sunday after Anna had delivered her news, she attended with her father at the family local church, St Patrick's in Donaghpatrick.

The beautiful old church dated from 1897 and Anna felt a very close link to it. During the sermon she mulled over not just the news she had told her parents with regard to Patrick, but also that she herself was now working for the Department of Trade, albeit as the Corpse noted, it was the best way to put her through the books.

It had been disclosed that she was to take up a teaching post in Madrid. The language school paid an adequate salary but Anna's income would be supplemented by the department in Ireland. They would say that they were having her language skills perfected and honed for future economic ventures. Anna and her father left the church together chatting with old friends, hiding the horror of what they really felt.

As Anna settled into the car with her father for the journey home, he turned to her and said, 'Anna, I know in my heart that this new position, this posting you are taking up in Madrid, has something to do with Patrick. Don't say anything, there is no need. I understand your life is outside of your control at the moment. However, no matter what happens, no matter how difficult things may appear, you are a very intelligent woman and you will work things out. You are resourceful and I hope you use that skill to your advantage along with your natural instincts.'

Anna, almost overwhelmed, but not wishing to make things worse, turned to her father whom she considered extremely courageous and hugged him. Nothing more was ever said on the subject.

Chapter 5

It was early April 1942 when Anna left Dublin for Beaulieu. This was a training school for the SOE (Special Operations Executive) which was based in the New Forest on the estate of Lord Montague. Here agents were trained in clandestine technique, how to maintain a cover story, self-defence and even how to pick a lock. The school also employed several ex-burglars.

It was without doubt a baptism of fire for Anna. Other SOE recruits regarded her with suspicion. Although Anna was Anglo-Irish she was identified as part of that country Eire, which had taken a neutral stance against the enemy. Initially most of the recruits were antagonistic towards her but the levelling of the playing field that the harsh training regime brought with it soon tested and proved her mettle. Anna was gradually accepted by the group.

The constant slog of the physical training, self-defence, weapons handling and use of radio communications; it was a steep learning curve. Yet something within Anna responded to the challenge, and it was not just the knowledge that she was helping her brother. A competitive edge had even developed between a few of the trainees and rather than separating them, it drew them closer. Anna got to know Mary Edgeworth and Tony Preston better than any of the other recruits. These three were the most competitive and in an odd way this bound them more closely together. There was one occasion in particular where all three of them were being bawled out by their physical endurance instructor as lazy good for nothing sissies, when a communal look passed between them and they all laughed outright. That response earned them all an extra hour's endurance.

On one of these training days Anna was being quietly observed by one of the instructors, 'Killer' Barnsby. He had learned his skills from subversive and nasty figures of the underworld. With him was Captain Malcolm Mortimer.

Malcolm Mortimer felt his almost recovered injured leg ache. He was blasted out of the war when he took a lump of shrapnel to his right leg. The surgeons had performed miracles with the twisted torn muscles, but the incident had left him with a slight limp which only surfaced when he was extremely tired. He had fought with the Eight Army as part of Operation Crusader, the Allied operation to relieve the besieged city of Tobruk on 17th November 1941 against Rommel's Panzar Army. His rehabilitation over, he was informed that a new role was imminent for him in undercover operations.

Barnsby was reluctant to speak while Malcolm Mortimer continued to use the field glasses provided to observe the agents in training.

Mortimer lowered the glasses and asked, 'When do you think she will be ready?'

'She's ready now. In our opinion she is one of three current recruits who are streets ahead of the rest of the group. Her ability to adapt is one of her main strengths, and her languages have been thoroughly tested. In this group there is no one to match that particular skill.'

'You paint a wonderful picture but if she has weaknesses what are they?'

The sarcasm in Mortimer's voice was not lost on Barnsby, but he declined to remark on it. He knew Mortimer and his record for bravery. He also knew Mortimer had been furious when he was informed of what he regarded as a babysitting role for an SOE operative. This tall sinewy, athletic man was still incredibly fit despite his injury.

The beard he sported was new and still relatively trim, and his hair length was gradually being allowed to grow for the benefit of his new role. Astute intelligent dark green eyes lay beneath well-defined eyebrows. His mouth was currently curved in a look of sardonic realism.

At the age of thirty-eight he remained unmarried, although there was almost a moment before the war had started when he had seriously contemplated it. In hindsight it had been a very good decision to let that moment go. Neither he nor Evelyn Sinclair were ready for marriage and war at the same time. No, that was not true, they were both ready for war. Evelyn with her sophisticated dry observations had commented, 'Darling, let's not do the obvious thing just because others are panicking about their destiny.' A tough journalist and realist, she wanted the opportunity to cover this war. He was somewhat relieved at being turned down, as he equally and fervently wished to fight. He admitted that perhaps the reality was that they were both equally ambitious and how better to prove oneself than on the field of battle.

Barnsby was measured in his reply, 'Her fitness and self-defence is good, well really good. She has learned fast and could even give some of the men a good run on that score.'

Mortimer felt something was left unsaid and pressed Barnsby. 'Well, what is it you are not saying?'

'She is extremely handy with a Browning HP and her target shooting is top rate.'
He hesitated before continuing, 'If she were directly put in a position where she had to kill another human being, we would have a concern that she might be reluctant.'

Mortimer lowered his field glasses.

'Unfortunately with a role like this realism does not always immediately come with training. If this woman is confronted in the field her true sense of survival will come to the fore. Let's hope for her sake that it rises to the occasion. There is to be no delay. At least we were able to by-pass sending her to Ringway in Manchester for parachute training. Your team are to instruct her to return to Dublin and from there arrangements will be made for her to go to Madrid.' What Mortimer did not add was that he himself was to be placed in Madrid.

Barnsby knew a reply was not required.

It was now September and Anna looked downward from the lovely long old sash windows of her family home. She loved this house with its stone walls, the beautiful old rooms with their wonderful high ceilings, and the approach just before the bridge that crossed the Blackwater River, the same river upon which she now glanced as it coursed through their land. The autumn colours on the trees were just beginning to declare themselves as they hinted at their arrival, their announcement of their inevitable progress. It was her favourite time of year.

Anna was to leave for Madrid in two days' time. On her return to Dublin, her meeting with the Corpse was approached in a business-like manner. He was impressed with what he saw but revealed none of this to her. Anna was to make contact with Halpin after she arrived in Madrid where a job had been arranged for her at the local language school.

This was easy to achieve with Anna's qualifications, and Tory Bartlett, who had tested Anna at the Corpse's request, had contacts and relatives in Madrid, and Anna was going to the school with her recommendation. At some point after her arrival she would meet with Seamus as if for the very first time. He was being placed in Madrid with the Department of Trade and Industry. At the appropriate moment, Seamus would invite Anna to undertake translation work for his department in Madrid.

It was hoped that no one would ever guess that this girl was a British agent. The language school was an excellent contact point for many internationals including German personnel from the German Embassy who needed to improve on their

Spanish speaking skills. It was known that the embassy was used by German engineers working in a safe haven for the war effort. It was also known that the embassy had very exacting demands with regards to the quality of translation work needed for these engineers. For this very reason there was quite a high attrition rate of local translators.

Anna's musings were put on hold as she joined her parents for breakfast. Imelda, who lacked a true mother's insight, twittered on at breakfast about the opportunities opening up for Anna.

Some of Imelda's completed canvasses were to go on the journey to Spain to an art dealer who had commissioned her work. Imelda felt obliged to take advantage of this opportunity and drew great comfort from the fact that the canvasses would be in her daughter's safekeeping. After all, Anna was to travel under a visa from the Department of Trade – what could be better? She did not seem to take into account that the sea journey alone could prove to be very dangerous to shipping. Margaret, their house-keeper who had worked with them for years had more insight into such things. She had a cousin in the Merchant Navy and he had related unsettling stories with regards to sea journeys over such troubled waters. Out of ear shout, she had said to Anna that she would pray for her. Anna had known Margaret all her life and they hugged each other but said no more on the matter.

Hugh had never confided his suspicions to his wife as to what he truly suspected about Anna's role and he had every intention of keeping it that way. Apart from Imelda's chatter, their final breakfast together that morning was somewhat subdued.

Returning to her bedroom Anna checked her luggage and deemed all to be satisfactory. She reflected back over two years ago on the almost romance with Jack Powell, of whom her mother totally approved. It was her first love and Jack had been totally committed to her but he felt a stronger pull to volunteer for the war effort. Jack wrote regularly for The London Illustrated News and was single minded about getting the story done.

After eighteen months of reporting, the news was received that he had met someone else. He felt he had to be honest with himself and Anna. In her heart she had seen it coming. The gradual introduction of a female journalist who was working with him, and then the final admission.

Anna wrote and wished Jack the very best.

As the car horn sounded outside, Anna surveyed her bedroom, forcefully imprinting the image of its warmth and protection on her mind. A new adventure was starting for her – one for which she hoped there would be a positive outcome.

Chapter 6

Sea journeys held many dangers throughout the war. During the Emergency, the Irish Mercantile Marine ensured that Irish Agriculture and other exports reached Britain, and that British coal arrived in Ireland. Ireland was a net food exporter. Ships on the Lisbon-run imported wheat and fruits from Spain and Portugal as well as goods already shipped from the Americas. Mercantile shipping followed a different line of longitude to that used by Allied convoys for obvious reasons.

Approximately twenty percent of seamen serving on Irish ships perished, attacked by both sides but predominantly by Axis powers. Often Allied convoys could not stop to pick up survivors because of submarine risk. Irish ships always answered SOS signals irrespective to which side they belonged. It was documented that in all, Irish ships rescued over five hundred seamen. Irish ships sailed with EIRE emblazoned on their sides and the tricolour was flown constantly in order to safeguard their passage. It did not always work.

Anna's journey to Lisbon was thankfully without mishap. She was not the only private passenger on board and indeed there were up to ten such people, who amazingly, even during times of war were venturing forth as entrepreneurs.

The voyage was interesting and thankfully without incident, and a certain camaraderie descended upon the group. Late in the afternoon, as the ship docked at Lisbon which in itself was a spectacle, Anna said her goodbyes to her fellow passengers, waving as she descended the gangway. The art work which her Mother had insisted should accompany Anna on her journey to Madrid was carefully brought ashore.

The ship's porter had very obligingly arranged for a local company to transport Anna along with the ten canvases to Santa Apolonia train station. This was the oldest railway terminal in Lisbon which originally opened in 1865, and is situated on the bank of the Tagus River in the historical district of Alfama. This station was the starting point for most international trains, and it was also where their journeys ended in the Portuguese capital.

Anna had been uncertain as to how the Corpse, as she now came to refer to him, would react to this request from her mother. In fact he appeared to see it as perfectly acceptable and plausible as it added an extra dimension to Anna's cover.

Imelda Fingal was a well-respected artist and international speaker of some repute. Why on earth would she not take the opportunity of her daughter's move to Madrid to showcase her current work when it was impossible to do so in the rest of Europe? Yes, as far as Patrick Herlihy was concerned, it added to Anna's cover and in no way detracted from it.

The truck was at the dock dutifully awaiting Anna's disembarkation and that of the artistic cargo. The canvasses were bound in a crate, and clearly marked fragile in several languages. The local driver and his assistant chatted away in Portuguese, trotting around Anna, and discussing the best way to haul the crate onto the back of the truck. A pulley was eventually located on the dockside, the crate was then lifted and suspended before finally making its way safely onto the back of the vehicle. Thus the journey to the train station commenced, and henceforth Anna knew that from now on she must always be on her guard.

The overnight sleeper to Madrid was a welcome break for Anna to collect her thoughts. It was the first time she had really been alone, and the weight, indeed burden of her mission seemed suddenly to descend and overwhelm her. She knew how everything she had learned would encompass her every move from this moment in time. She reminisced over her carefree boarding school days, her friends, her joy at attending Trinity College, and above all her love for her family, and in essence what she believed to be Patrick's survival. The Corpse had intimated that Anna's cooperation would guarantee Patrick's release.

At her final meeting the Corpse had emphasised the importance of her cover, but also that its beauty lay in the fact that most of what she would be doing in Madrid was in line with all her current skills. She was not using a false name and she was an Irish citizen, and to add weight to it all, her mother was truly a well-known artist. Even if the Germans chose to delve into that, they would uncover nothing.

There was also a major playing card in the pack; Anna's brother. British intelligence had passed on information to German agents supposedly originating from Patrick. It was verifiable information and it was leaked prior to Patrick disappearing under the radar into the confines of Bletchley Park. Anna, was not to speak about Patrick to anyone during her assignment. However, it would be made known that her brother had been arrested as a spy, his whereabouts unknown.

Chapter 7

Anna would never forget her arrival in Madrid. It was 9.30am on Monday 12th October 1942. The smoke from the train engines, the noise, the smell of food, the mass of people as they hustled their way through the Estación de Atocha train terminus.

The station itself was a huge structure which was originally built in 1851. It stood out in its distinct and unique design, its huge edifice towering over all. Various traders and newspaper boys were vying to sell their goods for meagre earnings – their sales cry, their never ending patter of buy, buy, buy. The throng of people was almost overwhelming, and as Anna gathered her senses and her belongings from her cabin she knew now how very different would be her new way of life.

As she moved along the train corridor she had two immediate concerns; firstly to commandeer a porter for unloading her mother's canvasses, and secondly, not to miss her contact here at the terminal. Tory Bartlett who had so expertly assessed Anna in

Dublin Castle had arranged for Anna to be met by her cousin Alphonse Bautista-Zabala. He would escort Anna to her new accommodation and help deliver her mother's paintings to the gallery.

With this throng of people arriving all at once, the train having been packed, and another now just arrived from Barcelona, the competition for acquiring the services of a porter was intense to say the least. She had just caught the attention of a porter who acknowledged that she was next in line. A few moments later as he approached Anna, the porter was intercepted by two men who appeared to be in the process of commandeering him. In sheer frustration Anna stepped forward and commenced to converse in fluent Spanish. All three men turned, the porter immediately apologising but stating that he had no choice. The smaller of the other two men spoke.

'We have large containers which require immediate transport without delay and we are with the embassy.'

It was only when the second man spoke in German that Anna realised which embassy was involved. The taller bearded man now spoke to his colleague, urging him to hurry up and not be delayed by an insignificant young woman.

Annoyed, but remaining very calm, Anna replied fluently in German stating that she had commandeered the porter first. Both men now gave Anna the benefit of their full attention – the smaller man spoke again, but very abruptly.

'Our need of this porter is urgent and I'm sure if you would have the patience to wait a few more minutes there will be someone else to help you.'

'Indeed, I have no wish to be rude but I would return your own comments and state that you also would need only to wait a few minutes. However, if you feel that your embassy rank gives you priority then there is nothing I can do or say to convince you otherwise.'

Christoph Beich, narrowed his gaze and gave Anna a very open and somewhat hostile appraisal which she was not inclined to like. He noted the trim figure, the good quality and well cut blue linen suit worn with an unusual bohemian elegance. A wide brimmed hat and a shoulder bag completed the outfit. His suspicions were raised as to the identity of this young woman who seemed to switch languages so easily.

Before he could form a response his colleague spoke.

'Really Christoph, don't offer explanations, let us go. Our porter is ready and this young lady can wait and that's that.'

Anna was being dismissed, and she felt the colour rise in her face with what Christoph Beich assumed and hoped was embarrassment, but which in fact was annoyance on Anna's part.

She knew it was better to let this particular discussion go in their favour as the likelihood of them meeting again was probable, if indeed they did work for the embassy. The taller of the two men had not even bothered to look in Anna's direction – as if her presence was of absolutely no significance. He was tall, lean, had brown hair and a short trim beard. His head was covered with a trilby style hat which made it difficult to see his face more clearly.

His shorter colleague on the other hand could only be described as quite good looking, but with a tough harsh expression which seemed to enjoy living on his face; he had blond hair and blue eyes. Although he had smiled when he spoke, Anna had sensed a toughness, even a coldness not to her liking. Barnsby had said if it was the only thing she remembered, it should be her instinct about people.

'You have a great natural instinct Anna, stay close to it. What your gut tells you, in fact it sometimes warns you, that you should never brush aside a good instinct. In your new role it might even save your life.'

Although Anna knew that Barnsby had trodden the wrong path prior to Beaulieu, she realised that her training had developed and been stretched to its limits by this man. She knew that he was a hard and brutal man, but his regime, although harsh, might one day save her life.

She stood observing the three men as they walked away into the distance, and it was then that Anna heard someone call her name. She turned, and recognised immediately from the photograph that

Tory Bartlett had procured for her, the picture of her cousin Alphonse Bautista-Zabala. He was a young man, probably in his late twenties, with a pleasant and open face, fully apologetic for his slight tardiness. And with him, there was a porter.

It was almost mid-morning by the time Alphonse, Anna and the canvasses were on board a truck and on their way. Their first stop was to be at the art dealer's premises in Calle de Alcalá, not far from Puerta del Sol. A pleasant companion, Alphonse made small talk along the way, experimenting and showing off his English language skills and also explaining life in Madrid.

'Anna, you must know Madrid is a much wounded city. Civil war is the worst possible outcome for any country. Raw emotions are still very close to the surface and you would be very wise not to discuss anything too political with people you do not know. You will learn that things are still happening here, things which we have absolutely no control over. Individuals disappear occasionally, during night raids by the pro-fascists. People wish to survive, they don't want to speak out. They have seen what has happened to those that do. Anna, do you understand what I'm trying to tell you?'

She had listened carefully to every word and knew that this young man probably thought Anna a naïve new arrival to Madrid. Although Tory Bartlett had arranged for him to assist Anna on her arrival in Madrid, she was given no indication of the true reason for Anna being sent there apart from honing her language skills for future use by the Department of Trade in Eire.

'You know Alphonse, Ireland, not as recently as Spain but again not too far back, had its share of civil war. Believe me when I say that the disparities between both our countries are not too great. Here in Spain, the atrocities, they continue for longer. We have all learned to adapt in order to survive.'

They both glanced at each other and nodded in communal agreement. At the next street corner they turned left and pulled up outside a shop front with the very proud title of Guillermo, it being named after its owner.

Despite the civil war this discreet art gallery had managed to negotiate and trade works of art from artists mainly based in Western Europe. Guillermo had an eagle's eye when it came to spotting talent, and to his mind Imelda Fingal's work came under that banner. He had attended two of her lectures over the years, one in Paris and one in London. He admired her style and the fluency of her work as it depicted everyday life with all its nuances and quirks.

The joy, and on occasion, the malice with which some of her characters were conveyed was striking. Yes, he was only too delighted when he heard that the paintings would be arriving, and with Imelda's daughter, Anna.

On entering the gallery, Alphonse and Anna immediately saw a balding portly man who was busy rearranging canvasses around the shop floor. He turned at the sound of the tinkling bell which was somehow linked to a bizarre doll style monkey, with grotesque lips and a very knowing grin It rotated ninety degrees and bowed as the shop door opened.

Anna was taken by surprise and Alphonse laughed having seen it all before.

'Welcome, welcome, and please tell me you are Imelda's daughter, Anna? You are most welcome to Spain, but to Madrid in particular which is the most beautiful capital in the world,' stated Guillermo.

Anna was charmed by Signor Guillermo Huerta-Melandez. He was a rotund man with an open gracious countenance. His dress was flamboyant, bright blue trousers, eclipsed by a silk harlequin style shirt worn with a cravat and red trouser braces. He stated how delighted he was to meet Imelda's daughter. He would honour her mother by placing the canvasses on prominent display and that he expected their appeal would entice many buyers even in this run down tortured capital!

Coffee was called for and Guillermo led his visitors to the back of the shop to meet his wife Carla who was the total antithesis of her husband. Dark features on a thin frame adorned with clothes greatly eclipsed by those of her husband.

She blended into the background, almost obliterated by Guillermo's siren colours. It was however clear to Anna, that they adored each other. Coffee was replaced by a glass of Sangria and a most welcome light lunch of omelette and salad. Anna felt enveloped in this household. Alphonse kept them all amused with stories about his mother's lack of success in procuring for him a suitable wife to help him run his up and coming jazz club.

Anna laughed easily and Guillermo and Carla were both delighted with Imelda's daughter.

'You know Anna, Alphonse tells me that you have gained a position to teach English and German to local students at Signora Arauzo's language school. She is an unusual woman, widowed now with a most beautiful daughter Karina who is about your age. She is fortunate in that she comes from a very wealthy family who have helped her maintain the school as a business venture. They look to the future. Karina does not live in the family home but in an apartment not far from here, and it is with her that you will be living during your time in Madrid. The language school also is not far from where Karina lives. I'm sorry I could not sort this for you sooner prior to your arrival in Madrid.'

Anna inwardly smiled to herself at her mother's adeptness in building up a relationship with Guillermo and Carla and involving them in her daughter's accommodation issues. Yet again the Corpse and Seamus Halpin saw it as part of Anna's natural cover story. The less, that anyone in Dublin or Madrid, or indeed anyone outside of Anna's family got involved in the minutiae of her stay in Madrid, the better.

'But it is perfect Guillermo, it could not be better. It means I can walk or cycle to the school, and transport will therefore not be a problem.'

'Ah, Karina,' said Alphonse. 'She has a beautiful voice and sings in my jazz club. The men adore her and the women they come along, but only to ensure their husbands are not enticed away by Karina's charms. They need not worry on that score.'

Anna wondered why Alphonse had said that, but she thought that he perhaps meant that Karina, although beautiful by all accounts, was not a siren in the true sense of that meaning. She thought it more likely the case that he had interests which lay in that direction.

Carla stood, and looking directly at Alphonse she stated it was time for Anna to get settled, and he should take her forthwith to her new accommodation. Guillermo would have his young assistant take the bags round later and therefore they could walk comfortably to Calle Jardines.

Chapter 8

Almost six weeks later and Anna was pleased with how she had settled into her new role in Madrid. Karina was everything Alphonse had stated. She was a classic Spanish beauty, with raven, wavy shoulder length hair. In addition to that she had a voluptuous figure, a tiny waist, and a devastating smile with which she easily captivated the men at Alphonse's jazz club. Anna felt dull in her presence but Karina hugged her and warmly welcomed her to Madrid. She was glad to finally have some sophisticated and intelligent company sharing her apartment as she herself had no gift for languages like Anna.

'You know Anna, when you have settled into your job as a language tutor you must come to the jazz club. It is such good fun, this city needs some fun and the music is the best in Madrid, some say the very best in Spain. But tomorrow, I will take you down to my mother's language school. You can walk easily or take a bicycle if you wish.'

Signora Arauzo's language school was beginning to flourish with the aid of investment from relatives. Based at 57 Calle del Carmen, the school attracted many and varied students. Some pupils were from wealthy families where languages were endorsed and promoted, and although some languages were taught in school there was not enough emphasis placed on them. The school was also a mecca for mature students who were mostly sent by their companies to promote links in the business world, or for foreigners who now resided in Madrid and needed to improve their Spanish for obvious reasons.

Anna took several classes, one, teaching English mainly to Spanish teenagers in the fifteen to seventeen year old group; the second, again for teenagers to learn German. Yet another group was for adults wishing to learn Spanish; and finally any adults wishing to learn German.

There were twelve teenagers in Anna's English class and they were all very responsive and eager to learn. As a teacher she knew it was very important not to have any favourites but she admitted to a soft spot for José Maria who not infrequently and

cheekily asked her, 'Where is it you are from –
Holland?' With utmost patience Anna would always
reply, 'Do they have leprechauns in Holland, José
Maria? I never knew this!' The group enjoyed these
little occasions, but more importantly for Anna, they
were enjoying her classes.

About the same time in a tobacco shop in Calle de
Atocha, a dark haired man was indecisive as to
whether to procure some Virginian cigarettes or a
few Tritons. He eventually decided in favour of the
small popular cigar which cost about thirty-five
centimos. As he rolled the cigar between his fingers
he looked out onto the street and saw that Madrid
was still hurting, still scarred, still trembling from
its war.

He had noted the wariness in people's eyes, but
such was not the case with this shop owner. A
shrewd business man, garrulous in his chatter and
nosy in his demeanour, Carlos Santiago had never
before seen this well-built dark haired man in his
shop. He had observed the large scar gouged across
the back of this man's hand but stayed wise in this

respect and said nothing. There were many scars left over from the war.

Seamus Halpin scattered the required amount of money on the counter and left the shop, turning right as he exited. He reflected that it was a well-stocked shop and that he would visit it again. Less than a block away in Calle Huertas he found the 'Magnolia', a café with exterior tiled walls blemished by bountiful bullet holes. He entered, ordered a coffee, lit up one of the Triton's he had purchased and waited for his contact.

There were only three customers. A young mother with a precocious child, a boy of about eight years of age, whose legs did not quite reach the floor from his seating position. They were discussing quite ardently an upcoming music exam and the fact that in twenty minutes approximately they must make their way around to the examinations hall. Seamus noticed some tightly clutched music manuscript for piano in the not unattractive mother's hand.

The only other waiting occupant was an old woman, whose dress and coat although of good quality had obviously seen better days. The war had not done her any favours but she still maintained a pride in how she looked and dressed. Seamus guessed correctly that this was more than likely an everyday haunt for this worn out poor matriarch. The café was extremely well kept, and its warmth from a very old but very efficient stove was no doubt the main reason for her presence.

The increasingly cold air of Madrid was winding its chilly talons gradually through the streets. Fuel was difficult for people to procure, and they were saving their somewhat feeble supplies for the very worst weather.

Waiting was not a good game for Seamus, not in Madrid. Here he thought of Sonsoles too easily, the only woman he had ever cared about. He reflected too easily on that past which he really only wanted to forget. He had tried to bury the images of that savage war deeply. To consign those horrors to that part of the brain which dealt with nightmares which he hoped would never resurface. However, that proved impossible. Just as his memories of Sonsoles sustained him, he knew that with those wonderful moments of respite came the awakening of other disturbing nightmares.

He had been fighting with the International Brigade at the Battle of Jarama. When Franco's frontal assault had failed, the Caudillo organised a Nationalist force of about forty thousand men, many from the 'Army of Africa.' They had crossed the Jarama River on 11th February 1937. Three International Brigades were sent to try and stop the advance of the Nationalists and Seamus was part of that group.

It made him jittery even thinking about it. The loss of life, the slaughter, the panic, those machine guns, and then there was the infamous Suicide Hill. It was here that he had seen many friends picked off by machine gun fire in that sunken road, mowed down, no reprise, nothing. He did not remember being shot, or much later when night fell, his removal down to a village called Morata de Tajuña. This village was being used as a base for immediate medical care and a young eager republican doctor removed the bullets from his broken ribs while mopping up the considerable blood loss.

Such scenes of chaos, and the screaming, well he would never forget that or the floors of the outhouses where they worked on the injured, so much blood, and yet worse scenes, of limbs discarded, now ownerless. What horrific sights they were, and how they sometimes returned to haunt him, as if he would ever completely forget.

And then Sonsoles, there was no memory like the memory of her. As he lay on a makeshift bed surrounded by other injured men, she had noiselessly approached and started to unravel and examine the wound for which there was no pain relief. His opening line was not one for the courtship books.

'What the fuck do you think you're doing? I've just had bloody bullets removed and now you're pulling off the bandages!'

The response was calm.

'Sir, perhaps if you were to scream at me in Spanish I might understand you better.'

He repeated it in Spanish.

'It is in fact five hours since you had the bullets removed and because you have lost quite a bit of blood it makes sense to check on your wound to ensure you are not haemorrhaging. In fact truth to tell, it should have been checked a lot sooner but you have hopefully gathered by now that you are one of hundreds, and we are doing our best. Also, there is a chance to move you out of here soon so I must know if you are stable. God help those who are not.'

Seamus's eyes started to focus properly on the young woman before him, and what a beauty he saw. Long dark hair tied back tightly but with small curls escaping under her headband. Black eyebrows, a broad forehead, flawless skin and when she finally looked up, what looked like dark hazel coloured eyes gazing steadily back at him.

He would never forget that moment, he was mesmerised, and for some reason they stared silently at each other for some time. Then a sudden call for assistance elsewhere drew her away and Seamus felt a feeling of almost immediate loss. He told himself not to be ridiculous and to pull himself together. No woman had ever had such an immediate effect on him.

Seamus was broken from his reverie by the unnoticed shortening of the tip of his cigar, which was gradually warming his fingers. He stubbed it out quite forcefully in the cracked ashtray. He looked up and registered the arrival of his contact who had quickly noted Seamus and the quiet corner of the café to which he had secreted himself. He was carrying, as arranged, a worn copy of Don Quijote, and he walked casually towards him, smiling as if they were old friends.

'Sit down old friend and take the weight off your feet. Coffee for my friend Signor, an espresso if I'm not mistaken.' Seamus had signalled the waiter who acknowledged his request.

As his contact sat himself in his chair both men made small talk until the coffee arrived. Seamus who faced the room ensured that as the waiter walked away that there was no one else within ear shout. It also gave Seamus the opportunity to size up this man whom he had never previously met. However, he knew he had the right man. Apart from the Don Quijote book which Malcolm Mortimer was carrying by way of identification, Seamus, whilst still in Dublin had been supplied with a photograph. He therefore had no qualms.

Seamus saw before him a tall man with brown hair and a well-kept short beard. He moved well and appeared very light on his feet. Even under the overcoat you got a sense of his fitness and a not unnoticeable toughness, a man who gets the job done no matter what the cost. Seamus mused how amazing it was that he was helping British Intelligence. Not a topic for a chat with the lads at home!

'Well, Captain Mortimer – I hear your journey to Madrid went according to plan and that you successfully caught up with the real Rudi Holtzman in Barcelona, eh and how shall I put it, disposed of him?'

Malcolm Mortimer, alias Rudi Holtzman quickly returned the compliment and sized up the man in front of him. His main concern being, just how co-operative this man might be in helping him towards his goal.

'Mr Halpin, we meet at last. I have to say Mr Herlihy paints a commendable portrait of you.' At this he noticed Halpin's smirk.

'Mr Herlihy, is not known to give praise Captain Mortimer so you will have to forgive my not so convinced look.'

'Noted. Look, let's dispense with the titles.' They nodded agreement.

'Our plans have gone well so far. How has your agent Anna Fingal settled?'

Seamus measured his reply, 'She has done so, remarkably quickly. I have to say that initially I was not really in support of her as the choice for this mission. I thought her too soft, but she is surprising in her qualities and very perceptive. Her instructors in Beaulieu rated her highly, but they did say that they would have welcomed a longer stint for her under their, how shall I put it tutelage?'

'Good. There is no doubt that she will be called upon to hold her nerve. What we like in particular in relation to this plan is that she is not here under an alias. We have to get her installed in the embassy. We have known for some time that this is where the engineers have been allocated a room where they can safely design their ballistics.'

At this point Seamus noticed the waiter approach their small table to ask if they required anything else. They ordered two more espressos and made small talk until the coffees arrived at their table. Seamus smiled at the pomp and ceremony with which this small act was performed. The man had a pride in his work despite the difficulties of everyday life in Madrid and of acquiring provisions. He mused that perhaps he got a good deal from the black market.

'We have a plan as to how we can get her into the embassy. How much contact have you had with her since arriving in Madrid,' asked Mortimer.

'Believe it or not, and although I speak fluent German, I've enrolled for her adult German language class which is aimed at people with a good knowledge of the language already. The emphasis in this class will be on speaking skills. It starts in two days and I'm hoping she does not act too surprised when she sees me. But it allows me legitimate contact with her without drawing any suspicions from outside. I will only attend until Christmas. My story, which is not untrue, is that I'm working for the Irish Department of Trade and Foreign Affairs trying to foster and promote economic relations with Spain. The plan is that we give an impression of a relationship, a friendship, and go out together to the few clubs that are functioning in this city. After all would it not be very natural, two lonely people abroad, finding comfort in a foreign country? Our department can even legitimately make use of Anna as a translator for projects without raising any suspicion.'

What Seamus didn't say was that in any free time that was available to him he fully intended to use it to locate Sonsoles. The outcome may not be to his liking but he had to know one way or another.

'Keep it that way. We have need of you also, but at this stage the less everyone knows of what is expected of them the better. That way if anyone is discovered they cannot reveal too much under interrogation. Another engineer from the embassy wishes to attend Spanish classes at the school, and it will be organised that it is not Anna who takes that class. He is not a pleasant character, quite dangerous in fact. Keep using your contact to keep watch, and by the way who is your contact?'

Seamus knew he could reveal the name of his contact but chose not to, simply for the same reasons that had already been discussed. Knowledge of this nature was best kept close to home in case anything went wrong. His response to Malcolm Mortimer was a shrug of his shoulders and a look that indicated that that particular bit of information would not be forthcoming.

Malcolm Mortimer knew when not to flog a dead horse. He noted this well-built man, and the deep jagged scar on his hand. His brief in London had revealed that Seamus had fought in Spain during the civil war and had been shot in action at the Battle of Jarama therefore ending his participation. The file also revealed a man who was prepared to step up to the challenge but also a man who knew his own mind. His language skills were excellent and this could be used to advantage later in this operation. But best for the present to keep what had not yet fully evolved in his own mind to himself.

As both men prepared to leave, Seamus had it in mind to ask one more question.

'I hear you have lost two operatives already on this venture. Have you any clues as to who is responsible for their demise?'

'No, none. But this operation is completely different. Our previous agents were left isolated. It will be different for Miss Fingal. Having only recently arrived as Rudi Holtzman, I have managed to be accepted as the German engineer they were expecting from Barcelona. They have extraordinary talent working on the plans. From where I'm positioned I can't sabotage the work, but I can ultimately discover and plan for where the documents are kept and how to get them out. Their work is incredibly detailed but they have momentarily hit a stumbling block as to how this missile may be perfected to be the ultimate weapon in turning the war in their favour. I admit that they have the best possible minds available to them and they are hopeful of a breakthrough sooner rather than later. It will be then that we must be ready to act.'

Seamus must have looked sceptical and for his benefit Mortimer spoke again.

'We will have another role for you to perform should everything go to plan. Ah, also please do not inform Miss Fingal of my true identity. At this stage the less she knows the better. It would also be sensible on our part if we don't meet unless there is an absolute imperative for us to so do. It's not an issue if we meet in connection with our work or socially amongst other people. You could get your contact to assist? I'm staying in an apartment in Plaza del Ángel so this café is easy for me to use.'

'Yes, but we can't openly meet with you, so how can we get messages through. That may be far too dangerous for my contact. Such people weigh up their lives very carefully, and believe me, they protect that at all cost. I for one don't blame them for that.'

Seamus hoped that the sarcasm dripping from his voice would not be lost on Malcolm Mortimer. Nevertheless, when his reply came he was stunned.

'Well, I have an alternative suggestion. You know that tobacconist shop where you just bought your

Tritons? Well Carlos Santiago works for us and is well remunerated and totally trustworthy. He has one of the best shops of its type in Madrid. He can take messages and pass them on in either direction in cigar or cigarette boxes.'

'You've been bloody spying on me, you bastard! I thought we were on the same side? And how do you know you can trust him for Christ's sake?'

Malcolm was not blind to the fact that this Irishman was upset and that his response had better sooth him. He leaned closer over the table as the waiter hovered nearby.

'His family was destroyed at Guernica, his wife and his daughter. He wants to help now when there was absolutely nothing he could do before. He could not control what happened to his family, and whatever you want to call it, a sense of guilt, a lust for revenge, anger against his sense of utter impotence in the light of what was going on around him; and finally I don't bloody care because he really is on our side.'

It was not lost on Seamus the passion with which this man now spoke. There was true fire in his eyes. Contrary to what he had said he did care as to why Santiago was willing to get involved in this dirty world of espionage. Both men tried to outstare each other, but Seamus relinquished when Mortimer went on to explain. Yes, he had followed Seamus prior to their rendezvous but not because he was spying on him. He needed to be completely certain that neither of them had been followed.

Mortimer now clearly felt everything was aptly explained. His final instruction about using the tobacconist shop was for Seamus to use it as a drop off or pick up for messages, but only on mornings and by eleven o' clock, no later. He, Mortimer, would only ever call into the tobacconist in the late afternoon as he strolled home to his lodgings. If a message had to get through very urgently for any reason, Santiago, who also sold chess sets would place the King in reverse position to the Queen. It was extremely discreet and it would stay unnoticed among the jumble of his window display. But both of them would have to make a concentrated effort to pass the shop almost on a daily basis.

Now Mortimer spoke.

'It's probably hard to believe that we are both on the same side, what with I shall say is the history between our two countries. That is the one thing we share even if neither of us like it. We both need to only know one thing and that is our mission is to achieve the one goal, get the plans and get out safely. This mission is going to be extremely dangerous for us all and in particular Miss Fingal. That's why these precautions are in place and that's why it's best we don't meet again unless absolutely necessary.'

Seamus acknowledged that what Mortimer had put in place so far was impressive. He certainly seemed to have covered all the bases as our American friends would say. Inwardly he was angry with himself rather than the man sitting opposite him. Angry that he had been so preoccupied with thoughts of Sonsoles that he had not spotted Mortimer in the background. It was a good slap in the face for him, even a good lesson. He would not let that happen again.

Seamus stood and Mortimer followed his example. Enough words had been spoken for the moment and both men nodded their agreement and shook hands. Gripping his hat and donning his coat before exiting from the café, it was notable how the weather outside, although bright, was also becoming quite cold. It was to be expected in late November. He departed the café first.

Malcolm sighed and took his seat again. He waited a further ten minutes idling the time away by reading the local paper. Then finally he called the waiter and requested *la cuenta*. He strolled casually from the café and made his way back to the embassy.

Chapter 9

Classes were progressing well for Anna at the language school. It was now Monday 7th December 1942. She had become an accepted member of the school as a part-time teacher and had gradually come to know her colleagues. Occasionally she had opportunity to meet with them in the teachers den as she liked to describe it. The owner, Señora Arauzo dropped in on a regular basis. She was an astute business woman who understood the importance of keeping her staff happy.

On this particular day as Anna entered the room for her welcome morning break, she noticed Señora Arauzo speaking to a new addition to the now gradually expanding school. All staff members were pleased and content in themselves that the school for the next few years was economically stable and thus their jobs secure. This was a miracle as far as most staff were concerned considering the economic plight and hardships endured in Madrid. Any stability for their families was welcome.

'Anna, there you are! Come sit with me. I have not seen you for some time so you must tell me all. How are you settling in?'

The speaker in question was Marta Villanueva-Ferrer who could only be described as a bundle of energy and fun. She was a good friend of Karina's, and both women did occasional work in the club run by Alphonse. While on the one hand Karina was a traditional Spanish singer, on the other, Marta was the essence of traditional Spanish dancing. They were both gifted in their chosen sphere. Karina frequently left the flat in the evening which she shared with Anna to practice routines for the jazz club owned by Alphonse.

'Ah Marta I'm afraid it's the same old thing for me. I'm not particularly feeling homesick despite having received updated news from home, but I do feel like a bit of light relief. Don't get me wrong, it's really inspiring to work here especially with my teenagers group, they give their best and they are really good fun. But some of my adult classes, they can become an effort.'

'I know exactly what you mean Anna. Why on earth do some of them come! They are a nightmare. There are a few who never improve and yet they return year on end. It's like watching the same movie over and over again!'

Here Marta paused.

'You know what you have just said is exactly right and you do need something to take you out of your routine. You must come to the club this Friday night with me and Karina. You need to get a taste of our local traditions and culture before you go home, get married and settle down.'

'Honestly Marta, you have me written off as a spinster already! I cannot have that and yes, I would love to go with you both on Friday, thank you.'

'That's great Anna. Now I will endeavour to sneak past greedy Raquel and grab some biscuits to go with our coffee whilst it is still hot. We don't see biscuits appear often in our restroom or is it just the case they do but somehow Raquel manages to target them first? You would think that as the latest addition to this language school she would have some respect for us more established members and at least leave our biscuits alone! You know Gabriel? He came into the restroom one day to deposit his lunch and Raquel was there. She could not speak, and Gabriel swears it was because she had stuffed in several biscuits just before he had walked into the room. She has hardly spoken to him since!'

Both girls smiled at the story. Raquel was in fact a good teacher but her sly way and the almost constant petulant look on her face did not draw friends easily. She taught Italian, and she had revealed that that talent was helped by the fact that her mother hailed from Naples.

Apart from that she only appeared to smile when she wanted something and on such occasions her curvaceous figure and not unattractive face were used to full advantage where her male colleagues were concerned.

Marta now headed on as one of her adult groups would be arriving in fifteen minutes and she had some preparatory work to do. She almost bumped into Raquel as she made for the door at about the same time. Anna relaxed for another five minutes amongst the lively chatter, then excused herself as she too was about to commence her new adult German speaking class.

Anna quickly made her way up the lovely old wooden staircase to the second floor where her classroom faced out onto the street front with its noises and everyday life.

She thought about life on the streets within the area she now lived and worked. On many occasions she would see what appeared to be extremely young, ragged, worn out children roaming and scurrying along the streets. They stopped occasionally, but furtively, and begged mainly for food, money and extra clothing. It was obvious they were living, no they were existing under extreme conditions. Karina had explained to Anna that in most cases they were the dispossessed children of Republicans who had fought against Franco.

Even now the homes of anti-Franco sympathisers and what were described as other unwelcome elements were raided. These night time raids still took place regularly striking deadly fear, and making neighbours who were once friends, suspicious, cautious and extremely watchful. It was exactly what the regime wanted to achieve, a sense of isolation and terror.

Anna shook her mind away from the despair of it all and entered her classroom which seemed like an island of comfort amid the ghastly happenings that surrounded them. The dichotomy of it all was not lost on her.

The entrance door was to the front of the room at the end where the teacher's desk was placed, and from where she would normally teach. It was a good sized room, well lit by sunshine even on a wintery day. This predisposed the room to be much warmer on such occasions. There was also an old stove in the room which had enticed the other occupants to stand close by, as its soft but welcome glow emitted a moderate heat.

No one noticed Anna enter into the room, and she was quick to scan the small huddle standing there. Her eyes caught the back of one particular shape and with immediate recognition she silently welcomed this man's appearance. Even if Anna's face had registered surprise no one in the room would have noticed.

'Good afternoon everyone.'

Immediately, eleven heads rotated, swirled and fixed on Anna. She continued to speak in fluent Spanish requesting if everyone would please take a seat so that she could check everyone's name against the roll and if they would then introduce themselves, stating who they were etc. Also, as this was a class for people who already had a good sound knowledge of German but who were wanting to improve their speaking skills, she would prefer if everyone would give their introduction in that language.

At once they all moved to their seats, scraping back the chairs over the well maintained wooden floor and now Anna saw more clearly the make-up of the group. There were four women and seven men and as a group most looked Spanish apart from three. The age range was interesting in that the youngest appeared to be in his mid-twenties and the eldest possibly in his late sixties or early seventies.

Anna now had the full attention of the group. She introduced herself and gave a brief history of her origins and her education. She could see some nods of approval for her breadth of Spanish and indeed her accent, and knew immediately that she was accepted by most. What surprised Anna was that it was not just one face which she recognised in the class. Apart from Seamus, there sitting to the right of her eldest pupil was Raquel, the sulky young teacher whom only a few minutes earlier she had been discussing with Marta in the tearoom.

It was almost imperceptible but Seamus did notice Anna's slight hesitation as she took in the presence of one of the attendees. She had not even batted an eyelid when her eyes fell on him, and he gave her full marks for that. He needed to find out what had taken her by surprise.

Anna took the roll call and asked everyone to introduce themselves with a very brief summary of their background. Most people were local to Madrid and working for foreign companies wanting to establish themselves and get a firm foothold on any future economic growth in this country. These companies were encouraging uptake of foreign languages and this was seen to be the way ahead for promotions within companies.

The septuagenarian was Portuguese and had come to live with his daughter in Madrid following her marriage to a Spaniard. He had a penchant for languages, a very active brain and he simply needed a hobby to fill his time. Seamus made light and short work of his introduction stating as planned that he worked for the Irish Department of Trade promoting economic links with Spain. Three more introductions followed and then finally Raquel who stated accurately that she was a teacher in the language school who wished to increase her portfolio of languages and that the school was sponsoring her to improve her German language skills.

Anna wished it had not been the case. Her instinct told her not to trust Raquel but she hid everything from her expression extending the same courtesies to everyone for the duration of the class.

Once the class session was complete and as the class filtered out, Seamus delayed his exit and in front of a few other stragglers he approached Anna stating how nice it was to see a fellow countrywoman from Ireland. He made a loud pretence of asking her questions to which he already knew the answers.

Anna reciprocated, and Seamus then invited her to go for a drink in a local café. As Anna prepared to leave the classroom she noted Raquel had seemed to linger longer than was necessary in the room, casting a sly glance at Anna before she finally made her slow exit. She was obviously frustrated as Anna and Seamus had switched from speaking in Spanish to English, a language with which she struggled.

When they were finally alone Seamus quietly cautioned Anna not to say anything of note until they had some distance between themselves and the building. Aloud he said 'I know of a pleasant café where the coffee is quite decent, let's go there.'

They walked leisurely together to the Magnolia café with Seamus making several discreet checks that they were not being followed. Some Falange youth were clustered in a slightly menacing manner at the entrance to an alleyway with obvious other intentions on their minds. They hardly looked at Seamus and Anna as they walked on silently.

Seamus cautioned, 'Don't look at them Anna – you know of what they are capable, and from what I've heard they remain very active in rounding up what this regime describes as undesirables. I can only pray they get their just desserts one day. They are vile and vindictive, intent on spilling blood for the sheer pleasure of it.'

He sensed Anna's silent agreement and felt her shudder slightly. Once inside and seated at a corner table Seamus ordered two coffees – he would have preferred something stronger but he had another rendezvous after this meeting with Anna and he needed to keep a clear head.

'Seamus, it's really good to see a familiar face. How long have you been in Madrid? I suppose you must have news for me as an old skinflint like you isn't taking me out for coffee for no reason!'

'Point taken Anna, and yes it's good to see you also. You seem to have settled in well at the language school, how is that working out?'

'Come now Seamus, I asked first what news have you? You have to know that all this waiting around for something to happen is very tedious.'

Seamus noted that Anna looked her usual composed self. Thank goodness she did not seem to unbalance easily, because based on the information

Mortimer had given him, he knew that this girl would be tested. He delayed his answer as the waiter hovered with their drinks.

'I've met with our British contact, or perhaps I should say handler.' Anna noted the slight sarcasm with which this was said.

'When do I get to meet with him?' said Anna

'Not yet. He does not wish for the moment to make contact with you. He feels that if anything were to go wrong that less knowledge is better than too much. If the wrong people were to really find out why you are here and you were caught then his cover remains secure. Sorry Anna, that's the way it works in this seedy world, but I'm sure they already explained that to you in Beaulieu. He's a very cautious man and I have to respect that.'

He noted a frown appearing on Anna's face. 'If it's any consolation I've had a communication from him only this morning stating that you should come into play very soon. But we need to know your movements this week.'

When Anna's reply came, Seamus immediately knew that a door was opening to get their plan off the ground.

'Well, you know I only work part-time at the language school. A full day on Mondays and half days on Wednesday and Thursday. This Friday I am going to Alphonse's jazz club along with Karina and Marta. They say it's about time I was educated with regard to Spanish dancing and music so I've taken up their offer.'

'Right then Anna, you've given me some helpful information. By the way, at your class tonight you seemed slightly surprised by the presence of someone else – who was it?'

Anna smiled slightly, 'You are quick Seamus. Yes, that was Raquel. You remember that she was the girl who stated that she is already a teacher at the school extending her portfolio of languages. She has a way of suddenly appearing around corners that makes me wary.'

'Well then Anna, you are usually quick with your observations. It may be nothing but watch your back,' he said to Anna whilst giving her a very measured look. Anna nodded her understanding.

A few extra stragglers were drawing into the café and Seamus correctly guessed it was most probably for the heat that the old stove was producing – why go back to a huge old apartment with high ceilings and no fuel to heat them when you could while a few hours here with some extra warmth.

'It's become quite misty and very cold. I think we should get you back to your apartment before all the stragglers start hovering.' Seamus quickly paid the bill and escorted Anna back to Calle Jardines.

In truth he was not so much worried about stragglers as he was about being late for his next contact. As well as that he would need to get a message to Mortimer in the morning with regard to Anna's movements for the rest of the week. And although she had said nothing, he knew Anna had not been fooled by his excuse. She knew from his attempts at small talk that his mind was now somewhere else. The streets were now quieter and they made their way quickly to Karina's apartment.

It was a relief to see that the Falange were not currently present on the streets. His obvious haste would have prompted them to stop and question him, and he certainly did not need or want that. He hurried to Calle Victoria which fortunately for Seamus was not too distant from where Anna lived. He earnestly hoped that he would not miss his contact, a man whom he had not seen in years, who played the game of survival very adeptly, selling his knowledge to the highest bidder, no morals, no scruples and whose only allegiance was to himself. Seamus could not stand him but he knew this man to be a major contact in the Madrid underworld.

As he entered La Casa del Abuelo the whiff of cigarette smoke gently billowed through the open doorway. His eyes quickly adjusted to the gloomy lighting inside. It was then he spotted his contact who was already seated with a wary waiter hovering at his shoulder.

Dec Buchanan smiled his lecherous, greedy smile. 'Well, Seamus me old mate, and what can a mere mortal do for you?'

Chapter 10

In Calle Jardines where Anna had taken lodgings, Karina had taken over Anna's wardrobe, or what little of it she had brought to Madrid from home. She was quite pleased with what she saw, and she directed Anna to try on a few combinations for their outing that evening.

Anna realised they were both enjoying the moment. Karina's not uncritical eye which on occasions spoke volumes without her having to utter a word – expression is everything as Karina would say. Eventually she seemed to find particular favour with one dress which was silver grey in colour.

'Perfect Anna, perfect! You must wear this to tonight's performance at the jazz club. It is a time for colour, for people to relax amongst all the horrible things still going on in Madrid.'

'But Karina, what colour? This dress is plain in colour. Yes, it has a lovely skirt that has a kick as you dance, but no colour!'

'Anna, have faith! You must trust me.' Karina shot from the room and returned hurriedly with a beautiful green shawl which had scattered colours of silver and black going through it. It went beautifully with Anna's dress and the matching green sandals which Karina had also managed to obtain.

'Where on earth did you get these,' asked Anna.

'Ah, the shawl is mine and the sandals belong to Mama who no longer has use for them. They are a little too big for my foot but for you I think they are perfect. What do you think Anna?'

As she looked in the mirror, Anna saw how beautiful the colours were against her pale colouring, and how they brought out even more the aquamarine of her eyes. Her figure was toned, and although she did not have the voluptuous figure which adorned Karina's frame, she remained pleased with her transformation. Beaulieu had done wonders for her in that respect.

'Do you not like it Anna?'

'Yes, Karina, I like it. I like it a lot. You know you are in the wrong profession?'

'Anna, wait until you hear my singing tonight and then you will know that is simply not true!' Both girls burst out laughing.

'Now Anna, you are sorted for the evening but I now need to prepare. If you would be so good as to open the door to Marta when she arrives in her full regalia?'

'Of course. Take your time and I will be on guard for her arrival!'

Anna settled with a book in the living room. It was a lovely old apartment with three shuttered windows adorning it. These windows faced to the front of the building and brought the various noises of the day into their midst.

The street carts delivering various goods, the street urchins begging for anything that they could either sell or barter for food. They were a pathetic sight. Karina had told Anna to be wary of them as many had turned to pick pocketing and were very adept at their new trade. Anna quietly laughed at that – she knew Karina had favourites among them. She frequently gave food and small amounts of centimos into their hands. They in turn adored her and declared they would do anything for her, anything! When she saw Anna slip money into an urchin's hand one day, she cautioned her not to encourage them, but smiled as she said it. She had an incredibly kind heart and she acknowledged that she and her family were lucky in their comforts.

Indeed the evidence of such comforts was clear to Anna. There was the wood which Karina's mother regularly supplied to the apartment. She gazed at the well burnt down logs glowing in the old Spanish grate, and felt the welcome glow of warmth it provided on this particularly cold evening. It made Anna reflect on home and how she missed her family and friends.

The noise emanating from the front door announced the arrival of Marta. She taught at the language school and performed flamenco dancing regularly at Alphonse's club in order to supplement her income.

She flung her arms around Anna and announced, 'Ah Anna, tonight we show you the real Spain. You will be transfixed, inspired and intoxicated! Tonight you will dance as never before! You know that

Alphonse has kindly set aside a table for us. He asks after you Anna, and how you have settled in. During the evening you know that either myself or Karina will be with you most of the time. However, there will be one occasion where we both perform a very traditional number and you will be alone. But you Anna, you are an independent woman and I think this will not bother you.'

What could Anna do but laugh at her friend's enthusiasm and joy of life. She was in fact really looking forward to the evening and already felt she was amongst friends who wanted to support her on this social occasion.

Karina now joined them. Anna could not see what either girl was wearing as their outfits were hidden by heavy winter coats. Then, as if on cue, the car which Alphonse had arranged was now outside their building. They could hear the hum of an engine. Marta confirmed its arrival by looking out through one of the living room windows.

Marta, forever the organiser announced, 'Anna prepare yourselves for an exciting evening of entertainment and dancing as you have never seen it before!'

As they departed from the building the cold night air enveloped them, but not for long as they hastily entered the car. Carlos, their driver, seeing that they were all settled slid the car into gear and struck off in the direction of the club. It was now eleven o'clock and the evening and early morning lay ahead of them.

Pulling up outside the club, Anna got a sense of what was a prosperous area. The building was old with wide curved steps leading up to it. She had anticipated a cellar somewhere but not this lovely old building. A considerate doorman rushed to the car and helped all three girls alight. Karina saw the questioning look on Anna's face.

'Alphonse's club is quite upmarket and Madrid has a lot of wealthy clientele who expect high standards. We have embassy staff, generals, politicians, and a myriad of business men from many walks of life. People want to prosper now, and in this one central location many deals are made. It's where a lot of wheeling and dealing takes place and Alphonse has hit the jackpot with his extravagant club. You will see inside.'

They entered through beautiful wide doors into a marble hallway of considerable size. At the furthest point of the hallway were two extremely large matching African statues, turbaned and with floating robes, the colours exotic and intoxicating in their vibrancy. Where these statues were positioned marked the start of another curve of elegant steps, ten in total, which on this occasion swept down to a lower level. Anna was so impressed with her surroundings that she hardly noticed their coats being taken and checked in.

As they reached the lower level, Alphonse appeared right on cue expressing warm greetings, as if they were his most prized clients. Anna was amazed at his suave appearance, his obvious pride in his business, and the ease with which he moved in such high powered circles.

'Welcome ladies to Club Alphonse. Marta, Karina, what have you done to Anna?'

'But Alphonse what is wrong, does she not look extremely lovely this evening?'

'Exactly, you rascal girls. You have turned her into a beautiful creature who will be stolen from us this very evening. Anna, I insist on a dance later, that is if you can cope with my stumbling feet!'

Anna, for the first time in years felt herself blush. She was not used to such open compliments. Alphonse then tucked her arm inside his and announced that he would personally escort them to their table.

Both Marta and Karina stood back and giggled at this performance, and they then strode purposefully alongside. As they moved across the room they were observed by many curious eyes. They made a striking picture, and although Anna had been initially embarrassed by the attention, Alphonse had skilfully managed to put her at her ease. Their table was placed discreetly near the stage. This was deliberately done for the benefit of Karina and Marta who would be performing at various times throughout the evening. As Alphonse seated Anna, he casually stated that there were many embassy staff present from numerous countries, but of particular note was the British and German contingent. They both had a significant presence for this evening's event.

It really was an impressive setting. Old Spanish traditional chandeliers hung from the high ceilings. The musicians all wore white jackets with black trousers. Their shirts were highly starched with point up collars encircled with bow-ties. There was no stage as such but a raised platform where a small group of musicians were placed and set well back to one side. Anna could see that this would leave ample room for performances of various sizes.

Scanning the room carefully, Anna was not surprised to see Seamus with two of his colleagues from the Irish Department of Trade and Foreign Affairs. They were sitting at a table which was slightly set back on the other side of the dance floor. Seamus immediately waved across, spoke something to both his colleagues, left his table and crossed the floor to where Anna sat.

'Anna, you must introduce me to these two beautiful young ladies.'

'Karina and Marta, allow me to introduce to you Seamus. He is a fellow countryman, a rogue and a star pupil from my German language class.'

At that very moment, the band struck up the first chords for the evening's entertainment and Seamus signalled for his two colleagues to join them.

'Ladies, this Irish contingent is getting the show off to a good start and we would be delighted if all of you would care to join us for the first dance?'

Anna immediately took Seamus's proffered hand as she knew this was a manoeuvre on his part to get her on her own. Several other couples had already commenced dancing, and as they circled the dance floor Seamus complimented Anna on her transformation with a raised eyebrow. Anna laughed and retorted that he had not scrubbed up too badly himself. Indeed Seamus looked every bit the representative from a foreign country. The stylish dinner jacket was very much in vogue and pressed to perfection. What surprised Anna was how adept he was on his feet.

'Thank you Anna, but it's down to brass tacks now. I finally got word through to our English colleague this morning. He is now aware of your movements for the rest of the week.'

Seamus had indeed gone to Carlos Santiago's tobacconists shop in Calle de Atocha the following morning and left a message for Mortimer. Carlos had adroitly taken the message from Seamus which was hidden within a folded bank note that Seamus had handed over for his triton cigars. The shop was busy as people who were scurrying to work rushed to buy their cigarettes or newspaper. No one noticed the exchange.

Once the activity had died down and the shop was empty of customers, Carlos rearranged the chess pieces in the window display and secreted the message into a box of cigarettes which he then put in his pocket. In the late afternoon, Mortimer made his habitual walk which took in the tobacconist's shop and immediately noticed the incorrect positioning of the chess pieces. There was only one other customer loitering and they did not seem particularly interested in the appearance of this newcomer. The packet of cigarettes was duly handed over.

'So, it begins,' said Anna

'Yes. Tonight we will arrange for you to meet with one of the German engineers who works in the embassy. They are frantic for extremely skilled translators and I will make a show of the fact that you have already agreed to do some work for our department. We will say how we met and that we are very impressed with how fluent you are in several languages. I've already sold your skills to my fellow Irishmen and they are keen to also get you on board for translation purposes. You need to follow my lead Anna when the moment arises for the introduction. Do you understand?'

'Of course, I'm glad the time has come to get this off the ground. This waiting has been the worst bit. How will you manage an introduction?'

'Ah, that will be a joy to behold Anna. If you were wearing a hat I would tell you to hold on tightly to it!'

Anna raised a questioning eyebrow, and Seamus smirked. The dance completed, all three girls were courteously returned to their table, and when the three men were seated back at theirs, they hailed the waiter, ordered more drinks and generously had some cocktails sent over to them. The girls acknowledged the gesture.

It was noticeable how Karina's dance partner could not take his eyes off her. Anna really only noticed then how stunning Karina looked in a gold and black tight fitting dress. Her beautiful dark hair was flowing down to just below her shoulders and she danced with great skill.

As the evening progressed, Karina made her excuses to depart from their company. The time was now drawing near to prepare for her performance. Marta nudged Anna and declared that their new acquaintance, Seamus, appeared to be drinking quite a lot and getting into boisterous conversation with the group of people at the table next to his. He then rose, stumbled awkwardly across one of the party concerned, and spilt a small amount of his whiskey.

Just as Karina was starting to sing, Anna could hear loud exchanges commencing. She rose from her seat and crossed the floor to see if she could help defuse the situation. Seamus on seeing her approach flung his arm around Anna's shoulder.

'Anna, Anna, Anna!' he declared.'

'This girl has just agreed to work for us and not only is she extremely talented in languages she's a fellow countrywoman to boot!'

On ensuring that Seamus, who on the surface appeared to have imbibed too much, was not going to fall over, Anna turned around to smooth the situation.

She looked straight into the startlingly cold eyes of the man from the Atocha train station, Christoph Beich, and sitting behind him was the same disdainful colleague who had made it very clear that he had no time for mere mortals like Anna.

In that very moment Anna realised that Seamus was unsurpassed at introductions. She also realised that in reality she had only a minute within which to save this situation and somehow ingratiate themselves. Anna turned to the German contingent.

'I believe, if my memory serves me correctly, that we have already met briefly before at the Atocha train station? You will remember that we were in competition for the same porter?'

Without waiting for an answer she turned immediately to Seamus, and said, 'Really Seamus you do no favours for us as a nation by getting out of hand. Is your role in Madrid not to build up relations in order to engage in foreign trade?'

'You are quite right Anna – perfectly correct in what you say! Gentlemen, I must apologise for my wayward exuberance.'

It was make or break in that moment. There were British embassy staff sitting at a distance of three tables away who were watching with keen interest the exchanges taking place.

The taller bearded German who had remained seated during the exchange was now casually lighting a cigarette. He now spoke quietly to his fellow countryman.

'Come Christoph, let us show how gracious we can be. This man is not British as you originally thought. That contingent are sitting some short distance away, and quite frankly they don't have the guts to engage with us. Besides this man has told us something to our benefit. We have need of a translator – let us use our brains and turn this to some benefit this evening. Now, let us move on and save the evening for enjoyment.'

Anna and Seamus both noted the furious looks particularly on the face of a young British attaché who was being carefully held back in check.

The moment was retrieved, and Anna inwardly breathed a sigh of relief as the German company introduced themselves.

Christoph Beich thawed slightly, then bowing to Anna in a stiff formal manner, he firstly introduced himself, and then his colleague, Rudi Holtzman. The two ladies in their company were not introduced. Anna correctly guessed that they were both Spanish and probably paid escorts for the evening.

Seamus did a fantastic show of ordering a round of drinks for everyone. Anna decided to remove herself and returned back to her table where Karina was now sitting, having completed her song. Karina and Marta were both looking concerned. As Anna sat, she could feel the eyes of Rudi Holtzman watching her closely. At that moment she was unable to decide which of these two men was the more threatening. She sensed a lot of malice in Beich, but not in his colleague.

Anna also noticed that Seamus' two Irish colleagues were aghast. They were both personally opposed to the war which Germany had waged in Europe. Their role in Spain was to encourage international trade, they did not want to appear to be part of a snub against the British contingent currently present in the club. When things had calmed down, the more experienced of the two Irish delegates approached the British embassy staff in order to smooth things over.

Marta spoke first. 'Anna, is Seamus crazy? Alphonse will go mad! He prides himself in this venue being completely neutral ground where people can leave at least their politics and their troubles behind.'

'Yes indeed, I have no idea what got into him. He perhaps had a little too much alcohol consumed,' said Anna.

When Alphonse got wind of what had happened and approached their table, his countenance was indeed stern, but Anna adroitly extricated Seamus and promised that nothing like that would ever happen again. She knew that he had a bogus understanding of their presence in Madrid because of his aunt, Tory Bartlett. She had been informed that they were on secondment to Madrid for various reasons to do with future trade agreements. Alphonse questioned the incident no further and remained seated at their table.

It was now one o'clock on Saturday morning. The musicians were preparing themselves to start playing for the last dance. Marta had excused herself as she needed to change in the dressing room. At that moment Christoph Beich appeared at their table with purposeful intent. He bowed and requested that Karina dance with him.

To Anna it had sounded more like a command, but Karina graciously accepted. As the music gathered pace, Alphonse gently took Anna's arm and led her in silence onto the dance floor.

'Herr Beich seems much taken with our beautiful Karina. I noticed earlier this evening that despite the fact that he has an escort, he could not tear his eyes away from her.'

'Are you jealous Alphonse?'

'No, not I, but she will need to be very careful. Herr Beich has the look of a man who gets what he wants. He is a dangerous man who would not be used to rejection. And you Anna, you also must tread carefully with my heart.'

As he spoke, Alphonse had continued to look over Anna's shoulder, but with this last comment he looked at her intently. Anna suddenly realised that Alphonse was attracted to her, and although she was not immune to his very handsome looks, something held her back.

On the opposite side of the room, Malcolm Mortimer cursed inwardly. He noted the caring look that Alphonse had given Anna and he was surprised at his own annoyance. She had been transformed tonight into a very attractive woman. Her eyes were a most striking feature, and her pale colouring contrasted well against the elegant dress and the exotic shawl that Karina had supplied. She had drawn admiring glances from many men.

He inwardly congratulated her on her handling of the situation that Seamus had created some time earlier. Quite a team in fact. They worked well together. He would have to have a quiet word with Seamus. There were not to be any unnecessary, emotional entanglements.

More importantly he worried about Beich and his sudden attraction for Anna's friend. He was a difficult man to read, yet he knew, he knew what the dossier on Beich had revealed; and its content did not make pretty reading.

The dance was finishing and without much delay Marta was duly escorted onto the stage for her interpretation of the flamenco. Her posture was superb, and her magnificent dress hugged her envious figure thus showing it off to its best advantage. The flowing arm movements when combined with the staccato tapping of her feet added a heightened vibrancy to the overall effect. That part of the audience which was Spanish was proclaiming its support by tapping their hands on the table surfaces. It was a wonderful and joyous moment which elevated everyone from the mire of what had been. Anna was mesmerised at her sheer talent and inwardly applauded the commitment it must have taken to achieve such a standard.

At that moment, Anna turned to look at Karina who was seated on the opposite side of the table. She was struck immediately by the look on her friend's face. It was a gaze of pure love, and the recipient was Marta.

Alphonse, understanding instantly what Anna had noticed, leaned towards her and whispered, 'Now, Anna, you understand why I am so concerned for Karina. If the wrong people discover what you have just noticed then her life may be in danger. She and Marta already know this. What they share is regarded in a very dangerous light by the current regime. It lists such relationships as undesirable. Both girls realise that they tread a very dangerous path, and that it would take just one vindictive person to destroy them.'

Certain things were now dropping into place for Anna. Karina's excuses of going to Marta's apartment to practice for their performances. The frequent evenings, particularly at the weekends when she stayed overnight, and then returning by late morning the next day.

It did not upset or disturb Anna. She had frequently heard her mother talk about people she knew who had these relationships, and she had occasionally met them among her mother's arty friends. At one soiree in particular, Anna had accompanied her mother to a well know art gallery in Dublin for the launch of an exhibition by a fellow artist. Anna had met and been enthralled by these couples and the secret lives they had to lead. It was not something that was spoken about in Ireland, as the consequences even there were grim. In Madrid, with its current political climate, the penalties for discovery would be brutal, and possibly even final.

Speaking again, Alphonse remarked, 'It's best you don't admit to either Karina or Marta what you now know. It may put your relationship with them on a different footing. They may unwittingly become more wary of you and even suspicious. You don't need that during your stay here in Madrid. Keep things as they are Anna. It will turn out better for you.'

'Thank you Alphonse. I believe you are right and there is absolutely no need to put my relationship with them in jeopardy. I have to say you are a loyal and amazing friend to them both.'

'And to you Anna, I am also loyal to you.'

Chapter 11

Having made quite a show the previous night of being the inebriated Irishman, Seamus was congratulating himself on his own performance. He had not a trace of a hangover. Indeed this Saturday morning, he was already washed and shaved and leaving his apartment at eight o' clock. He had another rendezvous with Dec Buchanan at Parque del Retiro.

It was a beautiful park studded with various monuments which had obviously sustained damage of various forms during the war. Originally built by King Philip IV as a retreat for the Royal family, this park with its 320 acre site was opened to the public in 1868.

He had agreed to meet Dec Buchanan at the northern end of the park, close to the lake, the Estanque del Retiro. Here, Madrileños would saunter when the weather was at its most agreeable. There you would find young girls who were becoming very aware of new emotions, flirting with their eyes as they ambled around the park. The bolder ones made an obvious show of their beautiful figures, teasing the young men, who like them were on a tight rein in this very conservative country. Families protected their daughters and advances by a young unwelcome man could be severely rebuffed. Seamus wondered at the number of broken hearts that this beautiful park had played a part in, unwittingly, unknowingly segregating what some families had decided was the chaff from the wheat. Social class and all its nuances were an integral part to society, especially here in Madrid.

Walking to the park was a welcome event for Seamus. It allowed him time to mull over how to deal with Buchanan. They had both fought on opposite sides during the Irish Civil War. That alone did not make them friends. Dealing with Buchanan was another thing. He knew that was going to be tricky. He had spun him a yarn which he hoped would fool Buchanan and not give him a true insight as to Seamus's real interest in Sonsoles. For Buchanan's benefit, Sonsoles was the sister of a woman now living in Ireland and married to a fellow Irishman.

She would pay good money to get her sister out if she was still alive. Seamus knew that Sonsoles had a sister named Alba, who did in fact, and by some miracle, escape from Spain during the war. However, no one now appeared to know the truth as to her whereabouts.

This did not bother Seamus. All he needed was to provide Buchanan with a story that was accurate to such a degree that if he were to make any furtive enquiries of his own, then the cover story Seamus had given would make sense and not make him suspicious. Added to this he had also sold the line that he was working in Madrid for the Department of Trade, which he was. In essence, he could not under any circumstances be seen to annoy any of the authorities in Madrid by making enquiries about a missing woman.

At the end of the day Dec Buchanan was a willing mercenary who sold his lack of ideals to the highest bidder, and it was obvious that he was more than interested in the money which the imaginary third party was offering. He seemed to accept the story that Seamus had carefully spun, but in all probability, the reality was that Dec Buchanan did not need to know the truth, only that there was a pot of gold waiting for him.

Into the park now, and Seamus shivered at the bitterly cold morning and he hunched down further into his coat. The bare tree branches and the twigs were covered in a spectacular hoar frost, each white frozen thread appearing to be individually defined as if they were arteries reducing down gradually to tiny capillaries. It reminded Seamus of winter tales on frozen nights during his own childhood.

He needed to snap out of such reverie and concentrate on the meeting about to take place. Buchanan had chosen this rendezvous deliberately as he knew that so early on a winter's morning it would be devoid of other people.

As he turned another corner, Seamus noticed a figure hunched on one of the wooden park benches. Also there, in front of the bench were two dogs in a stand-off with each other, growling and baring their teeth quite viciously.

It was as despairing as it was gruesome. The old woman exposed to the elements with her meagre ragged blankets must have died during the night. There were large numbers of homeless and dispossessed people in Madrid, and this poor woman's family must have been deemed to have done something to upset the ruling regime. Therefore homeless, without any hope and not long before all savings are spent, what else was there for this poor woman – nothing but despair.

The dog closest to the woman must have been her loyal pet, which was now trying to defend, protect, the body of his mistress. The other dog looked to be feral and was making slow circling advances towards the body. Seamus could see that the wild dog was the stronger and more cunning of the two and that it would be an uneven short fight. Neither dog had noticed his approach as they were so intent on each other.

Picking up a rock to hurl at the feral dog, Seamus was taking aim when he heard two low consecutive, almost silent whooshing noises. He turned slowly and there was Dec Buchanan, gun in hand with a silencer to boot. Both dogs lay dead on the ground.

'Good target practice for a Saturday morning Seamus. No point in leaving any of those two bastards alive. Once the smaller dog was dead that feral one would call in his mates for a good old feed and knees up. Anyway Seamus, you should know better than to help. If that feral one had jumped on you and got his salivating teeth round a juicy hand like that, you might not be the better of it for a long time. They carry nasty disease.'

Seamus knew the colour must have drained from his face. Initially, when he had first heard the shots, he thought he was the target. He had to recover himself quickly and not let Buchanan see the total look of contempt on his face. He struggled with the fact that shooting both dogs in the long run was probably the kinder thing, but in his heart he knew Buchanan enjoyed killing. After all, during the war back home, Buchanan was infamous as the man who had very ruthlessly shot dead his own unarmed brother. There were people on both sides at home who hated him for that fact alone, and it was probably the chief reason why he had left Ireland after such a particularly gruesome episode. He was a man with a target on his back.

Controlling himself carefully, Seamus spoke, 'Your intervention was very timely, but what about informing the authorities about the body?'

'Come now Seamus, let us be pragmatic. You call the authorities, it's us who will be taken in for questioning. Who are you, why were you in the park at such an early hour? You need that attention like either of us need a hole in the head. Leave well alone. Besides, I have news for you with which I think you will be pleased. Let us walk now and put some distance from this place.'

He knew what Buchanan had said made sense. As he walked away, he looked back. He knew that the only possible outcome for that old woman was the likely appearance of more feral dogs if someone did not find her body soon.

Seamus maintained the silence and let it stretch between them for some minutes. He did not want Buchanan to have an inkling of what this Sonsoles meant to him, and to seem too eager might alert this dangerous man.

They stopped at another park bench and remained standing as it was too cold to sit.

'It seems this woman Sonsoles was captured towards the end of the war and accused of treason for working in a field Republican hospital. Apart from that they tried to throw the whole book at her and falsely implicated her in the spread of Marxist ideology. Luckily for her, her parents were already dead and the one sister she had escaped. Otherwise they also would have been rounded up and falsely accused. My source has had it confirmed that she is still alive but incarcerated in a psychiatric hospital some distance from Madrid.'

There was huge relief in hearing that she was still alive. He felt such horror in knowing that his beloved wife was in fact a prisoner in one of those horrific hospitals. It was well known that the regime experimented on people that they termed as miscreants, undesirables, and delinquents. He had to keep calm and not show his true feelings.

'Well, where is this place?'

'It's a sanatorium called San José and it's based approximately twenty-two miles south of Madrid. She is in the women's section for what we might equate to the criminally insane, but of course she's not. Sedation and hypnotics are used quite regularly. They are always being interrogated by psychiatrists who are, shall we say, supportive of the regime. They are questioned frequently. Their replies are turned around in the most illogical manner and used to protect the status quo. It gives credence to their incarceration. Eventually they wear their minds down to such an extent that they don't even recognise themselves anymore.'

'How likely is it that we could get her out and when?'

Buchanan, at this stage had taken a plug of raw tobacco from the inside pocket of his overcoat. The knife he produced was not a pen-knife as would have been expected, but it did resemble a small butcher's implement. It was horrific looking in its sharpness. Buchanan manipulated it very skilfully, and all the while he was slicing away at the tobacco, he was very carefully making Seamus aware that only he could control this woman's future.

'You know Seamus you've just asked me how to perform a miracle. For me to get people I trust in place is going to cost a lot more money.' He then mentioned a sum of money that made Seamus whistle through his teeth.

Inwardly Seamus knew that at some point the blackmail for more money would commence. When Seamus had dangled the first carrot of money he had deliberately gone well under with the amount of available funds he had. He knew exactly what he had in this man, this ruthless, gruesome, cunning excuse of a human being. But then he knew that when it came down to survival, he could in his own way be ruthless.

'Right you need more money. It's a hell of a lot but I'll get word to Alba. She's determined to do what it takes to get her out, but Dec be sure of one thing, this is the final demand. No more money.'

Buchanan smirked, 'Don't worry Seamus. Now that I know for whom you are working in Madrid, it seems to me we could strike up a loose working relationship over the years to come. I have ideas for quite a few deals that will be beneficial to us both. You scratch my back etc.'

He nodded his agreement and said he had like-minded aspirations. He could almost feel the bile rising in his throat. They continued talking for about ten more minutes. Timelines were discussed as to when would be the most opportune moment to make a move on the sanatorium, and as to how the whole move could be realised.

They parted by shaking hands. Seamus then made his exit from the park via another gate and made his way back to his apartment. A quick shower was badly needed after that encounter. He now had to concentrate on the other job at hand and offer the support that Anna and Malcolm Mortimer required. Besides he needed to get clear of this park before any *civiles* arrived and started to ask questions.

As prearranged, Guillermo's art gallery was putting on a viewing of Imelda Fingal's art work along with items by two local artists. Guillermo Huerta-Melandez and his wife had carefully invited quite a range of people to the event. Money still flowed and there remained very wealthy families in Madrid who had an eye to future investments. The event was to start at twelve noon, and from Guillermo's point of view it was only natural that he would invite the daughter of his client. Embassy staff from various locations were also par for the course, and Seamus could discreetly include himself with the Irish staff from his department. The play was about to be made to get Anna working within the German embassy. Seamus could only hope that it worked.

Chapter 12

Christoph Beich had not been in a good mood about attending any art gallery. He was nursing quite a hangover from the previous night and he felt quite woozy, in fact almost disconnected from the occasion. However, his fellow countryman, Rudi Holtzman, had firmly stated that the embassy needed to be seen to support local business. After all Spain might yet enter the war on their side.

The model of the bizarre monkey with the grotesque lips and grin was the only thing that raised anything remotely resembling a smile from Christoph Beich as they entered the premises in Calle de Alcalá at 1pm. It was somehow connected to the door bell and thus announced any entrance to the premises. The final bow which the monkey made after its ninety degree turn seemed to appeal to Beich's warped sense of humour.

It was obvious that the viewings were in full swing, and indeed Mortimer was surprised at the level of attendance. Paintings were displayed in various and idiosyncratic areas of the room. This display area appeared to contain miscellaneous objects. Everything from Arabian style statuettes to Greek goddesses in flowing and abundant robes. Varied groups in various forms of dress were in attendance. There were also numerous fur coats being worn which were of outstanding quality. Malcolm Mortimer was amazed at how within such intimate environments the notion of a war raging in Europe could seem incredibly distant.

He and Beich were now approached by a waitress carrying a silver service tray which was laden with crystal glasses containing pink champagne. Beich eagerly grasped a glass, commenting as he did so that it might cure his headache.

Malcolm scanned the room. He noted Guillermo in high attendance with Anna, waving his arms to emphasise his admiration for the work in question. Standing slightly off to the side was Alphonse. 'That man is everywhere,' he thought to himself.

Standing with glass in hand towards the back of the room, Seamus registered the arrival of the two men and went into action.

'Herr Beich, Herr Holtzman it's good to see you both again. Have you both come with an eye to a good investment?'

In return to this greeting, Beich gave a formal, stiff bow.

'Art has its purpose in life Mr Halpin. Back home in Hamburg my wife and I are fortunate to have quite a collection of Flemish and Dutch art. It was for the most part inherited from Greta's side of the family. Besides, like you, we are here on a mission to create, or should I say maintain good relations with local enterprise.'

Seamus had more than noted the condescending tone that Beich used when he spoke about the Irish presence. The tone implied that he had a view of a scrawny backward little country, and how could it possibly have anything to offer society in general. However, Seamus knew he had to play the game so he kept what would have been his true response to himself.

'Well, Herr Beich you really should take a look at the work here by Imelda Fingal. She is an Irish artist and highly regarded by collectors who are currently snapping up any of her work. By the way, you met her daughter Anna Fingal at Club Alphonse last night. Allow me to introduce you both to her properly.'

Seamus with both men in tow headed towards Guillermo and Anna.

'Anna, you remember Herr Beich and Herr Holtzman from yesterday evening? Gentlemen this is Guillermo Huerta-Melandez, owner of this enterprise.'

Introductions made, Guillermo commenced to wax lyrical on Imelda Fingal's work. Even Beich acknowledged an interest in the style used and he questioned Guillermo closely as to the likely increase in the value of such a painting if he were to make an investment.

Malcolm Mortimer, standing alongside Seamus and Anna, kept a watchful eye on Beich, whom he could see had almost completed his conversation with the owner of the art gallery. As Beich returned to their group, Malcolm made a point of asking Seamus if he and Beich could have some time with Anna to discuss if she might be willing to help out in their embassy. Seamus obliged and said yes, he had just spotted someone else in the room with whom he needed to speak.

'Miss Fingal, as you know we need interpreters for our embassy and Herr Beich and I have both been impressed by your skills, indeed your fluency in many languages. We were wondering if you would be willing to leave the language school to work with us?'

Anna paused slightly before her reply.

'Herr Holtzman, what you are offering sounds interesting but I enjoy my work at the school which is part-time, and besides, I cannot withdraw from that. You must also know that Seamus has asked me to help occasionally within his department. I'm not sure that I can offer you the time you need.'

Beich now stepped closer and said in a quiet controlling manner, 'You know I phoned only this morning, very early I might add, my colleagues in Berlin. Within three hours they were able to get me some very interesting information about your family. Your sister Marion, she works for the International Red Cross, a neutral organisation of some merit I suppose. But it's your brother Patrick who is the gem. A German sympathiser incarcerated I believe by the British Government. Very tricky for your family no doubt, not knowing where he is or what might happen to him. He did manage to send some useful information to us before he was caught.'

Anna knew from Seamus that this information was to be divulged to these men. She had to look askance at the fact that they were in receipt of such knowledge. They knew they could blackmail her if necessary. A word dropped to the British embassy in Madrid, might impact on Patrick even more back in England. If the British embassy were to let the authorities in England know that Anna was working as a translator within the German embassy it would also implicate Anna as a sympathiser. Would Anna seriously want that to happen?

Mortimer watched Anna's face closely. Her response to this announcement was of an appropriate level. The fact was he knew the truth with regard to Patrick Fingal and his work for Bletchley Park. Yes, information of a useful nature had been leaked to the Germans, but not by Patrick. That particular perpetrator had been caught. When brought to trial, he was charged and found guilty of treason. Following incarceration at Pentonville Prison, the sentence of hanging from the neck until dead was duly carried out. Yes, war was a very ugly business.

He had contrived that Beich should make the call to Berlin. He needed him to be more convinced than anyone else that she was the right person to bring into their embassy. Also, he had ensured that the last drink of the evening, which Beich had consumed, had a very mild hypnotic added to it. This mixed with all the alcohol he had taken throughout the evening had made him more malleable than normal, and slightly less interrogative.

'Herr Beich, you know this is blackmail and that you are leaving me little room for manoeuvre. However, I must keep my work at the language school. If, in the future you no longer require me to work for you then there would be no employment for me to return to at Señora Arauzo's school. Working for you full time means they must replace me. Besides, I am there to perfect various language skills for my department at home. I insist that you accept this accommodation.'

Beich's face showed he was not used to any mere mortal insisting on their own demands. That anger was becoming evident in his face was obvious.

Mortimer intervened.

'Come Christoph, let us come to an agreement. What time have you available after your work in the language school Miss Fingal?'

Anna regarded Herr Holtzman carefully. He seemed more amused by the exchange than his colleague and she sensed he was more willing to move ground to fit in with her wishes.

'Christoph, I know you have other things you wish to do. Let me complete these particular negotiations with Miss Fingal, and hopefully next week we will get full clearance from our embassy. Also the language school will have to be informed that no more time, apart from that already devoted to them, will be forthcoming.'

This response seemed to calm Beich who now waved his assent to this conclusion.

He turned to Anna and remarked, 'You know Miss Fingal, it will be interesting to get to know you within the environs of our embassy. Don't let my colleague Herr Holtzman fool you that he is a pushover. I know him to be a loyal subject to the Reich.'

Beich sneered knowingly as he said this, and he then turned and headed towards Karina and Marta whom he had just seen arriving together.

Anna knew immediately that Beich, who was very attracted to Karina, was manoeuvring to form a closer relationship. She hoped these girls would handle this man with extreme caution and not rebuff him in an obvious manner.

'As you can see Miss Fingal my colleague has such a subtle way, particularly with women. We would be glad of your coming to work at the embassy. Now, would you mind escorting me and showing me the works of art which I hear were executed by your mother? Also we can talk about your available time for working at the embassy.'

Anna was surprised at the lucidity and knowledge that Rudi Holtzman displayed with regard to her mother's paintings. He showed particular interest in one and asked Anna about it. It showed the bridge at Donaghpatrick, near Navan in County Meath.

Crossing the bridge was a wedding procession. It was a bright day as the bride walked with her father to the church. It was a family of modest means but the painting displayed beautifully the detail of a bridal dress that had known many owners which was now worn with such pride. The father of the bride walked with a stick and a debilitating walk, but not incapacitating enough to stop him escorting his daughter to the church. He may have been stooped but his head was held high. Behind them chatting and carrying their small posies of wild flowers were the two younger sisters of the bride. Their faces shone with expectations for their own futures. Off to the side stood their mother almost apart from the entire grouping, her look forlorn and unattached, adding an obvious dichotomy of feeling within the entire grouping.

'I see this painting has a story to tell. What is this woman's story?'

'Well, we know this family and they have a tragic history from the civil war at home. The mother stands out because of her own personal suffering. It was a tragedy that affected her more than anyone else in her own marital home.'

'She had only two brothers. They chose different sides during the civil war and both were killed. She felt a particular responsibility with regard to the death of the younger of the two brothers. His name was Fintan and he was only twenty-seven years old during this awful period when he chose his side. The day he was killed he had called to his sister's house for food and shelter. That is the woman you see here. She refused him entry as she totally disagreed with two brothers fighting against each other, and she was refusing to take sides. They argued quite fiercely and he left. Ten minutes later he was dead. He had walked into a patrol from the opposite side and refused to surrender. He fired his gun and was killed. The body was brought straight to his sister's house. She felt such guilt and never recovered. Only a year after this painting was completed she died a very broken woman. My mother was trying to show what this wedding day should have been for this woman, but it couldn't be. She would never know what it was to be happy again.'

'Your mother has ingeniously shown amazing insight in one painting. It's quite a feat. It shows the damage of war but in a much more clever way than normal. You must be very proud of her.'

Anna, nodded her agreement and would have responded more but just at that moment Guillermo joined them.

'Ah, Herr Holtzman, I see you are quite taken with this painting and who can blame you! The wedding party and all its nuances, the story it can tell. You know Imelda Fingal's work has become very well-known and several of her paintings have already been sold this evening. This one is a bigger canvas and commands a much higher price, but for the right person it is a gem and a price can always be negotiated?'

Inwardly Anna applauded Guillermo. She had watched him throughout the afternoon and it had to be said he was like a whirlwind in the room. His more than colourful attire, his cravat and trouser braces, displaying exotic birds of every colour. Then there was his wife Carla who quietly went about her business making sure every guest at the exhibition was supplied with drinks and hors d'oeuvre. This whole event reminded Anna that she must write home and tell her mother how well her exhibition had taken off. Just then a sudden sense of feeling homesick came upon her.

'Herr Holtzman, I will not give up on you,' said Guillermo, and taking Anna's hand he bowed to her and said he had other urgent matters to which he must attend.

Anna was left standing with the man she knew as Rudi Holtzman and for some reason she felt a connection with him. He, for his part looked at Anna and smiled. That he was very attractive was obvious to Anna but she could not allow herself to think in any way like that. He was the enemy and there was a job to be done. They got down to discussing Anna's available time for working at the embassy.

'Miss Fingal, I think this will work for my staff at the embassy. When you return to the language school on Monday you must inform them that you will also be working for us. This will ensure that your time-table is not interfered with. You will only be able to gain entry to the embassy on allocated days. As you can imagine we have very strict security and tight controls are kept on those entering and indeed those leaving the building. So, next week you must make everything clear to Señora Arauzo and the following week you will also commence your translation work for us.'

At Anna's raised eyebrow he added, 'You will be satisfactorily recompensed for your efforts.'

'Yes, but are you able to give me an inkling of what exactly this work will involve?'

His response was sterner, and he had switched to speaking in his native tongue. He had noted that Beich was now standing slightly off to one side and on his own, giving the impression of sizing up some of the art work but in reality standing within eavesdropping distance of their conversation.

'No Fraulein Fingal, such matters will not be disclosed in any more detail. Once you have commenced, then and only then, would such detail be discussed. This is necessary for security reasons and giving out such information in advance of your commencement date is not an option. All will be explained at the appropriate time.'

He then mentioned terms of payment which Anna felt was remarkably fair. In fact she would be receiving better remuneration than that which she was receiving at the language school. Anna could see that Beich had a slight sneer of approval on his face, obviously pleased with how his colleague was dealing with this Irish woman from a country he regarded as backward and unsophisticated.

It occurred to Anna that Beich's toleration of her would only go so far, but that if he wanted to get to Karina, he perhaps should not alienate her flatmate completely.

At this point Holtzman called to Beich and announced that they should take their leave of the exhibition. Clicking his heels and bowing stiffly towards Anna, he then joined his colleague and both men then left the premises.

Anna was glad that the encounter had come to an end. On the one hand she was surprised at how well he appreciated and seemed to understand her mother's work, but then his sudden change from speaking Spanish to German had alerted her to be more cautious. He was difficult to read. What she had initially thought to be a display of impatience with her, now in hindsight seemed more like an energy that he was deliberately keeping in check. A man with a mission.

Standing alone with her thoughts and a welcome glass of wine in her hand, Anna turned at the sound of her name to see Alphonse.

'You look glad to see the back of those two Anna. I have to say on the surface Beich appears to be the more dangerous of the two. His advances towards Karina are most unwelcome and I can only hope that it does not completely get out of hand. To my mind he is not the type of man to accept rejection too easily. What say you Anna?'

Anna paused before she spoke, and looked up at the suave sophistication of Alphonse.

'Yes, I agree, he makes me feel uncomfortable. He is like a trapped wounded tiger, dangerous to encounter and more than likely lethal when ready to pounce. He is not a man who would be taken in easily. Yes, both girls must be very cautious.'

'Without doubt you are correct. You look a little tired Anna, but before I escort you home we could go to a wonderful tapas bar that I know. It will hopefully give you respite for at least this evening?' Anna gratefully nodded her agreement.

They found Guillermo, thanked him for his attention, and congratulated him on the success of the viewing. Imelda's work had sold very well, and indeed there were only two of the larger canvases still available for sale.

He was delighted with the success of the exhibition. 'Anna, I will phone your mother this evening to tell her what a success she has been! I can see many more commissions coming out of this. Her style is quite unique and events of the past in Ireland mimic events here. People relate to that. You can be proud of her.'

Guillermo embraced Anna, and in a mock stern voice informed Alphonse that he take good care of her.

Without any further delay, they left the venue and strolled towards Alphonse's car.

Anna now knew that in approximately nine days she would be entering a true hornet's nest and the trick would be not to disturb it too much.

Chapter 13

It was now Tuesday 23ʳᵈ December 1942. With only two days remaining before Christmas, Anna was making her way to the German embassy. The previous week in the language school had been busy and difficult. When she told Señora Arauzo about her new position at the embassy she did not speak, but the fact that her eyebrows almost disappeared showed how surprised she was.

Marta was complacent and noted that people had to do strange things these days in order to survive and if Señora Arauzo was not raising an objection then why would she? She did however advise Anna not to mention it to any of the other staff.

The tram was very full that morning and the drifting of cigarette smoke was causing a mild haze. It always surprised Anna how just one carriage of a tram could contain so many smokers. In fact as she observed her fellow passengers she realised that she was one of the few anomalies on board; except for four people, every other passenger appeared to have a singular attachment to their cigarettes. Having used the tram for as much of the journey as she could, she descended and continued the rest of the journey on foot.

There was a persistent light rain, and the cobbled streets were becoming quite slippery because of a heavy coating of frost from the night before. Keeping her footing was difficult at times. She noticed how the beggars and homeless seemed to emerge from nowhere, and with complete silence, but fortunately for her on this particular morning she was left in peace. She occasionally had small amounts of change in her pocket and if there was only one beggar present she would slip the coins into their hand. Karina had warned her never to take her purse from her handbag and it was easy to see why. Since coming to Madrid Anna herself had witnessed three purses being snatched with incredible ease, and the escapee then usually making their way down a narrow side street where they knew no woman would follow them.

On one such occasion, a very thin boy of about fourteen years of age had made a particularly audacious move. Unfortunately for him, he was spotted by some Falange youths who were adept at dispensing their own version of justice. They did not care who witnessed the brutality they meted out, they knew no one would complain, and if they did, well there were usually repercussions. On this occasion the beating this young teenager had received was incredibly brutal. For that particular event Anna happened to be in the company of Seamus. He warned her not to interfere, or pass comment, as it would do no good.

They both witnessed the assault from the safe confines of a café, an assault that lasted some considerable time with numerous and ferocious kicks being delivered to the head, chest and more delicate areas of the pelvis. Even the woman whose purse he had stolen tried to intervene, but her charitable attempts at halting this barbaric treatment were met with contemptuous and sickening laughter. Once this pack of young men had sated their unprovoked fury, they stood grouped and laughing for about five more minutes and then slowly and nonchalantly walked away.

Someone must have got word to a local curate. A small church was embedded so discreetly into one corner of the square that one would hardly even notice it. It was however known as a church which quietly helped the homeless and dispossessed.

To the rear of the church were some old stone buildings with several dormitories. It was rumoured that there were hidden tunnels surviving from medieval days beneath these buildings. The curate was known as quite a rebel who had more than once irked the patience of his bishop. The Catholic Church supported Franco as a protector against the evils of communism, but like all institutions there was thankfully always a little cohort of those who were not quite in step or in agreement with the status quo.

Anna knew of Father Ignatius and had great respect for him. It was he who had then approached the still body of the youth who had been badly beaten. He was still alive, and silently and quietly three other figures emerged and lifted the boy, carefully carrying him between them. Then, just as silently as they had appeared, they slipped down along the side of the church.

Anna, consciously jerked herself from her reverie as she noted the German embassy gates looming before her. The outer railing had several *civiles* on duty there. Her identity card was silently surveyed and with a slight jerk of his head, assent was given for Anna to proceed. It seemed to Anna to be one of the longest walks of her life, that short distance from the gate to the front door of the embassy. She knew how much her performance had to measure up for this operation to succeed.

Through the door at last and then onto the first of a series of three further security checks. That she was expected was obvious. The first two checks went very smoothly, but at the third and final one she was asked to wait. A few minutes passed and then a woman of a similar age to Anna arrived. No introductions were made and she merely asked Anna to follow her into a back room. Her passport was taken and Anna was requested to stand still as a photographer took her photograph. Forms were filled in, and Anna noted that they asked her to confirm many items such as her address back home, her date of birth, where she went to school and university, where she lived in Madrid and with whom. She realised it was a form of interrogation, a test to see if she slipped up on any of the information they already had. This form of questioning lasted fifty minutes but in the end her interrogator appeared satisfied.

As her inquisitor finally leaned back in her chair she cast a very fierce and penetrating gaze over Anna.

'Fraulein Fingal, my name is Frau Meyor and I am responsible for the vetting of all new staff. I can't say that you are the first outsider that we have employed here but you are certainly the first Irishwoman. What I need to emphasise to you, and I suggest that you take it on board very carefully, is the level of security we operate in this building. We always check all personnel and all bags going in and out of this building, and on occasion we may request for no particular reason a more, how shall I put it, oh yes, a more personal body search. I hope we fully understand each other Fraulein Fingal?'

'Certainly Frau Meyor I understand your position perfectly. I am here as you are no doubt aware to offer my services to your country. I am pleased to have been offered the position to use my language skills.'

Frau Meyor did not reply. She abruptly pushed back her chair and ordered Anna to follow her.

As they walked down the corridor Anna could see it was a building of considerable size. They took the back stairwell to the next floor and emerged into another corridor lined with numerous doors on both sides. It was at the fourth door on the left that they stopped, and with a swift knock on the door Anna was led into a large office and asked to sit. There were three secretaries seated behind their own desks and all were intent on processing documents. The swish of the typewriter carriages, and the energy with which these girls worked was impressive. Eventually, one of the girls looked up, smiled as she spotted Anna and said, 'Are you Fraulein Fingal?' Anna stated she was, and then the young woman in question rose and said she would immediately inform Herr Beich of her arrival.

It was now or never Anna thought. If Beich were in the least bit suspicious of her, now would be the most obvious time for him to show it. Inwardly she had hoped that her first meeting would be with Holtzman, and was irritated with herself for thinking that way. Why would it be any different with him, he was also the enemy.

'Ah, Fraulein Fingal, you find us on a very busy morning so if everyone appears distracted it is because there are stringent timelines to be met. Hopefully you will have the capacity for the work here. Please walk along with me now.'

Anna followed as instructed, and Beich, pleased with the reverence that the secretarial staff had duly, and as he thought deservedly bestowed upon him, was almost cordial in his conversation with Anna. This time Beich took Anna through from the front office where the secretarial staff worked into a much bigger room. As they entered the room she noted immediately that there were four people working quietly together, three men and one woman.

Apart from this there was a supervisor who sat alone at his own desk and who was currently just finishing what on the surface appeared to be a conversation fraught with tension. As he dropped the phone receiver back into its cradle, it was obvious that the phone call in question had left this man in a very unreceptive mood.

'Beich, what the hell do you want now?'

It seemed to Anna, that Beich was enjoying the irritation being experienced by the other man.

'Herr Huber, allow me to introduce Fraulein Fingal. We have promised you for some time an interpreter of vast skills. She is fluent in Spanish, German and I believe French. That should go well for any work or translations that you need help with here. And, yes she has been cleared by security, you need have no qualms on that front.'

Anna observed a man of medium build, with fine but dark flyaway hair to the point of unruliness. She estimated him to be in his late fifties and there was indeed a strained look to his face. He was observing Anna with curiosity and undisguised relief.

'Fraulein, apologies for my abrupt manner. Our work here is very intense and our previous interpreter's skills fell very short of the mark. Our team of engineers in this room are Spanish and German. None of us are fluent in the other's language and we cannot afford to have anything misinterpreted as we work.'

Anna took a deep breath and launched herself by saying how pleased she was to meet Herr Huber and would she be correct in guessing that he was an Austrian national and not German?

Both men looked surprised and Huber responded by saying Anna had won the first point with her observation but he would like to test her language skills further.

He explained, that of the three engineers that worked in the room, two men were Spanish and the only woman amongst them was German. The issue was in accurately convoying to the Spanish engineers exactly what needed done. They were highly skilled engineers but the previous interpreter had misdirected them on several occasions and they were therefore not always working in tune with one another. This had wasted considerable time and effort before the error was noted. It would be Anna's job to accurately translate all correspondence both verbally and in written form for the engineers.

'Please Herr Huber, to satisfy your doubts why don't I translate something for you now with your two Spanish engineers?'

Huber now looked at Beich who shrugged his shoulders.

'Herr Huber, it is for this that Fraulein Fingal is here. You and Rudi know what needs done and this woman is supposedly up to the task. Test her for goodness sake and let that be an end to it. Rudi is content for you to make the decision as he cannot be here this morning.' There was almost a sneer on Beich's face as he said this.

'Thank you, Herr Beich. You may leave Fraulein Fingal with me. By lunch time I will know if we can all work together.'

Anna knew what he really meant was that by that time he would know if she was up to the job. Beich looked like he had swallowed a wasp. He did not like being dismissed like a schoolboy in front of Anna, and she was surprised that he had allowed Huber to get away with it. This man must carry quite an amount of sway.

Huber then handed Anna some German and Spanish documents and told her that she had three hours, as did the engineers, to produce the exact same drawings from her translations. She introduced herself and set her mind to the task.

Herr Huber returned to his desk and continued with his work. The three hours passed quickly and Anna felt that she had done well with her translation work. Both Spanish engineers and the German engineer expressed a great sense of relief when they heard Anna's level of fluency and one went so far as to comment, 'Thank goodness, I thought we would all have been shot after the hole that other translator left us in. If Beich had his way we probably would have been!'

There was a nod of agreement from all concerned.

At this point Huber approached their work tables and commenced his testing and appraisal of the drawings that had been completed. Each engineer had exactly reproduced what he had based the test on. He was impressed with Anna and his face visibly relaxed.

'I am impressed Fraulein, you will do very well here. Rudi was correct in his assessment of your skills. Also I can see from the faces of my fellow engineers that they also feel relieved. We have a lot to live up to here and we are not in the habit of wasting time. It is intense work. There may be occasions where you will be required to stay late for which you will be remunerated.'

Anna replied, 'I'm pleased to be here Herr Huber. Is it Herr Holtzman you are referring to when you say Rudi?'

'Yes indeed it is. He is a highly trained ballistics and armaments engineer. This small group of engineers here have some of the most talented in Europe amongst them. That is what happens in this room. Our work is for the Reich and you can now see

179

why it is so imperative that any translation work is of the highest and most accurate calibre. We are a tight team in this room. Did Herr Holtzman not tell you this?'

'No, no he did not mention that at all,' Anna responded.

So, thought Anna. Here she was transported to the lion's den. The documents were inundated with comments about wolfram ore which yielded tungsten. This was a critical material as hardened steel alloys had many military applications in steel tools, ballistics and armour piercing projectiles. She could see how incredibly important this work was to the war effort. She just wondered why she was here helping with translations for such work. This seemed madness. She was right in the middle of aiding the German war effort. Seamus had questions to answer.

As Anna puzzled over the meaning of her new position, Captain Malcolm Mortimer, alias Rudi Holtzman, was secretly arranging to meet Seamus to discuss their strategy on the afternoon of that very same day. He had spoken with Herr Huber at lunch time. Anna's arrival was very timely. The Reich had not been pleased with the delay in the drawings and the lack of cohesion among the small group of engineers in the embassy. A knowing look passed between both men.

Seamus had secreted himself to a back room on the premises of Carlos Santiago's cigar and tobacco shop. Mortimer no longer deemed it safe for them to meet too regularly in a café or any other public place for that matter. Occasionally yes, that would not be a problem as even Seamus had somehow managed to charm Beich with his 'gift of the gab' – he was quite an act when he got going.

Seamus smirked as he saw Mortimer enter the room.

'Well, you must be pleased to have Anna in situ at last. Are you going to give me a bit more insight regarding our time scale here? The less time we have to spend in Madrid the safer for us all. Besides I've been getting word via my contact that the Corpse is none too pleased as to the lack of information on the progress of this operation. He is a man who normally likes to know all the nuances and moves but he fully understands that you are in charge here.'

Malcolm shook hands with Seamus.

'Good to see you Seamus. You look strained. Is everything all right?'

Seamus could only hope that Mortimer never got wind of what he was up to. He was certain that he would probably pull a gun and tell him that it was definitely a non-starter.

He responded, 'I'm fine. We're just worried about our girl on the ground.'

Mortimer nodded. 'You can get word through to Mr Herlihy that Anna has ingratiated herself with the language school and seems to have passed the first test today in the German embassy.'

Seamus sighed. It was sometimes like pulling teeth with Mortimer. Information was on a strictly need to know basis, and he appreciated and understood that, but now his interest lay much closer to his heart.

'We know how good Anna is. What I mean is can you give me an indication as to when this team will pull out of here? You've not told me exactly what you want to achieve, and the Corpse would still like a time frame.'

Seamus hoped this blatant lie was never discovered. The Corpse merely wanted to know of Anna's progress, and not for how long she would be on the ground in Spain, and quite frankly Seamus was already able to provide any information about her progress. It was Seamus who desperately needed to know what timescale they were working within. If Sonsoles were to be rescued it would be vital to have this information in order to balance the timing for getting themselves out.

'Well, I do feel you need to know that at least. It could be within the next three weeks. There are a few elements involved here. What we have to get out, how we get it out and by what routes. It will be complicated but at the same time it needs a simple solution brought to it.'

Seamus was stunned. He had perhaps only three weeks. He had felt the breath almost leave his body. He had no realisation that it might be as soon as that. He felt a slight edge of panic rise in him and hoped that it did not show on his face.

'What's the plan then,' asked Seamus.

'It's not fully come together yet in my head. It's mostly there but I have to allow for contingency plans should anything go wrong. There is something else I want to talk to you about and that's Beich's interest in Karina.'

Seamus looked sharply at Mortimer. 'What do you mean? Apart from the fact that he's already married, we know that. He's dangerous when he does not get his own way, we know that. Frankly, I would have thought that you above all people were not here to worry about his bloody liaisons.'

Mortimer slipped the dossier he had with him across the table to Seamus.

'Read that,' he said. 'And then tell me not to be concerned.'

Without further ado Seamus did as he was bade. He couldn't believe what he was reading. This excuse for a human being would actually make a good bedfellow with Dec Buchanan. It seemed depravity came easily to them both. Nastiness of this level was not the prerogative of any one nationality. However, it was a level of nastiness that one did not often come across, and when you did, what came with it was the realisation that with such people came gigantic egos. You only needed to look at the current war raging in Europe to see the egos at play. He slowly handed the dossier back to Mortimer.

'Well, what are you going to do?'

'This needs careful managing. As you can see he goes off the rails if a woman he feels particularly attracted to rejects him. He usually fuels up on quite a bit of alcohol when he makes his move, and then the violence starts. Apart from that, and based on previous form, he becomes more paranoid, and from that I mean with regard to everyone around him. That could make our job here extremely dangerous.'

Seamus nodded his agreement. 'Do you want me to have a word with Anna so that she can at least warn Karina?'

'Yes. I think that would be wise. How soon can you arrange a meeting with her?'

'Oh, I will be seeing her sooner than you might imagine,' said Seamus. 'The Spanish have their big Christmas meal on Christmas Eve and I've been invited along with the girls to Guillermo's. Everyone believes that Anna and I are just two Irish people glad to know each other away from home; friends and nothing more. Karina's mother will also be there and that chap Alphonse who seems to have taken a shine to Anna.'

As he finished saying this, Seamus thought he detected a look of sheer annoyance on Malcolm Mortimer's face, but as soon as it appeared, it vanished. He must have imagined it.

'Right,' said Mortimer. 'We are agreed on that plan. It's time we left here. Give me ten minutes before you leave by the back entrance and enjoy your dinner tomorrow. Oh, and by the way, be particularly alert to our method of communication over the next week.'

Mortimer, without any further ado abruptly left.

'Moody so and so,' thought Seamus. 'What got on his wick?'

Chapter 14

The apartment in Calle Jardines had been a happy place for Karina and Anna over the Christmas celebrations. It was now Monday 28th December 1942 and the language school remained closed over the holiday period. Marta, unusually for her, had dropped in a lot more frequently over the holiday period, but she never stayed overnight. It was always Karina who took that opportunity when she visited at Marta's apartment. Anna thought that they were merely trying to keep what they thought was a secret under wraps, or perhaps spare her blushes. It did not bother her. They were now good friends and they had gone to a lot of trouble to make Anna feel integrated and welcome.

She thought about the Christmas Eve dinner at Guillermo's which was a great success. Señora Huerta, Guillermo's wife, was feted by her husband on the spectacular display of her table, the quality of the food and luxury over all luxuries, pink champagne! The girls squealed with delight when they saw the pink concoction with its beautiful froth being poured into the wonderful flutes that had been placed on an ample sized silver tray.

Alphonse had generously supplied the beverage in question and was thanked on all sides for his welcome contribution. Anna had used a recipe from home and baked a small traditional Christmas cake. The cake stood splendidly on Señora Huerta's beautiful old oak sideboard and was much admired. A fruit cake like this was not part of a typical Spanish Christmas.

Seamus had brought an excuse for mistletoe, and that turned out to be another tradition that had to be explained. They all laughed and Alphonse took the opportunity to gently kiss Anna as he said he would not want to be the one to renege on this fine tradition. Anna responded to a very attractive man, but she was unsure in her heart if she merely saw him as a good friend and nothing more. At the moment she could never imagine him as her lover. Something about him held her back. She only hoped Alphonse was not too deeply involved with her.

As they sat in groups after the splendid meal, Seamus tactfully manoeuvred Anna to one end of the room where he discussed what Mortimer had told him, without letting slip who Mortimer was. Anna was astounded as to the time frame, but what she had just been told about Beich made her very afraid for her friend. Should she tell Seamus the truth about Karina and Marta? She decided she must. A life, perhaps lives were at risk here.

Seamus looked at Anna and said, 'Christ Anna, you had better pray, if you believe in God you had better pray that Beich never finds out about that. Keep a careful watch and let me know immediately if his pestering starts to become more regular.'

Anna silently nodded and then asked Seamus did he know why she was aiding and abetting the German war effort.

'Ours is not to question Anna, but I do trust the man in charge. It may seem very strange to you that you are helping with these translations but there is an objective. I think its meaning will become very clear.'

Anna was keenly observing Seamus's face as he spoke. She thought he looked a little strained lately which was unusual for him. A strong man, whose physique at times gave him an air of cocky confidence. She did not see that now. He also appeared to be rubbing more frequently at the scar on the back of his hand.

'Is your scar painful Seamus? Does this cold weather set it off?'

'No, it's almost just a bad habit with me now. I do it all the time.'

Anna thought, 'Not true Seamus,' and she said, 'Something is bothering you. I've never seen you work that scar quite as frequently as you do now. What's the matter?'

'Really Anna, nothing. It's maybe just the fact that things may need to take off very quickly and we all need to be alert and on our toes. You need to tell me if you feel under threat in any way at the embassy. They in no way should be suspicious of you. Your cover is fantastic, especially from the British perspective. Come now Anna, don't read too much into everything when you have more than enough to concentrate on as it stands.'

At this point Seamus announced he had to take his leave. He would see Anna at her request or if they bumped into each other socially. The fact that Anna, in any spare time she had, did some translation services for the Irish Department of Trade in Madrid was perfect cover, and the German embassy already knew she was involved in that. He also wished her luck going back to the embassy on 29th December. Taking leave of Anna he made his way over to where Guillermo and Carla were standing, thanked them warmly for their hospitality and left waving to all as he departed.

It was late now and very cold outside. Seamus' departure was a timely reminder to everyone else that their hosts deserved the rest of the evening to themselves. Alphonse gallantly offered to drive all the girls home which he did in his 1938 Packard convertible.

It was a sleek and elegant car, mid-blue in colour with a cream canvas style hood and beautiful matching car tyres. As an import it must have cost

Alphonse a lot. He merely stated that he was extremely lucky that the club was so successful. As Alphonse also noted, it was a delight to drive. The girls laughed and teased him, as his pleasure in this beautiful classic car was obvious.

Anna concluded her reflections on her first Christmas in Spain and prepared for her work for the following day.

It was now the 29th December 1942. As she approached the embassy Anna needed to ease herself back into her true role and discard the holiday feeling that the festivities had induced in her.

Minutes later she entered the office on the second floor having passed all the security outside and on the lower level. The three secretarial staff greeted Anna as she walked through into the large back room where the engineers worked. There was a small rest room to the back of this area where all the staff could sit and take their breaks. Off to another side was a cloakroom where coats could be abandoned. It so happened that the coat rack was positioned above a large radiator and this meant their outdoor garments were in fact lovely and warm when it was time to go home and exit to the extreme cold of the Madrid winter air. The embassy was obviously not restricted where fuel supplies were concerned.

The restroom had two large windows which overlooked the garden to the rear of the embassy. It was quite large. It had some lovely trees, borders that were obviously well cared for, and a moderate sized fountain in the centre of which stood a beautiful Greek goddess who was holding an urn. It was from the overflowing urn that the water cascaded into the fountain. The walls surrounding the garden, indeed the entire embassy, were very high. Barbed wire glistened and curled its way along the entire length of those walls. Anyone attempting to scale them would encounter broken shards of glass which had been embedded as an extra deterrent. Anna hung up her coat and returned to the hub of this nucleus from which all the engineers worked.

They were all already stationed at their respective boards working at their calculations and drawings. Huber nodded towards Anna, who only then noticed another man in the room, Herr Holtzman. He appeared to be assisting one of the engineers with a mathematical problem. At this point he asked Huber to join them and after some discussion there was some clapping of shoulders and congratulations.

Looking up, Huber now called Anna over. 'You are acquainted with Herr Holtzman? We are very glad of his services here. A fresh mind adds a new dimension to our work and we have just in fact overcome what we thought might be a major obstacle. It's something we had hoped for and now it's come to fruition.'

Anna smiled at Huber, and noticed that Holtzman had not yet acknowledged her presence. He continued to discuss the drawing with one of the engineers whilst at the same time helping to finish the dimensions.

At this moment Beich entered the room, ignored everyone and went straight to his overlarge desk, in fact the only one of such a considerable size in the room. He picked up the phone on his desk and phoned through to one of the secretaries in the outer room, barking demands, and then finally slamming down the receiver. The poor girl in question almost fell into the room and scurried into his presence. His mood seemed particularly foul this morning. He wasted no time in reducing her to a quivering mess, and she wasted no time in exiting the room as quickly as possible.

Anna noticed how all the engineers had tensed but they did not intervene. It was Holtzman who spoke first as if nothing had happened.

'Well, Miss Fingal, we have quite a bit of work for you this morning. Plenty of translations to be sorted. There is some French paperwork which we managed to get our hands on. I'm afraid my skills are not quite up to it, but then that is why you are here.'

Beich looked up and added, 'Indeed Rudi, your Spanish is excellent but as you say your file agrees that French is not one of your languages. Nor English for that matter. Whereas I, you realise I speak fluent English with a perfect accent!'

What Beich said was true with regard to his fluency in English. Anna herself had heard him practice with Seamus who had indulged his notion of the perfect accent. It indeed fell short of the mark and was heavily accented.

At this point Rudi Holtzman turned to Beich and said, 'I'm glad you find my file so interesting and that you went to the trouble of doing so. Remind me to return the compliment sometime.'

The sarcasm appeared to be lost on Beich who merely grunted and smirked. He gathered up his briefcase, stuffed it with papers and marched from the room. They could hear him shouting at his secretary as he walked out into the corridor and slammed the door.

Silent looks were exchanged between the three more junior engineers but nothing was said. They were not going to indicate anything in front of Holtzman about a colleague.

At this point both Anna and Huber were requested to take a seat at Holtzman's desk.

'Otto, you hopefully are very impressed by Fraulein Fingal's skills?'

'Yes, indeed Rudi, I have no qualms at all. Indeed I think she has saved our skin. We can concentrate more easily on the job in hand now and not have to worry about inaccurate translations.'

Anna observed a slight smile on Rudi Holtzman's face, and he nodded his head before turning his attention to Anna.

'Did Otto explain that you may be required to work late here some evenings, and would that be a problem for you? You need have no worries about getting back to your apartment late in the evenings. We would arrange transport,' he added.

'I can certainly work late, and as you say transport home would be most welcome,' replied Anna.

'Good, then we all know where we stand. Otto, please take Fraulein Fingal and get whatever it is you need done today. Time is short and we don't want to keep our friends in Berlin waiting.'

There was almost a hint of praise in his voice, and a slight smile emerged.

Anna silently reminded herself not to respond too readily. She found Herr Holtzman a very attractive man. Tall, obviously fit, with an impatient manner at times. She did sense that his character was nothing like Beich's. True, he appeared a very determined man, but in a much different manner to Beich from whom sinister vibes exuded. She also noted that unlike Beich, he had no personal photographs of any type on his desk. She wondered if there was a woman in his life.

At the same time as Anna immersed herself in her work, Seamus was fulfilling another meeting with Dec Buchanan. He had delayed contacting him again about his request for more funds towards the task of freeing Sonsoles from the sanatorium in which she was incarcerated. If he was seen to return with the funds too quickly, Buchanan would certainly be suspicious. He had to pull this off and not give any intimation that his interest was of a much more personal nature.

Seamus had heard stories about 'The White Terror,' which was the name given to executions and to a regime of starvation and deprivation in prisons. His fear was that Sonsoles may also have been subjected to some of these conditions, and even if they could get her out, in what state would her mind be. His Irish colleagues in Madrid had said that it had been going on like this since 1936. He knew it was true and that the Falange were up to their necks in it.

He had now reached Calle Victoria and without delay he entered La Casa del Abuelo. It was a lovely old atmospheric bar which was opened in 1906, and it was still run by the same family. Originally it specialised in sandwiches, garlic sausages and anchovies but now it was renowned for its prawns; 'Gambas a la Plancha,' fried or grilled in their shells; 'Gambas Gabridino,' battered and sprinkled with salt. Another speciality was churros. These were twisted pieces of fried batter sprinkled with sugar as they are taken from the hot oil. In winter these churros were very popular with adults and children particularly as they were served with hot chocolate.

It was lunch time and Dec Buchanan was feasting on one of the famous prawn dishes. He was shovelling up the prawns like a man who had never seen food before. Seamus recognised the dish as 'Gambas al Ajillo'. They were cooked in boiling olive oil and infused with garlic, chilli and parsley; a hugely popular dish. Dec Buchanan had oil dripping from his chin, and cared not who noticed. He looked up and nodded his acknowledgment of Seamus' arrival but continued to eat.

Seamus sat down at the table knowing that it was a waste of time waiting to be invited. Again he reminded himself not to show any sign of impatience with this man.

Signalling the waiter, Seamus ordered some coffee, not a meal as he did not want to have to spend too long in Buchanan's presence. Just as his coffee was brought to the table, Buchanan shoved his plate aside, leaned back in his chair and lit up a cigarette. He did not offer one to Seamus.

'Well Seamus, you were a bit slow in getting back to me. What's the delay?'

Good, Seamus thought, if he's irritated by the delay he won't suspect a more personal interest.

'Come on Dec, are you joking? Christmas holidays and everything else. It's probably not easy for this woman to put this money together at such short notice. In fact I think it's even a miracle that it has already arrived.'

Buchanan with a large shrug of his shoulders and a sneer on his face replied, 'Don't be so sensitive Seamus. Aren't we all in this together, aren't we both taking risks for this woman? She's lucky I'm doing it at this price and a good one at that.' He winked with this last comment and Seamus could have easily, and in fact wanted most eagerly, to land one on him there and then.

Instead Seamus passed a small package across the table. Buchanan had the string unravelled and the money counted in less than a minute. It was the first time Seamus saw a genuine smile appear on the bastard's face.

'Well done Seamus. I told you that sisterly love would make her cough up more. They always claim that it's the last possible amount they can pay, but people need a little push in the right direction, don't they? Dig deep that's what I say. After all I'm the one taking the risks.'

'All right Dec you're a saint,' Seamus responded.

Buchanan's mood had lifted once he had counted the money and he was now much more receptive even to a quip or two from Seamus.

'Well do you know anything further? How you might be able to get her out and when? Also what is her condition like?'

Buchanan did not immediately respond as he was too busy creating and blowing small circles of smoke above his head.

'Patience Seamus. Yes, there is a plan in situ and our best time will be, believe it or not, on a Monday morning in three weeks time.' Buchanan noted the look of surprise on Seamus's face.

'I know you are thinking why not night time but it's fifty times more risky then. That place goes into total lock down. I got my hands on some plans and there are too many doors to get through. Mondays are best for several reasons. There are deaths, even suicides at the weekends and the bodies are never removed until Monday. It's also an extremely busy day for deliveries to the hospital. Everything is checked in and out through the one security area. It can get a little bit hectic on that day and papers are not checked as consistently as they normally would be on other days of the week. Also, the one insider we can avail of only works at the weekend.'

Seamus saw why Buchanan was respected or should he say treated with caution by friend and foe alike. Here was the master planner. He had obviously done his homework but there were questions he needed to ask without desperately seeming to be too involved!

'So how can you get her out, and what about this nurse, how on earth do you know you can trust her? If this goes belly up, it's one occasion where even you Dec, even you will need to be extremely worried. Remember that working relationship you said you would like with me when this is all over, well if that's going to succeed this will need to be managed extremely well.'

Dec Buchanan actually rolled his eyes and said, 'You worry too much. You're a man of the world Seamus and I can't hide from you that this won't be without its dangers. The woman in question, this patient, she is very weak. She has been interrogated and she has been mistreated on quite a regular basis. They wear them down until they admit something that can get them classified as deviant. Also malnourishment is a normal factor within these places so physically she's very weak, but if my contact is right her spirit is not yet broken which is incredible under the circumstances.'

Seamus paused before he added, 'Well, at least we know she is alive which is good news for her sister. I still don't know how you will manage to get her out?'

Buchanan now leaned in towards Seamus and lowered his voice even further.

'Look Seamus, her relative only needs to know we are getting her out. Our nurse contact just happens to be pretty nifty with the medication. Sonsoles will have to be, well how to say this, extremely heavily sedated. So sedated that it will appear as if she has stopped breathing. Our nurse will have her declared dead and have her removed to the hospital mortuary as close to 7am as possible and there are two reasons for that. Firstly, if she is removed too early to the mortuary she could die from hypothermia, it's like an ice room in there, and secondly at 7am the night staff change over with the day staff. Once the night report is handed over by our nurse, she will accompany the ambulance to the city mortuary. They get extra allowance for doing this. At the city mortuary a next of kin is declared for claiming the body for burial and someone can be put in place to do that.'

He had to admit, it was brilliant. The greatest risk would be with the medication, in the giving of it and in its wearing off. If this nurse gave too much of the cocktail then it would kill Sonsoles, and if she did not give enough the city mortuary would witness a corpse coming back from the dead! God almighty, could it work? Could it?

He drew back from these thoughts and said, 'What about the woman, has she been told what might go wrong?'

'Put it this way. She is very willing to take the gamble, she has no other choice except this one. It's this, or remain incarcerated in that hole and never see the light of day again. What would you do? I believe she is an intelligent woman and was in fact training to be a doctor before the war intervened.'

'Yes,' agreed Seamus. 'I believe you are right. If it's a choice between barely existing and living, well then there is only one choice. I have to congratulate you Dec, it's a brilliant plan.'

Dec Buchanan looked extremely pleased with the compliment smirking and shrugging it off at the same time.

They moved to finalise their conversation. Buchanan stated that once the so called body was claimed from the city mortuary, Seamus would have to arrange where the handover would take place.

As Seamus departed the café and struggled with the icy wind outside, he felt at last, hopefully, in approximately three weeks time, he would be with the only woman he had ever been truly and deeply in love. He hoped that it worked. The scene was set for Monday 18th January 1943, when he and Sonsoles should be together again. He could only hope that she had retained some semblance of her former self and that he would not be meeting with just a vacuous shell of the woman he once knew.

If events could coincide with Malcolm Mortimer's timings for getting out of Madrid then luck might be on his side. Now he needed to get back to the department where he was to meet his two Irish colleagues. There was to be a New Year's Eve party at Club Alphonse and the Irish Department of Trade and Foreign Affairs was insisting that their boys were in position to carry out some business negotiations at the venue.

Chapter 15

The language school was not starting back again until the New Year, but in the gap between Christmas and the New Year celebrations Herr Holtzman had asked Anna to work some extra days. She had agreed to do so. This was the last day that her presence was required before the New Year's Eve party and she found herself looking forward to the upcoming social event.

Anna liked Otto Huber on many levels. He was an intelligent man who spoke about his wife and family with great affection and an obvious wistfulness in the hope of seeing them sometime soon.

When Anna had first asked why his family had not come to Madrid with him, he had remained silent on the subject. However, on Thursday, as Anna and Otto were taking their break in the rest room, he confided a little more information to her. He looked less strained than he had done the previous day, and there did seem to have been some kind of breakthrough in their work with which they were all pleased.

'Anna, we are all delighted with your translation work. You know Rudi told me that you would be excellent and he was correct.' He remained silent for a moment and then continued.

'You know something Anna, none of us are what we seem.'

Anna raised a quizzical eyebrow as she tried to casually sip her passable cup of coffee, and silently wondered if he had somehow found her out.

'What I mean is that your perception of us is not who we are. I do not support the war and nor do the two more junior engineers with whom I work. We are in this awful quandary of having no control over our own fates. I lived with my family in Austria when the war broke out. They wanted to enlist me and I refused. I would have been shot as a traitor to the cause but for the fact of my engineering skills. So whilst I work here in this fractured city, my wife and family are practically under house arrest in Austria. So you see Anna, even though I have no wish to work here, the fact is I have no choice in the matter. Herr

Holtzman, who is also a gifted engineer is for the war effort and has been sent to ensure that we deliver what the Reich requires. As for Herr Beich, well he is the complete overseer. He watches everyone.'

'I'm sorry Herr Huber. This is a terrible predicament for you. Hopefully some of the burden has been lifted from you. You did all seem pleased with something a few days ago?'

'Indeed, but it took both Rudi and I to sort it together. He is a very gifted man. Anna, you must call me Otto and I will hope that you are not offended if I return the compliment?'

Anna smiled at Otto and said, 'Not at all and I'm pleased that you have chosen to break down the formalities, but I'm afraid my break time has come to an end, and I must get back to my translation work. Besides I can hear the girls from the outer office approaching and we will not be heard above the din of their voices once they arrive!'

At that Otto Huber got to his feet and stated that Anna had made a very valid point and perhaps he also should get back to his station.

As the morning wore on, Anna communicated constantly with the team in the office, clarifying items and completing correspondence that needed to go to Germany.

As lunch time drew nearer, Malcolm Mortimer entered the room and stood observing the diligent manner in which everyone in the office was working. There was, he noted, unusually for this environment, a certain amount of laughter and he could hear Otto and Anna had resorted to using first names. He could see that Anna was weaving her magic. She looked very pretty today in a red skirt and red striped blouse. Her wavy, and at times unruly hair was tied back with a colourful scarf. This accentuated her wonderful large eyes and the bone structure of her face. She was a very attractive woman.

'I see that everyone appears to be getting on well with their work,' and as he announced this four pairs of eyes turned to look at him. Not one of them had noted his entry to the room.

'Ah, Rudi you are here. I need to talk to you about a certain matter which will require us all to stay late this evening. Well, no I don't mean us all, the two junior engineers may go home. They have worked very hard and they need a break.'

The two younger engineers looked pleased at not being included.

'Anna has already agreed to this arrangement. Are you able to do so Rudi, or had you made other plans?'

'No, that's fine by me. If however you don't require my assistance this afternoon, I will be attending to something with Herr Beich, but I should be back at five-thirty. Have you arranged for some food to be dropped in this evening?'

'Unfortunately food won't be possible, but really we should be finished by seven-thirty and most of us I think can last until that time,' remarked Otto as he looked at Anna who nodded her agreement.

The rest of the afternoon moved on quickly and as five o' clock approached, the junior engineers who were obviously glad of the respite prepared to depart. As they departed, the man Anna knew as Rudi Holtzman returned. Again he had quietly entered the room. As Anna stepped back she almost collided with him, an action which caused her to lose her balance. His arms immediately enveloped her and he easily brought her to her feet again.

Anna noted that he looked quite intently at her as if he was trying to bore right through into her thoughts. She brushed aside how protected she felt within his arms. She sternly cautioned herself not to be ridiculous, to remember that he was the enemy.

Having regained her composure she apologised for her clumsiness.

'It's nothing Fraulein. Perhaps you are just tired and would prefer not to work overtime this evening?'

'No, really I'm perfectly all right. Whenever you and Herr Huber are ready then so am I,' Anna stated with a look of annoyance on her face.

She disliked being confused by her reaction to this man. Furthermore, it caused her to reflect on her previous relationships. Not one of them had raised the same level of awareness in her that this man did.

'So, let us get down to work. Otto, what is it you would like me to look over?'

As both men got down to tackling the matter in hand, Anna could see that there was obviously another stumbling block. Several lively discussions commenced as to how this particular area should be negotiated. Whilst they parried ideas with each other, Anna completed several translations. The two hours passed very quickly and it was only when Otto approached Anna's desk and said that they had hit an obstacle which would require fresher minds, and therefore it was time to call it a night. They all needed food and some rest.

They collected their hats and coats in preparation for the cold air outside. The last three nights had been very severe. Anna had heard from Karina that some homeless, destitute people had been found dead from exposure.

After passing through security they eventually found themselves at the main entrance to the embassy grounds which was guarded by the *civiles.* They always gave the Nazi salute to anyone entering or exiting the area. Anna found this particularly difficult but knew she had to comply as part of her cover.

Otto lived nearby and excused himself by saying he really needed an early night. As the following evening was Thursday 31st December 1942, and as he would not be attending the celebrations, Otto wished them both a happy new year.

A freezing fog was descending on the city and Anna was left standing alone with Malcolm.

'Come, we both need food and I know quite a nice little restaurant near here, or do you have other plans,' he asked.

Anna suddenly realised that she had hardly eaten at lunch time and therefore agreed. Their conversation was sparse as they walked the few streets to the venue in question which was a small restaurant hidden up a side street. As they went inside, the warm air from a burning log fire threw out welcoming waves of warmth.

For some stupid reason she suddenly felt tearful, and thoughts of home crept into her mind. There was little news in her mother's letters about Marion. As far as they were all aware she was still safe, but reports as to her whereabouts were mixed and could not be taken as accurate. Nothing was ever mentioned about Patrick and she knew this was as much a cautionary measure as it was an acknowledgement that there was no further news on the subject.

They were both now seated and had quickly ordered food. The restaurant was not busy as most people were keeping to their homes until the following night when the New Year would roll in.

'You look tired Fraulein Fingal. Is anything the matter?'

'You will have to excuse me Herr Holtzman but thoughts of home at this time of year seem to ingratiate themselves quite often and easily. I do love this city but there is a lot to mend here.'

'Rather like where you come from Fraulein,' Malcolm remarked.

Anna was surprised at this man's knowledge of her homeland. He spoke with obvious clarity on the subject, but she thought it unusual for a German to be so knowledgeable about Ireland.

'How is it you know so much on the subject? A lot of what you have said is true but the civil war in Ireland is not as recent as here. The point I'm trying to make is that there does seem to be continual repercussions here from its aftermath.'

Mortimer could see almost a fierce look come into this woman's eyes. She did not reveal herself often, but when she did you could sense a passion that remained well checked. Instead he replied that it was perhaps wiser and better if they did not talk politics and just enjoy the food which had now arrived to their table.

As the meal progressed Anna realised that this man had skilfully questioned her about her background and where she grew up. He reintroduced the subject of Anna's mother Imelda, and her obvious skills and collectability as an artist. She noticed that whenever she tried to enquire as to his own history that the answers were short and not very revealing at all.

The subject of the New Year's celebrations came up, and Anna admitted that she along with Karina and Marta had been invited by Alphonse to the club. They were all looking forward to it. She then asked what the embassy staff would be doing.

'To my knowledge we are also attending. Herr Beich is very keen and has already booked a table,' remarked Mortimer. He added, 'Perhaps your good friend Alphonse is making arrangements for a car to pick you all up and return you home?'

For the first time, alone in this man's company, Anna felt herself blush. Mortimer, not unaware of her reaction, interpreted it as an acknowledgement of her feelings for this man.

To cover the moment Anna asked if he were in a relationship, and he said no, there had been someone, but it had come to a natural conclusion. He added in a very joking manner which surprised Anna, 'Perhaps I'm just not lucky in love.'

At this Anna laughed outright and accused him of looking for sympathy, and Mortimer caught suddenly off his guard stated it just needed the right woman who would be honoured to pamper him. They both suddenly locked eyes and the realisation dawned on them both that they were hugely attracted to each other, but neither admitted the fact. The waiter arriving to their table broke the moment.

Malcolm Mortimer decided it was time to end the evening. As he paid for their meal, Anna thought he looked regretful for having suggested it in the first place. He no longer looked like he was enjoying his surroundings. Once *la cuenta* was sorted, the waiter was requested to order transport to take them home. When they stepped outside it was notable that the fog had lifted to quite a degree, and a beautiful moon now shone through in the Madrid night sky.

Anna gazed upwards wondering how it was that even in times of warfare, of pure ugliness, of dictatorship and unease, you could still look up at the night sky with its moon and stars, and draw a sense of calm and awe from such beauty. How easy that was to say for a person who had their liberty. For the incarcerated, the prisoner looking out over the night sky, did it give succour or just embed an even harsher reality that you would never have the opportunity to walk under its beauty as a free man again?

'Our car has arrived Anna. We must go and as you are aware the embassy does not require your services tomorrow. Besides I'm quite sure you and your friends will enjoy the anticipation of the New Year's Eve Party at Club Alphonse.'

'Thank you for the meal. It was enjoyable after such a busy day. And you are right, it will be hectic with everyone preparing for the huge event at Alphonse's. If Karina is correct there will be quite a show.'

'Well then, until tomorrow.' Whereupon he bowed to Anna, and opened the car door.

Anna mused as to why he did not share the lift as she knew his accommodation was not that far away from where she lived. Perhaps he had other arrangements he was just not prepared to discuss.

On entering the flat Anna realised she would be on her own this evening. There was a note on the kitchen table informing her that Karina was staying that night at Marta's, but they would like to meet with Anna in the morning for hot chocolate and churros.

Waking at 7.30am Anna was quite surprised at how well she had slept. She was looking forward to meeting the girls at a local café. It would distract her from thoughts of Rudi Holtzman and how he had inadvertently used her first name.

It was a cold but bright morning and as she walked towards her destination, in the distance ahead she was almost certain that it was Raquel from the language school that she could see, and she had a companion. They had just exited from a bakery and were deep in conversation. Some minutes later they took their leave of each other. Anna could see that their discussion had been quite intense, but as the man had turned and walked away in the opposite direction she was left unable to identify him. The overcoat he wore with the turned up collar and the fedora went some way to hiding his identity. Who was Raquel's companion?

Fortunately for Anna, neither of them had seen her as she had darted into the doorway of a shoe shop. Besides, with her hat pulled well down she would not have been easily recognised.

Anna was preoccupied as she continued towards her rendezvous with Karina and Marta. She could not allow them to see that she was distracted.

The premises was buzzing with activity but amazingly the girls had managed to get a window seat. Anna noted the glorious smell of the hot chocolate coming from a large silver pot already standing proud on the table. It was truly welcoming and inviting.

At a wave from Marta to the waiter, plates were brought to the table. This was shortly followed by the arrival and wonderful aroma of freshly cooked churros. There was silence for a moment as they savoured the wonderful tastes after dipping the churros into their hot drinking chocolate. Then the serious chatter about the evening ahead commenced.

'Marta, Anna, I know a wonderful hairdresser who has agreed to see us all and will perform miracles with our tresses. We are all booked in for the early afternoon, and no, you will not make any objections. My mother uses this girl a lot and it is she in fact who is treating us to this pampering session. Therefore no arguments!'

The girls laughed and held up their hands in mock surrender.

Some hours later they arrived back at Karina's apartment. The afternoon had been a welcome treat for them all. The drawing room fire was quickly lit and was soon sending welcome waves of heat throughout the lovely old room. Anna had made some tea for them all to drink prior to the car arriving. Reluctant at first to try this very British beverage, both girls had now acquired quite a liking for it.

As Marta, leaned out from the upstairs window for the umpteenth time, her call of, 'At long last, our car. He is late!'

'No Marta, he is not late. You are worse than a young teenager on her first date, calm yourself,' responded Karina, and they both smiled lovingly at each other.

On arrival to the club the car stopped directly in front of the old majestic building. A red carpet hugged the steps and a silk rope railing was provided on either side of it.

Once inside the foyer, the girls were greeted by the hostesses, presented with small beautiful posies and guided to a very well positioned table. It was evident that Alphonse had gone to a lot more effort for this special night. There were flowers festooned more widely around the dance floor, and each table had a complimentary bottle of red and white wine along with a small elegantly wrapped parcel of handmade chocolates.

The table was for six people, and Seamus and both his colleagues from his department were already there and seated. They rose and greeted the girls warmly as they arrived. Seamus knowing that Karina and Marta were in a relationship had warned his colleagues that the girls' hearts lay elsewhere so they were not to push their luck.

They lost no time in asking the girls up to dance as the music was already in full flow and the dance floor was bustling with many eager couples. As Anna danced with Seamus she wondered if she should inform him about seeing Raquel with an as yet unknown companion, but then decided against it. Tonight was for enjoyment.

Anna had noted that Herr Beich was holding court at one of the largest tables, and as the evening progressed they could hear his raucous laughter become louder, and his demands to the waiters became more strident. He was making frequent sorties to the gaming tables where his luck appeared to be holding. His poor mistress, who looked quite elegant, seemed fraught, and Anna did not blame her.

In about ten minutes the New Year would be rung in, and it was at this moment that a very drunken Beich approached their table demanding that Karina should dance with him. He was sweating profusely in his tuxedo and looked like a man who would not take no for an answer. Seamus leaned over and whispered to Karina.

'You can refuse him. He is behaving like the bully he is.'

Karina glanced at Marta who looked tense and worried, but she turned to Beich and allowed him to lead her onto the dance floor.

'Seamus, if we do anything we will bring his wrath down on top of us all and it could jeopardise our operation here. Karina is struggling with him as they dance and he is holding her far too tightly.' As Anna stated this Alphonse joined their table.

'I don't like this, his temper is notorious and I don't think I've ever seen him quite this drunk before. Marta, this is distressing, go backstage and prepare for your number. I promise you that I will not let anything happen to Karina,' said Alphonse.

At this, Marta who did look upset but was doing her utmost to hide her feelings, left them. Alphonse had signalled to the band leader to shorten the number. Beich was so drunk he would not notice. A few chords later and the dance ended. Karina was obviously having problems detaching herself from Beich, and Seamus stood to intervene. But another man, unnoticed by them, had approached the struggling couple first. It was Rudi Holtzman. Beich's face was purple with fury, but whatever the other man had said seemed to work. He marched from the dance floor and headed over to the cocktail bar to order another drink, and it was Holtzman who led Karina back to her table.

As he bowed to Karina he said, 'My apologies Fraulein. My colleague as you can see has imbibed too much and his behaviour is unacceptable. I can only hope he has not completely ruined your evening.'

'Well, well,' said Seamus. 'You have just made yourself a very dangerous enemy.'

Looking at Seamus and acknowledging Anna, he replied with a smirk, 'Thank you for your concern for my welfare Mr Halpin, but I can more than take care of myself. It is regretful what happened but fortunately not too many people noticed.' At which juncture he turned on his heel and rejoined his embassy table.

Karina was now visibly trembling. Seamus put his jacket over her shoulders and hugged her. It was at this point that the band struck up to welcome the New Year. Balloons billowed from craftily concealed nets on the high ceiling and voices joined together to proclaim a hopefully brighter and kinder new year.

At that moment Karina saw Marta standing at the entrance to the performance area of the floor, and throwing caution to the wind, she ran to Marta and flung her arms around her shoulders as she sobbed. As Anna turned to see if she could offer assistance, she noticed Beich. He was now nursing and imbibing a large cocktail, and he had a clear view as he observed the moment when Karina had run from the table and across the floor to where Marta stood.

Anna grabbed Seamus's shoulder and whispered, 'Look Seamus he knows. Look at his face!'

Beich's face was a revelation in showing a display of first disgust, then anger, and finally the realisation of what he was witnessing. But the worst moment was when he smiled, so repugnant in its intensity. Anna could only compare it to a vengeful poisonous snake with the intent of grave malice.

Alphonse had also noticed and turning to Seamus he said, 'Look I will arrange for my car to be brought around now. Anna please get Karina to the changing room and I will ensure that Marta goes on and performs her number. It's her only performance this evening, but the moment it is finished be ready to exit from the side door of the club. Seamus, do you mind seeing the girls home?'

A silent affirmative response from Seamus was given.

'Look Seamus, don't say goodnight to your colleagues. The quieter we do this, and with the least fuss, the better it will be for everyone.'

'I agree,' said Seamus. 'Hopefully, once Beich recovers from his state of drunkenness he will think his memory has played tricks on him.'

'I know you're trying to make us feel better Seamus, but I have a very bad feeling about this. Very bad,' replied Anna.

Chapter 16

It was now Monday 4th January 1943 and there
was so much to think about since the drama of the
New Year's Eve party. Anna's thoughts returned to
these events as she cycled to the language school
which had now reopened after the festivities.

It had been so dreadful for Karina who of course
and understandably had stayed at Marta's house
that night. In fact she did not return to the
apartment until the Sunday evening. She appeared
to be her normal composed self, however, she made
it clear that she did not wish to speak about it. When
Anna had asked if she had said anything to her
mother, Karina responded no, that her relationship
with Marta was not something to which she could
admit. At this point she looked sternly at Anna and
asked, 'And you Anna, how do you feel about me
now?'

Anna smiled, 'You know something Karina. I feel
exactly the same way now as the day we first met,'
and she hugged Karina and affirmed their

friendship. There were tears in Karina's eyes as she thanked Anna for not judging her.

Entering into the busy reception area of the language school, the porter took Anna's bicycle and stored it for her until such time as she would require it for going back to the apartment. It was a bonus to know it was safe as anything left on the street was silently spirited away by those a lot less fortunate.

With many people milling around, eagerly anticipating their language classes recommencing, the hall and stairs areas were a hive of activity, but Anna quickly made out Raquel as she descended the stairs and headed for the staff rest room. Now would be a good time to carry out some detective work of her own. There were at least twenty minutes before the bell would ring to announce the start of the first class, and Raquel was taking the opportunity to imbibe a cup of coffee and secrete a few biscuits from the cupboard.

'Oh, good morning Raquel. Happy New Year! I hope you had a pleasant holiday break. Did you attend any parties during the festivities?'

Raquel for once appeared receptive to Anna's questions.

'Yes, my mother has relatives here and they were kind enough to include me in the celebrations,' she replied.

'Well that is good. It must be lonely for you as it is for me on occasions. Have you a boyfriend, or friends with whom you can go dancing or indeed go with to a jazz club?'

Raquel was still receptive to Anna's questions.

'I have some cousins and they include me on occasions, but no, as yet no boyfriend. Besides I am here to teach and learn. Men can sometimes want too much of your time if you get my meaning?'

At this juncture Anna noticed the old sly coyness descend over Raquel's face. She noted that she could be quite pretty when she was not thinking nasty negative thoughts about someone.

Keeping her tone light, she asked, 'Well, what about New Year's Eve? Did you go out and about then with your cousins?'

'No, I stayed at home all day but joined the celebrations that evening.'

With that response Anna knew that Raquel must be working for someone else who had no connection with the language school. She now knew for certain that it was her she had seen outside the bakery that day, and the added proof was the coat and hat that Raquel had thrown over the arm of one of the sturdy chairs in the staff room. It was the self-same coat and hat. A blue fitted coat with black turn up sleeves, and the hat, also black, had a small brim which was pinned back with a sea-horse brooch. This on its own was distinctive and for Anna it more than confirmed that Raquel was lying and that she had met with someone that she was now unwilling to mention.

It was also interesting that Raquel did not bother to return any questions to Anna as to what she had been doing over the holiday period. The only conclusions that Anna could draw from this was that she already knew the answers, or she did not care.

At this point the bell rang announcing five minutes to class start time. They both left the room together and headed their separate ways to different classrooms.

Meanwhile Seamus had plans of his own. He had to find a safe hiding place for Sonsoles once she was freed from the hospital; and from his previous sojourn in Madrid he knew the perfect location. He just had to ensure that the curate in question would return the favours that Seamus had completed for him.

The man in question was Father Ignatius whom he had last seen when he and Anna had both witnessed the brutal beating of a young vagrant thief. Seamus had not disclosed to Anna that he already knew the cleric and the secrets of the small labyrinth of crypts beneath the church of Santa Cruz. He was now about to meet him following a funeral Mass for one of his recently departed flock.

It was just after two o' clock in the afternoon, and as Seamus entered the church he immediately took in the smell of incense. A young altar boy was tidying up like a busy bee and Father Ignatius was merrily complaining about the lack of funds for the church that were not forthcoming for repairs. His boundless energy was amazing. It was as he turned for the umpteenth time to point out yet another area of the roof that required repairs that he noticed Seamus who was leaning against a pillar towards the back of the church.

'My good friend, my good friend, how are you? Your absence has been keenly felt.' All said as Father Ignatius descended upon Seamus, embracing him, then slapping him on his shoulders.

He looked sharply at Seamus and then regarded him quietly before saying, 'You have returned for a favour Seamus. I know that look. I've seen it on many faces both during and since the civil war. Your face has not changed but your eyes tell a different story. Is this about Sonsoles?' Whereupon Seamus merely nodded and his friend the curate noted it was time for confessions.

Back at the German embassy Malcolm Mortimer was also planning his move. The time would soon come for Seamus to be informed of the 'package' in question that somehow had to find its way out of Madrid, and eventually out of Spain to Britain. The timing of when to inform Anna of his own cover would need to be carefully considered. Firstly, he needed to meet with Seamus and he was hoping to do so on Wednesday evening at a reception at the Hotel Ritz Madrid. There would be numerous consulate and embassy employees there on behalf of their respective governments. Many industries and trades would be represented, and in fact there would be numerous journalists from various European countries. This reception was being hosted by the Spanish leadership to boost economic links and trade with various countries. Economically Spain was in a mire out of which it must elevate itself.

The Hotel Ritz Madrid was iconic, a glorious landmark building. The official opening was performed by King Alphonse XIII at the turn of the twentieth century. It was built as a rival to the Ritz Hotels of London and Paris. Its central location between the Retiro Park, the Teatro de la Zarzuela, and the private garden facing the Prado Museum made it a monumental success. It was the place to be seen in by anyone who felt a need to be noticed. Its amazing sculptures, architecture, paintings and total approach to every idiosyncrasy of its valued guests was what made it an institution. For the coming reception every government official worth his salt would be there at his own behest or as a direct order from a superior.

Unfortunately for Malcolm he would have Beich in tow at the event. There was no choice in the matter.

He ruminated on just how dangerous this man might become. His temper had certainly not improved much since the events of the New Year's Eve party, nor his impatience with Otto Huber. His staunch opinion was that Otto should have had a more significant breakthrough by now for the German cause and his patience was noticeably wearing thin.

Malcolm also noted how he always kept a gun close to hand. But he had to keep his own thoughts on track and not allow himself to be distracted from his own plan which had been approved by London. Nevertheless, his thoughts turned to Anna and the fact that she would be returning to work in the embassy tomorrow, and he was rather looking forward to that.

As Anna finished her classes for the day, she felt that she had achieved a lot with her various groups. Some of the younger pupils had remained behind. They wished to question Anna further on some nuances with which they had not quite got to grips. She enjoyed these occasions as they allowed her to get to know each individual a little better. They in turn were always offering little bits of advice to Anna about where to eat, and which jazz clubs were fashionable at the moment. More important for a stylish woman in Madrid was where to find a really good seamstress, one who could perform miracles with your older dresses, or indeed make one from scratch at a reasonable price. Anna had taken up their advice and to her delight she found an amazing woman who could do just that.

Gathering her books, Anna called out her various farewells, and on leaving the lobby area to reclaim her bicycle she found Alphonse waiting outside with his car. He immediately jumped out and invited her to a small soiree at Guillermo's which was due to start very soon.

'How well you are looking Anna. I thought you might enjoy a reprieve from your apartment and anyway you know what first days back at work are like? Everyone hates them!'

'Alphonse what makes you think I can just jump into that car and while away the evening with you and Guillermo,' she quipped. But she knew full well that she was extremely keen to see how successfully her mother's paintings had been received.

Reading her thoughts Alphonse replied, 'Come Anna, is your curiosity not roused as to the sales of your mother's work? Ah, yes I see it is, and you are only teasing me. Jump aboard you mischievous young lady and I will spirit you away in my horse and carriage without delay. Your bicycle is not a problem and you can collect it when you are next working at the college.' Holding the car door open he bowed to Anna, who could only laugh in appreciation at Alphonse's flamboyant mood.

When they arrived, it was Guillermo's wife, Carla, who greeted them.

'Welcome Anna,' and kissing her on the cheek she beckoned her further into the gallery to see the latest exhibition.

'You see that we have only one of your mother's paintings left? She has made her mark here. Even the larger ones were very popular, in fact they sold out ahead of the smaller canvases. Your mother, she must be very pleased. Guillermo is adamant that he will approach her for more commissions.'

Anna could not remember seeing Carla so enthusiastic about anything. She had always just seemed to blend into the background in her muted clothes which were in sharp contrast to the extravagant ensembles that Guillermo favoured.

The only painting by Anna's mother that remained on display was of a small group of three young girls standing together under the famous clock of Clerys Department Store in Dublin.

This had over the years become a famous rendezvous and landmark for people meeting up in Dublin. Their faces shone with the excitement and anticipation of 'The Day Trip,' as the painting was titled. The scene brought a small lump to Anna's throat. She had such wonderful fond memories of this famous emporium, an institution which she hoped would last for many years to come.

'I'm delighted for you both that it has been such a success. I see that my own favourite has obviously been claimed and hopefully it has gone to a good home? I mean the painting of the wedding,' said Anna.

Arriving just at that moment and overhearing the end of this conversation, Guillermo announced that that particular work had drawn keen interest from several parties, and he hoped that the new owner appreciated its worth.

'Now Anna, I leave you in Alphonse's safe care. Enjoy our latest exhibition even though it is very divergent in taste and much more abstract, but you know I think you have an open mind and will like it,' stated their host.

As they mingled Anna observed that it was a smaller gathering of guests as opposed to the evening that she had previously attended.

Alphonse was very attentive and introduced Anna to several small groups, announcing her connection to the well-known artist Imelda Fingal. This was an easy ice-breaker as Alphonse knew it would be, and it was not lost on the many guests how smitten Alphonse appeared to be with this girl.

At 9.30pm the buffet supper had almost ended when Anna decided that it really was time to get back to the apartment. Settled into the comfort of Alphonse's car her thoughts drifted to what a wonderful companion and host he was, but why was it something always held her back? A nagging doubt that made her cautious.

'What are you thinking Anna? Hopefully something about me for you must be aware that I have very strong feelings for you? You must be honest with me. I am a man of the world and I realise you are a very independent woman, but even independent women need to plan for the future. What do you say Anna?'

Anna looked at this caring and successful man and said, 'Any girl would be delighted to be in your company Alphonse. But I don't want to say something that I will later regret. What I feel for you is great friendship but I cannot say it is the true love that you are looking for although there are many that would say from friendship comes great love. I have no wish to disappoint you, and for that reason I cannot commit to a deeper relationship with you. I hope we can continue to be friends?'

'Anna, you have been honest with me and I also truly value your friendship. I have no wish to coerce you into a relationship that you don't feel right about. But I do note that you have not dismissed me totally out of hand which gives me some hope.'

At that moment they drew to a stop outside Anna's apartment. He turned to Anna and taking hold of her hand, he asked, 'Anna, is there hope for us?'

'There is always hope Alphonse. You are a very attractive man and I believe quite a few girls would give their eye teeth to be in your company. Can we leave it at that for now and not rush anything?'

Leaning over to Anna, he gently held her chin and planted a small kiss on her lips. They both looked at each other and smiled. He then alighted from the car, assisted Anna in getting out, and then seeing her safely into the building his parting comment was, 'I live in hope Anna. Sweet dreams.'

For some minutes after Alphonse left, Anna remained leaning against the wall in the hallway. Why was life so complicated? Here was a wonderful man ready to do anything for her, and although she admired him, enjoyed his company and found him attractive as a man, she knew in her heart that something held her back. Was that one defining spark just not there? Why on earth was she more attracted to Rudi Holtzman, her enemy, perhaps even her nemesis?

Shaking these thoughts aside, Anna went upstairs to the apartment with the intention of getting some papers corrected. She could see that Karina had already gone to bed and without any further delay she dealt with the work in hand. It was well after midnight before she settled into her bed.

The next day at the embassy was hectic. Quite a bit of work had obviously piled up over the holiday period. Otto kept everyone busy but also insisted on breaks being taken.

Anna found herself admiring his intelligence, diligence and concern. She hated what war did to

244

people by casting them against each other. How the hatred, greed and power of a few men could turn Europe into such an inferno. Everyone had said that the carnage and slaughter of the Great War would be the war to end all wars, but to no avail. Did the world never learn from its own experiences and that winners and losers were terms that were mostly meaningless under the clouds of utter despair that were left behind? How and why did human beings allow themselves to be lulled, fooled and beguiled by their own leaders?

Lunch time arrived and went and as Anna returned from the staff room she noticed Rudi Holtzman in conversation with Otto. She was surprised at how she had missed his presence and reflected on the fact that she had enjoyed his company the evening they had dinner together Otto called to her.

'Come here Anna, a moment of your time. Would you please clarify some translations here for us with regards to these engineering instructions which are in Spanish? Rudi's grasp of Spanish is excellent but I think your expertise is called for on this occasion.'

Smiling at both men Anna responded, 'Of course Otto, leave it with me.'

'I will stay with you Fraulein Fingal as there are some areas that are confusing,' added Rudi Holtzman.

So, thought Anna, we are back to formality again, but as this very thought went through her mind, she believed that perhaps this was better within the working environment of the office. She noted that although he had addressed her formally, he had smiled and was not otherwise behaving in a distant manner.

They worked at his desk at the furthest end of the room away from the other engineers, and they were almost finished when Beich thundered into the room. It even startled Otto who was normally unflappable.

On the plus side Beich's mood was not as foul as it had been on more recent occasions. He approached their desk, and ignoring Anna, he spoke to Rudi.

'Tomorrow night we have the reception at the Hotel Ritz and we cannot be outshone by any of the other embassies. You must go Rudi, but it's important to remember that we liaise closely with the Spanish government. You know how much the Fatherland wants this. We must of course bear in mind reports we have been receiving about our troops on the eastern front. There are concerns there. We are aware that the Red Army has surrounded twenty-two German divisions in Stalingrad. We must continue to entice Franco with promises. Our U-boats continue to be refuelled in Spanish bases, radar is of course vital and we continue to receive safe locations for our agents to operate freely on Spanish soil. None of this can be ignored. We need to keep all channels open in order to also avail of the export of valuable raw material.'

Malcolm Mortimer was somewhat astounded at Beich announcing so much in front of Anna. He could only think that of late his alcohol consumption was more excessive and this was resulting in a somewhat less discreet Beich.

His reply showed his caution and mock anger.

'Perhaps Herr Beich we should continue this conversation in your private office?'

247

With a nod of agreement from Beich both men left the room.

Anna had also been amazed at this monologue. She was learning little from the Spanish press which was very pro Axis. Seamus if he knew some of this information was not telling her, but she correctly sensed that they were both very much in the dark where that knowledge was concerned.

Meanwhile in Beich's office, Malcolm Mortimer wondered what the hell was wrong with Beich. He did not actually seem overly concerned about the current problems that the Reich and army were facing. He seemed much more excited about something else.

'Herr Beich, I think we need to be more careful about what we speak of in front of Fraulein Fingal.'

'Nonsense Rudi. She has full clearance and her little brain can probably not get round what I was saying.' As he stated this his mood changed and he glared at the other man.

'You engineers have no end of excuses for delays in your work. The Fuhrer's secret weapons must not be delayed. The development of new rockets and aircraft are essential to our cause. Long range means long range. So why the delays?' This was all stated as he now looked menacingly at Malcolm.

'We're doing our very best with the rockets. We have already overcome many problems but there is one rather annoying obstacle. We feel we are close to a breakthrough and you must recognise that in Otto Huber we have a brilliant mind.'

'Rudi, I'm telling you now no more delays will be tolerated. I cannot speak for the safety of Herr Huber's family if we don't have results soon. I hope you understand me fully?'

With a wave of his fat hand and as he leaned against the bureau blowing circles of smoke up into the air, he added, 'You must cajole him along. You get the best out of him. If I threaten him about his family he will underperform, and we don't want that, do we Rudi.'

This was a statement and not a question. Beich then looked at Malcolm and said, 'Time is running out for a few people here. You know what you have to do, results or else. I can't spell it out any more clearly than that.' As he had said this he glared at Malcolm in a most vindictive and nasty manner.

Not wishing to appear cowed, or on the other hand brazen, in front of this dangerous man, Malcolm responded, 'I'll do my best to fulfil your wishes Herr Beich.' He then turned on his heel and left the room.

He had to keep calm. He knew Beich was now fingering him for that New Year's Eve debacle, or embarrassment as Beich would interpret that evening in Alphonse's night club. Beich had been made to look a fool in front of embassy staff and indeed in front of anyone of any importance in Madrid. Seamus had been correct. His actions that night had turned Beich against him.

It was more essential than ever to have a solid plan ready and in place. In fact almost everything was already in place. What the meeting with Beich had just taught him was how much more imperative it had all become to put the plan in motion. Hopefully nothing else of note could upset this.

As he returned to the engineer's room, he appeared on the surface to be very calm. Now that Anna had cleared up a few misunderstandings with regards to some translations, he resumed his work with Otto.

It was now late afternoon and almost four o'clock. It was starting to snow outside. The younger engineers moaned as they all knew that with the ground so dry this snow would settle and not melt away. By six o'clock the landscape outside was already transforming itself into a totally different image.

Exiting the building and rushing for the tram, Anna thought how cleansing the effect that the snow gave to the city. Shop fronts looked more inviting, the lighting from the streets lamps cast a mock glow of security and comfort, almost beguiling one into the belief that all was well in this city. But no, it wasn't. There were still atrocities being carried out that no amount of snow could ever whitewash. Strain showed on the faces of weary workers who had jobs but were scared of losing them. There was very little security where employment was concerned and very few rights for the common man on the street.

Anna was descending from the tram when she heard her name being called. It was Marta whom she had not seen since the incident on New Year's Eve. Her friend looked tired.

'Anna, have you a moment? I wish to speak to you about Karina. Do you mind if we go to this café for a quick coffee and before this snow gets too settled on the ground?'

'Of course not Marta. A hot chocolate is what I would really like as quite frankly my hands are freezing despite my wearing gloves,' replied Anna.

As they entered the café, they noticed a few stragglers. Three school girls were productively finishing their homework. The café owner was used to them and their occasional loud chatter. They waited two evenings a week after school for their lift home and had enjoyed their own treat of hot chocolate.

Marta signalled to the owner and gave their order only to be told that unfortunately the school girls had consumed the last of the chocolate, however coffee was still an option. Marta and Anna both nodded their agreement.

Anna regarded Marta closely and thought how pale and drawn she looked.

'Marta, is something troubling you? You seem anxious about something?'

'You know something Anna? I believed more than anyone that what Karina and I meant to each other was a well-kept secret amongst a few close friends. I include you when I say that Anna, and I know from Karina that you do not judge us. However, there are others that do, and I'm frightened for us both now because of what happened that night.'

'But what's different Marta? It's true as you say that very few people know of your relationship so why do you now feel more concerned than usual?'

Marta appeared to tense even more as she said, 'I know I'm being followed.'

She looked intently at Anna to see how she reacted to this information.

'Since the new year, as I've gone about my business, I've sensed on several occasions that I'm being followed. I'm not imagining it Anna. I can see the doubt on your face but it's true.'

'Marta, I don't doubt that you are worried but perhaps you are a bit oversensitive since that evening. Have you seen anyone or is it just a feeling?'

'It's little things. On two occasions on my return to my apartment I noticed a man standing on the opposite side of the street, in the shadows, carefully avoiding any street lighting and therefore not illuminated enough for me to recognise him. Another time I'm certain I was being followed by a woman. The footsteps were a lot lighter than a man's. You know what the streets are like Anna? When they are quiet you can tell the difference between a man's footsteps and a woman's. They seem to be watching and checking my routine.'

Anna was convinced that Marta was not imagining things and she asked, 'What precautions are you taking? Is the street very quiet when you make your way home, or are there other people about?'

'In this atmosphere Anna no one hangs about or delays too long. Besides the weather is so cold that people want to get home as quickly as possible. However, the streets are busy enough at that time and that gives me a bit of comfort.'

On the one hand Anna did not want to add anything that would weigh more heavily on Marta's mind but she felt she had to ask, 'What about Karina? Has she stated anything similar to you?'

'Nothing. She appears unworried and I do not want to burden her with my thoughts. There is something else.'

Marta was now visibly upset and found it difficult to go on. Anna waited and allowed her to compose herself. Fortunately their coffees had already been delivered to their table and Marta was sitting with her back to the rest of the room. The three school girls, as the only other occupants of the café, apart from the owner, had been more interested in getting their homework finished. Added to this, their driver had just arrived to take them home. The noise they made was a welcome distraction and gave Marta an opportunity to gather her thoughts.

'Anna, someone has been in the apartment. I swear to you that there was the lingering scent of a perfume that I know neither Karina nor I use. No one else has a key. I asked the landlady if she had been doing any checks and she said no. She had only done a check the week before Christmas and she was happy with how all her tenants were caring for their apartments.'

A horrible silence hung between them. After some moments Anna spoke, 'Have you any idea who it might be?'

'Yes, I have ideas but even I don't want to admit it to myself,' responded Marta

'What do you mean? Can you not tell me? What about Alphonse, you could confide in him. He has always been discreet and concerned for you both. He may know what to do.'

This thought seemed to settle Marta somewhat and as she leaned back in her chair she said, 'You are right Anna. I'm not thinking clearly and yes, Alphonse might be able to guide me in this matter.'

'Good. Please contact him as soon as possible. Would it not be best for you if you were to spend a few nights with us in our apartment?'

Marta hesitated before replying, and Anna could see that the offer was tempting to her, but then she said, 'No Anna. The arrangement has always been that I never go to Karina's apartment. It's just that, well occasionally, as you know, Señora Arauzo does sometimes drop by the apartment to have a chat with Karina. They are very close and Karina enjoys the independence that the apartment offers, and frankly, she does not want her mother to know about us. It is the same for me. I could never admit our relationship to my family.'

Anna nodded her understanding and Marta thanked her for listening to her mad ravings. They parted a short time later as both agreed that for Marta's sake it was best for her not to delay the return to her apartment at too late a time.

As Anna completed the walk back to her accommodation, she mused uneasily about what Marta had confided. Marta was not highly strung or given to outrageous comments. Neither of them had spoken about what the other had truly thought, and that was the likelihood of Beich having a grotesque hand in the matter. She needed to talk to Seamus and confide her concerns.

Tomorrow evening loomed with the forthcoming evening of enterprise. Guillermo was taking an exhibition stand at the Hotel Ritz and he was beside himself with excitement. He had implored Anna to attend as a translator for the evening. Many people spoke English but Guillermo was by no means fluent enough to deal in multiple languages. Besides he thought the possibility of launching himself on the international art scene was more likely if he had someone of Anna's translating talents in tow. Moreover he would only be delighted to pay for her professional time.

As she was settling down for the evening, Anna acknowledged that tomorrow night would be a welcome distraction. There were her classes to take in the morning, but apart from that she had the afternoon to prepare for the events ahead.

Chapter 17

The day for the Hotel Ritz Madrid event had quickly arrived. It was Wednesday the 6th January 1943. As the evening ahead grew closer, Anna mused that it would give a perfect opportunity to mingle without drawing any untoward attention to herself, or to others. She knew Seamus would be attending so contact with him was inevitable, but she wondered how he would react to her concerns for Marta. He would probably remark, as he sometimes did, that they needed to keep to their game plan whatever that was going to be.

It was the one aspect of her role that she disliked, and that was being constantly kept in the dark about the details of their mission. She did accept that it was for security reasons and that above all it was personal safety that was of the utmost concern.

Putting the final touches to her ensemble for the evening and gathering up her warm coat, Anna was pleased with the end result. Her skin glowed and her new dress made by a young artisan who had her own workshop was amazing. At home this dress would have passed for haute couture. One of Anna's older students had recommended Yaiza and she had to admit that she was a gifted young designer with an extraordinary talent which would not remain secret for much longer.

Confirmation that she had heard the arrival of a car outside was followed shortly by the sound of the doorbell. Anna descended from the first floor to be heartily greeted by Guillermo. He was ebullient and nervous with excitement and talked non-stop on their journey to the Ritz Madrid. As they alighted from the car, Anna had to admire the glorious edifice before her. This hotel had an amazing location and was famous for the guests that had passed through its doors over the years.

As they entered the foyer they could hear the orchestra playing 'Concierto de Aranjuez' by the spectacular Spanish composer Joaquín Rodrigo. Although politically neutral himself, the traditional yet colourful conservatism of his work had endeared him to the ruling Nationalist regime. Anna loved his music as it evoked tapestries of life in eighteenth century Spain.

Guillermo was now very aware of his environment as he noticed for the first time the interested faces of the assembled guests as he made his way through the foyer with Anna on his arm. He realised that Anna looked particularly lovely this evening and she was wearing what looked to be a very expensive dress, and that the glances being shot in their direction were all due to her presence. He chuckled silently to himself and realised that apart from the artwork he would be exhibiting at his stand this evening, that another draw would be Anna. Her obvious foreign pale colouring stood out, and he counted his blessings that Imelda Fingal and her lovely daughter had dropped into his life. Yes, he was very pleased.

The waiters and staff had been well tutored earlier that day by their manager as to what an important event this evening was for trade between Spain and the rest of the world, even if trade was somewhat curtailed by the war. As for the staff, they were all only too pleased to do everything they could.

Employment was difficult and managers could be fickle in their favourites.

Having just been served glasses of pink champagne, Anna spotted Seamus who was moving through the gathered contingent with his Irish colleagues, hailing and greeting people he already knew. He gave a nod in Anna's direction and a quick sign that he would catch up with her later.

At this moment Guillermo guided Anna towards a small group of people. As they neared the group he explained that they were Italian clients who had already procured two works of art by Imelda Fingal. Introductions were made in Spanish and the small party were delighted to meet Anna. They expressed an interest in more personal commissions from her mother.

A group of local reporters and photographers approached their group and requested an interview. All were happy to oblige. Guillermo was in heaven with all this publicity. It was at this moment that Anna observed that there was also quite an international presence of reporters and that some were extremely loud in making their presence known.

She then noticed Seamus. She was about to make her way over to him when she realised that the man he was speaking to was Rudi Holtzman. Their conversation seemed somewhat strained and intense. Seamus spotted Anna and beckoned her over.

'Anna, you lovely rascal. What a dress! Obviously Herr Holtzman is paying you very well for your services,' he remarked with a twinkle in his eye.

Malcolm Mortimer had observed Anna for some time after entering the foyer of the hotel. He now admitted to himself that he was very attracted to her, and how she looked this evening was yet another revelation. Unlike other women he had known, who knew they had beautiful figures and the clothes to match, Anna never gave an impression of being as aware of such things, and that was what he felt made her all the more attractive. She looked stunning in that dress.

At that very moment, amongst all the noise in the room, a voice which appeared to be drawing nearer, was calling out someone's name.

'Malcolm Mortimer, above all people is that you?' They could see a woman who was struggling to make her way through the now large gathering.

The man Anna knew as Rudi Holtzman froze.

'Who the hell is that woman,' asked Seamus.

'Good grief Seamus, it's an ex of mine. Her name is Evelyn Sinclair. She must be here with the press corps. Do something or we are dead here and now,' uttered Malcolm.

Seamus grabbed Anna who was trying not to look bemused. 'Anna, I'll explain later but right now we have got to pull off the greatest act of our lives or we are dead.'

With only yards to spare, Evelyn Sinclair was almost upon them when Seamus walked directly into her path. He grabbed her in his arms and said, 'Evelyn you gorgeous bird and what the hell are you doing here?' Whereupon he added for all to hear, 'You were always hopeless with names and may I remind you right now it's not good for a man's ego to have his name forgotten, and by the way darling, it's Seamus.'

Whereupon Seamus kissed Evelyn Sinclair for all and sundry to see. Hugging the somewhat taken aback but amused journalist, Seamus quickly explained in low tones just what a dangerous moment was upon them.

As he glanced sideways he almost froze himself, because there standing within feet of them was Beich. He was staring in their direction and had obviously heard some of the exchange, but how much? Had he heard Evelyn Sinclair call out Malcolm Mortimer's name and had he seen at whom it was directed? Hopefully he was true to his usual form lately and had too many drinks on board.

Remarkably Evelyn Sinclair pulled off the moment and allowed Seamus to keep holding her. Guiding her towards Mortimer and Anna, he continued a flow of absolute verbal tosh to cover up their dilemma as best as possible, whilst at the same time displaying an appearance of delight at seeing an old girlfriend.

'Herr Holtzman, Anna, allow me to introduce an old friend of mine, Evelyn Sinclair. Our friend, Herr Holtzman, is attached to the German embassy here in Madrid and Anna apart from being an Irish colleague, she teaches here in a well-established language school as well as carrying out translation work for Herr Holtzman at the embassy.'

Seamus noted that while the introductions were being made, Christoph Beich continued to regard them, and in fact appeared to be edging closer.

Evelyn Sinclair rose to the occasion and smiling, extended her hand firstly to Anna, and then to her ex-fiancé.

Anna observed an incredibly lovely looking woman and could understand why a lot of men would be drawn to her beauty.

'Miss Sinclair, what brings you to Madrid,' asked Anna.

'Oh please call me Evelyn. My editor back in London felt I needed a break from the front line of war reporting and he thought this might amuse me for a while before he throws me to the wolves again.

Such a darling Tom with his wonderful sense of humour,' she drawled.

Anna heard the timbre of an incredibly husky voice. A woman who seemed to have it all and who acted like a magnet to men.

She had just turned her gaze unto Malcolm Mortimer when they noticed that Beich had manoeuvred into their group, and he immediately introduced himself whilst bowing over Evelyn's hand.

'Why Seamus, you old dog, how did you become friends with such a beautiful woman?'

As Seamus pondered how to answer this question, which he was sure Beich would try to verify, Malcolm Mortimer came to his rescue.

'Miss Sinclair has just revealed that she was in Madrid towards the end of the civil war reporting for her newspaper when she met Seamus.'

Mortimer knew that Evelyn and Seamus had both been present in Madrid at approximately the same time, but he was uncertain if in fact it had been at the exact same time. He hoped that Beich would be suitably if at least only momentarily satisfied with this answer. He knew better than anyone that he could not trust him one jot.

'How amusing for you Seamus and what a coincidence, you both showing up here again in Madrid. What are the chances of that,' asked Beich as he carefully tried to assess everyone's reaction.

Seamus laughed and hugged Evelyn close stating that if the group did not mind he would momentarily like to capture Evelyn to himself and catch up on old times. Also he needed to know for how long she intended to be in Madrid. He added that perhaps if Beich behaved himself he could make up a foursome and they could all go out to dinner together if time permitted.

As Seamus had intended, this invitation took Beich off his guard. He replied that he would be delighted and he would leave the arrangements to Seamus. Now glancing beyond Seamus he had obviously seen someone else with whom he wished to meet, and bowing in his stiff and formal manner, he took his leave.

An air of relief enveloped the group. Anna was about to speak when Evelyn Sinclair practically stole her very words.

'Why boys, I believe someone, if not all of you, have a lot of explaining to do, and you know a girl does not like to be kept waiting,' she declared with one hand resting on her hip and the other on Seamus's shoulder.

'Yes, you're right,' said Malcolm. 'But it's best Evelyn that you go with Seamus now and he will fill you in to the extent that he can; and in the meantime Anna, you also need to be brought up to speed, but not here. You now already know that I'm obviously a British agent and that's all I can say about that for the moment. Besides, I will meet with you on Friday at the embassy and we can arrange something there. We should not give Herr Beich any further reason this evening to keep us under his regard. It's best if we separate now. But remember that outside of this group no one is to know who I really am. It's uncertain if everyone in our daily environment can be trusted. Even those whom we think we know well. Be very careful.'

And with that he formerly bowed to Anna and took his leave of her. To say that these events had left Anna somewhat bemused was an understatement. But one thing she now knew for certain; the man whom she had thought of as the enemy was actually, quite amazingly on the same side. Just as her heart had lifted at this revelation, it almost immediately plummeted. Anna could not believe that the gorgeous Evelyn Sinclair no longer meant anything to Malcolm Mortimer. For goodness sake, they had at one time been engaged. Her normally regulated thoughts were in a swirl and she fought with herself to not allow her personal feelings to disturb her too much. Even with or without the presence of his ex-girlfriend, why would Malcolm Mortimer be interested in her, particularly if his usual taste in women extended to such sophistication?

Dragging herself back to Guillermo's side, Anna acted out the rest of the evening as best she could. Even Guillermo gently chided her for her wandering mind.

'You see here this evening Anna? Would you know that there was a war happening in the rest of

Europe? This is what our country needs, these entrepreneurs. Tonight we have many groups, global business leaders from many industries, various international art dealers, and in the middle we have little Guillermo trying to make his way in this hierarchy of business. And you know what delights me? They are interested. They want this art. They have a nose for it – for a good investment for the future. We are all part of this Anna, including your mother.'

'I promise you that my mother will be delighted if she receives private commissions. It's a bonus to her when a prospective client knows what they want and she is excellent at sending sketches for approval prior to the execution of any detailed work. Guillermo, you already know that the one thing that has driven my mother to distraction has been the restrictions to her travel because of this war. She almost takes that personally, as if no one else is affected! This will boost her no end. Guillermo, I thank you on her behalf.'

Anna could see that this gallery owner was buoyant with what he saw as an extremely successful evening. He guided Anna to the spectacular buffet of fish, meat and salad dishes. The displays of food were an art in themselves and each table was adorned with incredible ice sculptures.

At various moments throughout the evening Anna saw Seamus with Evelyn and noted that occasionally Malcolm Mortimer somehow managed to join them. At the close of the evening, as various groups took their leave, Seamus had returned Evelyn to the company of her fellow journalists and photographers who were in the process of gathering up their belongings and scurrying to make editorial deadlines.

By now Guillermo had reclaimed their coats as his car had arrived and the driver was waiting patiently outside. There was no requirement for small talk as Anna was driven home. Her fellow passenger filled the void with his excited chatter. He courteously escorted Anna to the front door and bowed graciously to her for her endeavour in securing such a successful evening. Anna could only smile her acknowledgement. She realised that she had missed out on the opportunity to inform Seamus of Marta's fears. This was something she needed to do sooner rather than later.

As it was now two o' clock in the morning and a day's work lay ahead tomorrow, Anna was thankful that the eventful evening had ended, and she went to bed.

Chapter 18

A light but sharp cold wind whipped colour into Anna's cheeks as she walked along to the language school. She thought about the previous evening's events, the success for Guillermo on the one hand, and what would have been the obvious dire consequences for them all if Seamus had not come to the rescue.

It was now Thursday the 7th January 1943 and Anna felt things might begin to happen soon. There had been a couple of close calls. Madrid was a dangerous city where many spies acted with impunity. She was also very keen to see Marta this morning and would do so during the tea break.

As she entered the restroom to hang up her coat and collect some papers which had been corrected, Anna could see that most of her colleagues were busy doing likewise. The start bell for the beginning of the school day rang out and a myriad of teachers headed in various directions. Anna was glad to be back in the environment of the classroom. More than anywhere else in Madrid, it was here that she felt a sense of normality with people who had no other agenda other than to learn a foreign language.

Feeling more at ease than she had done for a few days, Anna felt the morning progress well, and she welcomed the mid-morning break. On entering the staffroom she casually looked about, but even after a further ten minutes, there was no sign of Marta. Perhaps she had taken a day off for some reason, or she could be ill? There was no opportunity to delve into it any further and besides she would be finishing her work for the day once lunch time arrived. She really needed to meet with Seamus and therefore would try calling to the office where he worked. She would do that once her morning at the language school was completed, and prior to starting work for the afternoon in the embassy.

The morning session now over, Anna did not delay in making her way to Seamus's office which he shared with his two Irish colleagues. A lax and bored security man nodded her through to the entrance of the building. It was easy to find their office as it took up a considerable area of the ground floor. As her knock on the door was acknowledged, Anna immediately entered to be greeted by Rory. He waved her to a seat and offered her some coffee and what looked like a slice of apple cake which Anna welcomed. She was quite cold and now realised that she was also in need of some food to give her sustenance prior to working in the embassy for the afternoon. Besides, she would have no spare time to buy a sandwich because of the diversion to Seamus's place of work.

'Whoa Anna, I can actually see the colour returning to your cheeks as you eat that cake. Did you not eat breakfast this morning?'

'No, we had eaten quite late at the exhibition the previous evening so I did in fact forego breakfast. Thanks for this Rory, you are a lifesaver. By the way where is Seamus today? He was to confirm if we were meeting for dinner this evening so I thought I would drop by to check if that was still the case.'

The lie was said easily, and Rory was not suspicious. Why should he be? He knew and liked Anna and he did not see a relationship other than friendship between her and his colleague.

'Ah Anna, our man Seamus is sometimes a law onto himself. Even we wonder on occasions where he is off to for the day. But you know the powers in Dublin seem to give him a high degree of leeway and they have stated that they are all happy with his work. The Spanish really like him and he has done well in closing out some contracts. Where he has trotted off to today, well I really don't know. His diary maintenance is also a law unto itself in that it's mostly unfilled, but Seamus does seem to know what he is doing. We don't quibble over it.'

This was stated with such a laid back attitude that Anna almost laughed. If Rory had any suspicion as to the real reason for Seamus's presence in Madrid, he certainly did well in giving nothing away.

'Well, would you just remind him of our proposed meet-up and ask him to phone me at the apartment when I get home later this evening?'

Rory stated that he would. Anna thanked him again for the cake, and like the true gentleman that he was, Rory escorted Anna from the building, waving her off and promising to pass on her message.

Anna knew that for the rest of the day her concerns about Marta would have to wait. What she needed this afternoon was to fully concentrate on her work for the embassy. She knew there was a plethora of work awaiting her presence but she welcomed the escape her immersion in it would offer.

The time went in quite quickly. Malcolm had not been present for the entire afternoon, or indeed Beich for that matter. She cleared up her paperwork as quickly as possible, said her goodbyes and exited via the security area. There had been several occasions when she had been stopped and her bags and coat checked, and today was no exception. No laid back staff on duty here. All was very efficiently overseen.

Walking swiftly towards the tram stop and seeing that one was about to arrive, Anna increased her pace. If Seamus had picked up her message, he knew it meant to meet at their usual café after work. There would be no phone call to her apartment.

The early evening air had deepened in its chilliness. Anna thought it must be one of the coldest since she arrived in Madrid and she found she was beginning to shiver slightly as she entered the café in Calle Verde. The small door-bell announced every entry and exit to the premises. The café owner, now used to Anna's occasional visits, had become quite friendly, and on seeing Anna he announced that there was still some hot chocolate if she was interested. She smiled and nodded an affirmative.

As previously instructed by Seamus, she declined a window seat and sat at a table further into the room. Discretion was paramount even though no one would be particularly surprised if they were seen together.

She was half way through her hot chocolate when Seamus arrived saluting the café owner before grabbing the seat opposite Anna. The café was unusually busy for this time of day but they both welcomed the background noise. The owner knew that Seamus was not a fan of hot chocolate and he sent the waitress over with coffee and a few churros. Seamus nodded, smiled his thanks and handed the young waitress some change with which she was delighted. It was a rarity for a customer to do this.

Seamus glanced around the room, and seemingly satisfied with what he saw, he turned to Anna with a slightly raised and questioning eyebrow.

'Well Anna, what's up? It must be important for you to call into the office. Don't tell me you think your cover is blown?'

'No, it's not that. Seamus I'm really worried about Marta.'

Anna recounted all that she knew to Seamus. What worried her most was Marta's absence from the language school.

'She may just be in bed with flu Anna, did you check with anyone?'

'Yes Seamus. After my classes finished I called into the school office to make inquiries. The administrator said there was a phone call from Marta to say that she had come down with flu and she would need some time off work. It doesn't feel right Seamus. Look, I believe Marta when she says she is being followed and that someone had been into her apartment. She is not given to hysterics. I think she has reason to be concerned.'

Seamus sat back in his chair. He could see the concern on Anna's face and he felt himself that there were genuine grounds here for being worried. But, they were here to complete a job. They were part of an operation and should not get embroiled in this. Anything that brought them to the attention of the authorities was dangerous.

Equally, as he was thinking this, he knew he was being a total hypocrite. Here he was conniving to free Sonsoles, an act which was just as likely to scupper their operation. He inwardly cursed and struggled with which answer to give.

'All right Anna. This is the only thing we are going to do, and I mean the only thing! We will grab a quick bite to eat here before we go back out into that freezing cold air. Rory has loaned me his car for the evening as he had no particular plans. It's now almost seven o' clock. By the time we have eaten and get over to Marta's apartment it will be about eight-thirty. But don't be surprised to find her tucked up in bed with flu. Only problem is how will we gain entry to the apartment?'

At which juncture Anna placed a set of keys on the table.

'I took the opportunity to borrow these from Karina. Well, in fact she does not know they have been borrowed. I did not want to worry her excessively, and besides Marta herself did not want Karina to know of her fears. Karina had also told Marta that she would be too busy to meet up with her this week and she therefore is not suspicious as to why Marta has not been in contact.'

Seamus smirked.

'You know Anna, I do believe that we have all underestimated you! Now let us order some food and then get over there. No one wants to be out too late in this freezing air. And Anna, if Marta is not there in the apartment, it is the end of our involvement. We will see how to handle things if we glean any information. Caution is paramount, we can't be drawing attention to ourselves. I don't think our Malcolm Mortimer would be too happy about any of this, but we are committed now.'

As predicted by Seamus, it was almost exactly eight-thirty when they arrived at Marta's building.

As they drove along the streets, Anna observed how quiet it was. They had passed only two other people who were walking briskly on their way. The street lighting was at best muted with several lamps not working. Long shadows, whose depths were difficult to penetrate, added an eerie air of foreboding. Anna was very glad to have Seamus alongside.

Seamus drove up and down the street a few times to get a feel for the area, and how best to gain access to the building. There were a few other cars and vans driving along the street which thankfully made their vehicle less conspicuous.

Eventually, he satisfied himself that the alleyway to the rear of the building was the best option for the car. He did not want the presence of a strange car to draw any suspicions from local Falange or *civiles* if they were strolling the streets. Once parked discreetly at the back of the building in a rear courtyard, they then made their way back along the alleyway to the front of the building.

Anna made sure that the correct key was to hand so that there was no fumbling with the lock. Entry to the communal entrance hall was quickly gained.

Seamus and Anna were more than relieved that no one else was present in the large hallway, which was almost square in structure. It was tiled like a chess board, and quite cold which they were both glad and relieved about. It meant that no resident would hang about before entering into their apartment.

It was a lovely old building. There were many *art deco* features and half way up the stairs, just as it turned, there was a beautiful stained glass window. The wrought iron balustrade, black in colour, was a lovely contrast to the marble steps.

There were two apartments on the ground floor on either side of the hall. From the one on the right, they could just about hear the strains of classical music being played, which was probably being used to drown out an argument currently in progress from the apartment on the left. Anna remembered hearing Marta talk about a newly married couple who had arguments on a regular basis.

They were both very glad of the cover which this noise offered. Seamus cautioned Anna not to speak. They ascended the stairs as quickly as possible to the next landing where there were two further apartments. Anna knew it was the apartment on the left. She was also aware that the other apartment was currently unoccupied and this was a bonus for them. Seamus saw the back staircase before Anna did and indicated that he would check it out. The staircase served this floor, and the two floors above to the back of the building as well as the exit to the courtyard on the ground floor.

Through a laundry room containing several laundry baskets, Seamus walked swiftly to the large back door which was bolted from the inside. Glancing through a side window he could see Rory's car safely parked in the shadows. He quickly ascended the stairs again.

'Listen Anna, there are obviously some occupants in the apartments downstairs. We need to get inside Marta's before anyone sees or hears us. I was going to put you on look-out, but it's too dangerous.'

Without further ado Seamus inserted the key and turned it gently. They were in. They both leaned against the door and took in their surroundings. A mantle clock was ticking into the eerie silence; its noise erupting into the room. The living area seemed otherwise undisturbed with nothing in particular seeming out of place. The curtains were closed, but oddly, a light had been left on.

'Anna, check the bedroom first. If Marta is in there asleep we don't want to scare the hell out of her. I'll check the kitchen and the back laundry area. Be very quiet, and don't disturb anything.'

Anna signalled her understanding and realised her training was now coming into play. She made her way silently and cautiously along the corridor to the bedroom. They were solid floors and thankfully did not creak too much. The door was slightly ajar, and as she pushed it gently open she could see that the bed was unoccupied but dishevelled. There were pillows lying on the floor and the bed was almost completely stripped. There was no sign that any drawers or cupboards had been opened to indicate if Marta had packed in a hurry. The dressing table looked untidy, but there was nothing out of the ordinary about that.

Next came the bathroom which was very large. It looked tidy, and Anna thought that in fact it was almost too tidy in comparison to the rest of the apartment. Strange there were no towels lying around. The bath tub which rested on elegant legs lay below the level of a large mirror, and it was as she glanced at the mirror that she noticed it. Tiny splats of red across the lower level of the mirror, some of which had trickled down into the frame. She felt herself tense, but immediately commenced searching around the area to try and confirm her thoughts. It was then that she felt it.

As she swept her hand along the floor under the bath she felt the dampness, not water but something more viscous. Drawing her hand back she was horrified to see that it was noticeably covered in blood. She felt the nausea build up. At that moment Seamus pushed through the bathroom door and was about to say something when he noticed Anna's face and her blood stained hand.

'My god, is she in the bath Anna?'

Struggling to speak, but knowing the impact of her findings Anna responded, 'No, Seamus, but whatever has been done to Marta they did it here. It looked too tidy and it was. I wouldn't even have searched under the bath but for the blood specks on the mirror. They must have taken her away.'

Seamus noted that Anna's composure was commendable but there was a more notable pallor to her complexion. He had witnessed his fair share of blood on the battlefields of Spain, and indeed during the civil war in Ireland. Anna had never been exposed to that in real life. Even with all her training for this mission it was not something that you could really properly prepare for, until it was a reality.

'Right now Anna, we need to get out of here. Wash your hand, and use this handkerchief to dry it. Don't use anything else.'

Silently, they retraced their steps. Seamus carefully opened the door of the apartment, and leaning into the corridor he noted nothing unusual. He beckoned Anna to follow.

Cautiously they made their way to the back stairs and descended to the lower ground floor. Since his earlier visit to the laundry room, Seamus now realised that someone else must have been there as a light had been left on. He was about to switch it off, as he did not want anyone to observe them when they opened the door to make their escape, but at that moment he realised something had been moved. It was one of the large laundry baskets. It had been placed nearer to the back door as if prepared for collection.

Anna was wondering why Seamus was delaying their exit. He was starting to lift the lid on a laundry basket and moving sheets aside. Why on earth was he doing that? Then she heard his sharp intake of breath and he suddenly stood still. He turned back to Anna.

'Whatever you do don't shout out. It's Marta .....'
Anna rushed to the basket before he had managed to finish what he was saying. There amongst the blood soaked sheets rested Marta's body. Naked, tortured, her face beaten to a pulp. At first it was nausea she felt, and then a rising anger at such mutilation and at the people who did this to her friend. Anna bent down to touch her forehead, and as she did, she noticed an almost imperceptible flutter of Marta's eyelashes. Was she imagining things? Bending closer she checked Marta's right

wrist for a pulse which was something her sister Marion had taught her.

'Seamus she's still alive, barely alive but it's there the weakest of pulses!'

'Are you certain Anna? She looks gone to me. I know you're upset but...'

'Seamus I'm certain. My sister taught me how to check for a pulse. It's barely there. We have to get her out of here!'

In his mind Seamus knew that someone was probably coming for that basket and pretty soon. The realisation that they'd had a very lucky break was not lost on him. Whoever had done this had probably only vacated the apartment a few hours ago. If Marta's body had been left there in the apartment at the time of the deed they would have been caught.

'Wait here. I'll reverse the car to the back door.'

A few minutes later and they found the strength to bundle the extremely limp form of Marta into the boot of the car, having cushioned it firstly with lots of sheets. Seamus then ran to the alleyway to check that there was no one in sight. Satisfied, he returned to the car and they slowly drove back onto the main street.

'What will we do with her Seamus? Where can we take her?'

Seamus already knew, but he could not bring Anna with him.

'Look Anna, you have to trust me with this. Firstly, I'm dropping you back to your apartment. Don't say a word about this to anyone, especially not to Karina. She's too emotional and will insist on seeing Marta. Just tell her the story you heard at the school. Are we agreed?'

Anna merely nodded. She knew Seamus was right. Their luck held. There were no Falange patrols. Thankfully the bitter cold air must have kept them indoors. They were soon back at Karina's apartment. Anna turned to Seamus and wished him luck.

As he drove away, Seamus thought he knew who might be responsible for this, but his anger had to be tempered with caution, and a large dollop at that. He was about to make a night call on his friend Father Ignatius. He hoped that he was not out on a visit to a dying parishioner.

Back in her apartment Anna sat with shaking hands while also trying to hold steady a small glass of brandy. She gulped it back quickly and felt the warmth of it cruise through her cold limbs, and for some moments she sat there contemplating the evening. Thank goodness she had involved Seamus. If she had entered Marta's apartment on her own she would have found the blood but perhaps not have searched the laundry at the exit from the building. She would have left by the front door and Marta's body would have disappeared forever.

The other bit of luck was a note from Karina to state that she and her mother were travelling to Valencia to visit a sick aunt and they were uncertain as to the time of their return. That was a relief. If Karina had started to ask too many questions the truth would have had to emerge eventually. The less other people knew for now the better. Anna also realised that Seamus had no intention of telling her where he was taking Marta, and she fully understood the reasons for that.

Gathering herself she prepared for bed. She mulled over her very first close encounter with the results of a very brutal, vicious and ferocious beating. She eventually drifted fitfully off to sleep knowing that whether Marta lived or died, that deep inside she wanted the perpetrator to be caught, identified and justice overseen. Such were her final thoughts that evening.

Seamus's final thoughts that night, or to be more accurate, early morning, were somewhat different. On entering his apartment he felt exhausted and feeling desperately in need of a wash. His clothes had notable evidence of blood marks in various locations. Marta was so close to death and yet it was impossible for them to take her to a hospital. However that spirited energetic priest, Father Ignatius, had contacts and would get in touch with them forthwith.

As he had carried Marta through to the secret bowels of the church he suddenly realised her eyes had opened for a mere few seconds and they conveyed a message of such pain, as of a scream that was locked within but with no energy to expel it.

He shook his head and as he turned to remove his jacket he noticed an envelope on the floor. The note inside should have thrilled him but the events of the evening had marred that. It was from Dec Buchanan confirming that Sonsoles would be freed on Monday 11th January and that he needed to meet with him that weekend to finalise the details. What next, thought Seamus, what next?

Chapter 19

The following morning as Malcolm Mortimer made his way to the German embassy, he pondered on the fact that time was running out with regard to Herr Beich's patience, and with what he saw as the lack of progress being made by Otto Huber.

Malcolm had reluctantly made contact with London a fortnight ago but that was in order to communicate the degree of importance and urgency he placed on the matter. After a few days of tense silence the order had come back to evacuate Madrid and get the plans out, but then it wasn't just the plans. No, it was far more complicated than that. He knew exactly what the order meant and for how many people he would be responsible. There may be casualties and that was part of war but one person in particular had become much more meaningful in his life, and he wanted more than anything to see her safely through.

He was more than impressed with the manner in which she had engaged with their subterfuge. She held her own with Beich and hid extremely well how she really felt about anyone, including him. But he had to push these thoughts aside. His task was to see this through at all costs.

That same morning Seamus left Rory's car at a private garage to be cleaned. He already knew that this particular garage owner was very discreet. It would not do if Rory found any spots of blood in the boot. By way of explanation he would just say it was his way of returning the favour by having the car valeted.

Striding purposefully to work that same morning, he noticed in his favourite Triton tobacconist shop, that in the display window, the king and queen chess pieces were in reverse order. He entered the shop and casually greeted the owner Carlos Santiago. As he paid for his Tritons which Carlos had placed in a bag, they casually made small talk about the slight improvement in the weather. This was for the benefit of a few straggling customers who seemed reluctant to leave and go into the still chill air outside.

Back out in the street Seamus muttered, 'Hell's teeth, what else in the space of two days?'

The note said to meet urgently later that day at the tobacco shop.

At the embassy that afternoon Anna noted how Malcolm and Otto Huber appeared to be in deep discussion about something. Although they had drawings out on display and were bent over them as if discussing a problem, she noticed they in fact never glanced at them. Otto in particular looked tense, but perhaps that was easily explained by the presence of Beich who appeared to become more menacing as the days rolled on. There was a nasty smug look on his face that was more chilling than any words he might care to speak.

Malcolm acknowledged Beich formerly and hoped that his then turned back invited no further approach from him. At this juncture he indicated to Anna that she should join them at their table.

'Fraulein Fingal, if you would please assist in these few translations for Herr Huber. He values your expertise in that area.'

'Anna, I would be a much happier man if you would. My three assistants need direction that has to be absolutely accurate. Sit here Anna and tell me if we have translated this correctly?'

As she sat to go over what Otto had indicated, Anna could sense Malcolm standing close and looking over her left shoulder. So close she could feel his breath in her hair. It was distracting but welcoming, and it made her wish that she could more openly spend some time with this man. After some minutes she clarified the written text for Otto, and as she turned she looked straight into Malcolm's eyes.

'Thank you once again Fraulein Fingal. You know we must be so careful in our work, so very careful.'

Anna returned his smile but noted how tired he looked. Was there something else in what he had said? Was he warning her about something?

Overhearing this comment Beich interrupted by saying, 'Indeed I could not agree more my friends. What you are being asked to do for the Fatherland is of the greatest honour. To aid and be at the forefront of the Fuhrer's grand vision is without doubt a noble thing.'

His tone changing, he added in a slow but much more menacing tone, 'Yes, you must all be very careful indeed.'

Turning on his heel he stormed out of the room. Anna noted that no one dared risk a comment, but Malcolm continued as if Beich had not spoken.

'Well everyone, this day is coming to a close. Please, as usual put everything away securely and as it is Friday we will see you all again on Monday. Fraulein Fingal, if you would remain a few moments longer?'

Anna nodded her agreement. It did not take long for the office to clear and Malcolm drew her as far into the room as was possible, away from the door in case he was overheard.

'You know Anna, things are beginning to move quite fast. In fact within the next week we will be leaving Madrid.' He noted the questioning look on her face.

'I don't want to say anything more except to forewarn you to be prepared. Have your papers with you at all times and when you leave them in the apartment ensure they are well hidden. As far as I'm aware no one has a clue as to what any of us are doing here, but Beich is a worry as he has become more dangerous and threatening, especially towards Otto.'

'I understand, but who will give the final word on when to move?'

'Come, let's get our coats from the cloakroom first.'

As he gathered their coats he helped Anna into hers, and when she turned around, he was standing incredibly close. She did not step back. She wanted to say something but not make an idiot of herself by expressing her true feelings.

'You look tired Malcolm.'

'Yes, I'm tired. I'm bloody tired and I've had enough of this pretence.'

In the very next moment he pulled Anna to him and kissed her. Anna did not repulse his sudden move. At first her response was hesitant, but then, and to his delight, she was leaning in closer. His arms had enveloped her and she could feel the sinewy strength of his limbs. She was more than willing to respond to her attraction for this man and she easily realised that any relationship before this was no match at all for the emotions she was now experiencing.

It was Anna who heard first the sudden noise of a door opening into the outer office, and she pulled back quickly from Malcolm and warned him. She composed herself by making a pretence of trying to find her hat and then announcing that she had located it and all was well. On exiting from the cloakroom area they immediately saw Beich gathering up some papers and stuffing them into his briefcase.

'Ah, still here, the dedicated team. Herr Holtzman, let us walk out together. A quick word with you about Herr Huber I think.'

Anna knew she was being dismissed and said her goodbyes. Perhaps it was just as well that they had been interrupted as she knew she would have made love to Malcolm Mortimer there and then.

Security was tighter that evening and every bag was being thoroughly searched. She wondered how on earth documents of any kind could be sneaked from this building. As far as she could ascertain it would be far too risky.

On the journey back to her empty apartment, Anna thought a lot about that kiss and what Malcolm Mortimer had said.

Having eventually taken his leave of Beich, Malcolm made his way to Carlos Santiago's tobacco shop where he would meet in the back room with Seamus. He thought about that kiss and to what it might have led. He mentally kicked himself for not concentrating fully on the job in hand, but one thing was for certain, and that was that Anna had responded to him. She had not repulsed him or turned away. He momentarily smiled at the memory, but as he had just arrived at Carlos Santiago's shop he had to put all thoughts of their encounter aside.

As he entered the shop he was followed by a young woman in her early to mid-twenties. She was not in a hurry to leave. Malcolm continued to browse and Carlos made an effort by showing him some new more expensive imports and extolled on the quality of the leaf used in its production.

A few minutes later the young woman in question made her choices, paid for her items and left.

Seamus realised that if he did not get a move on, he would be late for his meeting with Malcolm, so he made a unilateral decision to use Rory's car. Not a decision he needed to worry about as Rory was back in Ireland on a well-earned holiday, his first in over a year. As he drove around the corner into Calle Atocha, he saw a woman exiting from Carlos' tobacco shop and almost stopped the car in its tracks. The street was very busy and she had not noticed Seamus. It was also fortunate that she had turned in the opposite direction. She then jumped into a car that was parked on the other side of the street.

Was it just coincidence that she had been in Carlos' shop? Part of him felt he should head to the meeting with Malcolm, but his curiosity was roused and he decided that he would follow her at a very safe distance. He did not want to admit it to himself but he was now feeling quite anxious what with the other events that had occurred over the past few days.

She drove smartly, and finally reached her destination which appeared to be a renowned tapas bar in Calle del Mesón de Paredes. Without any further delay she entered the building.

Seamus knew the taberna and its great reputation for hearty meals. He decided to park his car a short distance away and up a side street to avoid drawing attention to himself. He then walked back briskly. He was deciding on his strategy while pretending to browse a shop window. It was then that he noticed another car draw up, and a man he knew only too well got out.

He had to confirm that they were meeting each other. Seamus waited, and then pulling his hat well over his face he entered the busy and noisy restaurant. When the waiter approached him he stated that he was meeting with friends and he was just checking if they had arrived. He could not see either of them. As the restaurant was fairly deep he headed to the rest room area towards the back of the building, and then, as he turned a corner he saw them.

It was Beich. And with him was Raquel. Smirking, sly Raquel along with that monster Beich.

He had to get out and back to Carlos' premises. At that moment the band struck up for the Friday evening entertainment and using it as a distraction Seamus got out as fast as he could.

A while later he was entering the tobacco shop and Carlos looked up and saw a very pensive Seamus.

'How are you my friend?'

'I could be a lot bloody better. Is he still here?' Seamus noticed the empty shop and registered a negative shake of the head from Carlos which confirmed Malcolm was no longer there.

'Tell me Carlos, when my colleague arrived did a young woman in her mid-twenties follow through after he entered your shop?'

'Well yes. She seemed uncertain as to what she wanted but eventually bought something small. Is there a problem?'

Seamus did not want to overly concern Carlos and hoped his reply went some way towards reassuring him.

'No, no, it's fine. I just thought I recognised her.'

With that he bade Carlos goodbye.

As Seamus took his leave, Carlos reflected on the look of sheer anger he had witnessed on Malcolm Mortimer's face when Seamus had failed to turn up.

Already back in Plaza del Ángel where he resided, Malcolm Mortimer was intensely unhappy. The rule which he had reiterated time and time again was to abandon a meeting point if one of the personnel involved was over 15 minutes late. This protected the person already at the location and hopefully got them out in time in case a colleague had been rumbled.

The walk back to his apartment had given him some time to think. He did not want to assume that something untoward had happened to Seamus. There were no indicators that anything was amiss, but it was very unlike Seamus to be late for anything. He acknowledged the fact that they had very different ways of working but Malcolm had certainly come to respect and trust Seamus. Besides, he also knew that G2 were very keen to play a part in this venture, and that Patrick Herlihy was held in considerable regard by those with influence in the War Office. If Patrick Herlihy sent someone into the field he would be very certain of his man, or woman, for that matter.

What he could not understand was why they had used blackmail to entice Anna to work for them. In truth he felt she would have played her part without being cornered with regard to her brother. Perhaps Herlihy needed Anna to believe it. But that was not his concern now.

Now back in his apartment, he needed something to eat and he was considering his options when he heard the creaking of the normally quiet floorboards outside his apartment door. He quietly and quickly pulled aside a loose plank which ran along one side of the kitchen sink. Wrapped inside a cloth was his Browning HP. He withdrew it from its holster and was just in position inside the door when a knock came. He did not answer but just waited. Someone was now trying to manipulate the lock, and then the door started to slowly open. As he prepared himself, he realised that firing his weapon would draw too much unwelcome attention. There was only one thing for it. He lifted the gun, pulled the door back violently, and quickly brought the gun down on the intruder's head. He then pulled the now limp body inside the room and closed the door.

It was not a position in which he had ever seen Seamus before, and he knew that when he did come round, that the headache he would shortly be experiencing, to put it mildly, would not be appreciated. He could see that Seamus was now gradually showing signs of recovery. Fifteen minutes later he was struggling to his feet and Malcolm assisted him onto the sofa in the living room.

'Seamus, you had better have a good reason for missing our rendezvous and now breaking into my apartment. What the hell has gotten into you?'

Feeling the lump on his head, Seamus quickly came to the conclusion that if the shoe had been on the other foot, then he too would probably have meted out the same treatment. It had not been the wisest move on his part.

'You were followed by that traitor Raquel from the language school. Anna was right about her all along.'

'What the hell do you mean? Who is she?'

Slumped on the sofa Seamus explained what he had witnessed. He also decided it was time that Malcolm was told about Marta and what had happened to her. He was now certain that both Beich and Raquel were somehow involved in the beating. Whether they had actually taken an active part themselves was another matter. He remembered Anna relating how Marta had sensed that she had been followed home by a woman one evening after work, and who better to do that than Raquel who worked in the same language school. It was also now obvious that Beich was using Raquel as a spy and that she had followed Malcolm.

'The cunning bastard. That's why he delayed me going there this evening. That woman must have been waiting outside as I left the embassy with Beich. It was so she could identify who she needed to follow and then ascertain who I met. It's pure luck that you were late and spotted her.'

'Your right. That's the only explanation. Beich has never forgiven you for embarrassing him that night at Club Alphonse. He is the type of man who harbours a grudge and always gets his revenge. I followed her to a restaurant a few streets away and Beich arrived to join her for dinner.'

'Seamus, this has made our plans a lot more difficult. Beich obviously does not trust me. I don't believe my cover has been blown but he is such a paranoid individual. Also, he is so infatuated with Karina that he would have Marta beaten to an inch of her life. Will she survive and where have you taken her?'

'To an old friend and that's all I'm telling you. It's better for everyone if it's kept that way. As to whether she will make it? I don't know. I've seen men pulverise each other whilst they were in a very drunken state, but this, well this went way beyond that. They were not there to teach her a lesson. The intention was to kill. They may have used the Falange who are totally against anyone they categorise as deviant.'

'Yes,' said Malcolm, 'Spain remains a very dangerous place for anyone on that very long list. Intellectuals, anyone liberal. The church and the State, hand in hand, are terrifying their own people.'

'Not all of them. There are still a few people prepared to put their head above the parapet.'

Malcolm did not disagree. It was more a weariness for what war, politics, and huge egos could make people become. He made some coffee and fetched a small ice pack for Seamus.

'By the way Seamus, this friend of yours that Marta is with? Is this the same contact you spoke about before or is this someone else?'

'Yes, it's someone else. Someone I knew from my time before in Spain. I know that Marta will be completely safe there and that everything possible will be done for her.'

'I'm telling you now Seamus, and you can relate it to Anna, we cannot afford personal issues to stall our plans. Our work here must be objective and we cannot allow anything to interfere with that.'

They drank some hot coffee and after a few minutes of silence Seamus spoke.

'What are you going to do? How will this affect your plans?'

'Seamus, we are going to have to get out of here sooner than we thought. It was to happen soon but in view of all of this we need to move it forward by a week.'

'All right but when is that meant to be?'

Seamus thought he might fall off his seat at Malcolm's reply.

'It has to be next Friday, the 15th January. By the way you might as well know now that it's not documents we have to get out, it's Otto Huber himself. All the information we need is in his head. He's been deliberately stalling in developing these weapons. He has no wish to be here working for the

Germans. However his time here has allowed him to develop and refine his expertise but also to withhold just enough, a miniscule of information which makes it look as if a breakthrough is about to be made. His family are under house arrest but we plan to coincide his evacuation from Madrid with their escape. That's the deal.'

'For Christ's sake, how will you get him out?'

Malcolm leaned back in his seat and looked at Seamus.

'That Seamus, is where Anna will come into her own. You will have to meet with her and tell her about this turn of events. Next Friday Anna and Otto must be prepared to get out of Madrid. In fact, it will probably be Saturday before they can leave. I just need to finalise a few things. By next Wednesday the plan should be firmly in place. In the meantime tell Anna that this coming Monday she is to inform the language school and us here in the embassy that she is taking a holiday for the week beginning the 18th January. That way there will be no concern about her not suddenly turning up to work. All right?'

On hearing Malcolm's words, Seamus hoped his expression did not look too stunned. If this man sitting in front of him realised that he had secret plans of his own with regard to Sonsoles he was certain he would put an end to them. He had to meet Dec Buchanan tomorrow. Why the hell was everything happening at the same time!

'Seamus, are you all right? You look a little stunned. Perhaps that knock on your head has caused more damage than I thought?'

Shaking himself from his reverie Seamus replied, 'I'm alright, I just need to get back to my place and get a good night's kip. Should be as clear as a bell in the morning. Help me up for Christ's sake and remind me to return the favour sometime.'

Smirking, Malcolm assisted Seamus to his feet. It was one of the elements of Seamus' character that he liked, his ability to lighten a situation, if only momentarily.

'I will drive you back in your car. Don't protest Seamus, it won't work with me. Once I drop you off I can get the tram back home. Let's go out the back way.'

A while later and Malcolm had returned to his apartment. He stood looking through the living room window into the night. Seeing but not seeing, examining several scenarios in his mind and judging the timing of everything. It had to work, it had to.

Chapter 20

The following morning was the 9th January 1943. As he looked in the bathroom mirror, Seamus had to admit that he was not very impressed with what he saw. He looked drawn, he had a headache, no surprise there, and he felt extremely tired. In fact it reminded him very much of some of his past hangovers.

Probably not a bad way to look in view of his meeting with Dec Buchanan this morning. His thoughts drifted to Sonsoles and the anticipation of seeing her again was wonderful, but also there was his concern as to how damaged she may be. However, that would have to be dealt with on a day by day basis. Let's just get her out first.

Twenty minutes later and feeling somewhat revived after a very hot shower and several cups of strong coffee, he donned his heavy winter coat and made his way to Calle Victoria and La Casa del Abuelo which he reached at ten o' clock.

Once inside he noted that Buchanan had not yet arrived and he ordered churros with hot chocolate. Not a drink he would normally take but this morning he felt he really needed a sugar rush. Anything in fact to keep him fully alert and on his toes when Buchanan arrived.

He was just starting into his penultimate churro when he noted the arrival of Buchanan. This was his haunt and you could immediately sense that some of the waiters were not exactly thrilled to see him. Seamus thought it amazing how you could smell trouble off some people.

'Jesus Seamus, you look awful. You look like a man with a very bad hangover and apart from that you are drinking chocolate. That can't be a good follow on for anyone's stomach.'

'What Dec, are you concerned for my health?'

'Now Seamus, I will overlook that sarcastic comment because my friend I'm in very good form today. Some very lucrative black market shenanigans on my part have paid dividends. Quite a killing in fact, and you Seamus, we could both be part of this for the future. We could both be wealthy men if we played our cards right.'

Seamus hoped that the loathing and contempt he was feeling inside was not translating to his face. What Buchanan more accurately meant, is that he would be an extremely wealthy man if Seamus danced to his tune and accepted a few crumbs in return.

'And I look forward to our collaboration together. What more news have you for me? I have to say your note was a surprise. I was not expecting any movement at your end for another while.'

Buchanan's large cigar was already lit and wafting circles of smoke in every direction. His coffee arrived and he grunted the waiter away.

'Well me boyo, believe it or not it was the nurse who asked for a change in timing to facilitate a family event.'

'Excuse me, is that a joke?'

Buchanan exposed his not too pleasant teeth and slapping his knee, he laughed.

'No, in all honesty I jest not. It really is the truth. But look Seamus, surely it does not matter to you if the timing is a little earlier, what's the problem?'

'Nothing, probably mostly my hangover and having to inform the family of a slight change of plan.'

'If that's a problem for them then they'll get over it. Now listen Seamus if we're going to be in business together you are going to have to get a lot harder about stepping on peoples toes. Now let's go over in detail again about what needs to be done and how you can arrange for the so called body to be collected on Monday morning. Remember timing is everything.'

For the first time ever in Buchanan's company he felt himself relax. Seamus now knew that Buchanan had no inkling that he, Seamus, had a very personal interest in this woman, in fact his wife. How good that felt.

He listened to Buchanan outlining the plan. There was absolutely nothing either of them could do if anything went wrong. If they were seen to be involved they would be dead men walking for several different parties. All Seamus had to do was arrange for someone, and they had to be Spanish, to collect the body from the mortuary by nine-thirty on the Monday morning. They had to be on time. From ten o'clock Señor Murez came on duty and if anything was slightly out of the ordinary, he would spot it. Worse still, he was a Franco man through and through. It would be best if the person nominated to collect the body had false papers, then every angle would be covered.

'Hell's bells Dec! Where am I going to get someone to collect a supposedly dead body and at such short notice?'

'For Christ's sake Seamus, keep your voice down! I'm taking the risks here, not you. You will have to bribe someone – all right? No more involvement for me, I've been paid and job done as far as I'm concerned.'

Seamus was pleased with his performance. That snake Buchanan did not suspect anything out of the ordinary. He already knew to whom he could go to arrange collection of Sonsoles. His secret contact here in Madrid could procure false papers and had a network of people in line to assist. It was quite amazing how past friends were prepared to help him. They parted some twenty minutes later with Buchanan promising to be in touch for future collaborations.

As Seamus stepped into the street, he reflected on a good morning's work. Then he remembered Marta. He needed to know about her condition. Best to phone though, and he would use the lobby of a hotel a few streets away from his apartment. Malcolm had cautioned him that phone calls were frequently monitored. However, phones in hotels were regarded as a safer bet.

Seamus nipped into the lobby and phoned through to the chaplaincy where Father Ignatius lived. The housekeeper stated that he was currently visiting some parishioners but she expected him back soon.

Seamus gave the number and found a newspaper and waited. Some twenty minutes later the phone rang. Seamus answered it quickly before anyone else responded.

'Hello, Father Ignatius, is that you?'

'Ah Seamus my friend I'm glad you phoned. I'm afraid that parishioner we spoke about before, you know the one you befriended at our services? Well she died last night. The doctor did everything he could.'

The old priest was being very careful. Seamus did not know the last time he had attended anything to do with a church apart from his marriage to Sonsoles. Marta was dead and he would have to break the news to Anna.

'I hope she was able to make a last confession Father.'

'Yes, indeed yes. She is at peace. Perhaps you would like to attend our evening confessions? It's at seven o' clock.'

He would see the old priest then. He was indicating that he wanted him there. He was certain Marta had named her killers.

That same morning Malcolm paid a visit to Guillermo's art gallery, and as he entered the premises the strange mechanical monkey performed its bizarre twist and bow as the doorbell chimed. He was there to speak with his contact. Unknown to Guillermo, his wife Carla was working closely with British Intelligence. Guillermo was prepared to ride the waves of war, to avoid betraying which side he favoured, and then no matter the outcome, their existence would go on as a thriving commercial enterprise. Therefore and unwittingly, Guillermo was perfect cover for his wife. Carla blended into the background, and always allowed her husband to be the negotiator and extravert dresser. She had her reasons for working with the allies, and that was the death of two brothers during the civil war.

Malcolm knew all of this. He had been very finely briefed on everything. He regarded Carla as one of those women to whom the phrase *'still waters run deep'* could be accurately applied. A quiet woman who kept her thoughts and opinions under close guard. She was perfect as far as he was concerned.

There were two other couples browsing in the art gallery and Carla was standing with them, but after some minutes she excused herself and approached Malcolm.

'Herr Holtzman, how nice to see you again. I'm afraid we don't have any current exhibitions coming up, but we have a few interesting individual pieces. Also Carlos is unavailable today as he is meeting with a young artist who lives in a village some miles out of Madrid.'

In a low meaningful tone Malcolm replied.

'It's you I've come to see.'

'I understand. It's almost lunch time and I don't think these customers are really interested in buying. Give me a few more minutes with them.'

Some fifteen minutes later both couples left and Carla closed up the shop.

'Well, Herr Holtzman, I was told you would only ever approach me if you needed to get out of Madrid, or if you required false papers. Am I correct?'

Malcolm nodded and their discussions began.

Back in her apartment Anna was somewhat at a loss as to what to do with herself this Saturday morning. Not knowing when Karina might return she decided she would do some shopping at El Corte Ingles in Calle Preciados. She had visited a few times before and had been impressed with the range of clothing it stocked. She had just left her apartment and was walking down the street when Seamus caught up with her.

'Good morning Anna, I need to talk to you.'

'Let's go back to the apartment then,' said Anna. She had a feeling that Seamus had not just happened to walk by on a Saturday morning unless it was something to do with Marta.

'No, just walk on together. It's not good for your reputation in Madrid to be seen inviting a man into your apartment. There is a café in the next street.'

Now seated and with some coffee ordered, Seamus prepared to tell Anna the news about her friend.

'Look Anna ....'

'It's alright Seamus. Marta must be dead or you would not be accosting me off the street close to lunchtime on a Saturday. We both saw the beating she took. I'm not surprised, but I am certainly angry at her destruction. How did you find out?'

Seamus paused as their coffee had just arrived.

'I got in touch with my friend. He is a great man working under very dangerous circumstances. I don't want to tell you any more than that Anna.'

Anna was silent for a moment and then said, 'Would it be possible for me to see her Seamus? To pay my last respects to Marta?'

Seamus hesitated, and then shook his head in the negative. He could not bring Anna to the very church that Sonsoles would be brought to after her hopeful escape.

'It's not possible Anna, but one thing I can tell you for a fact is that she did regain consciousness long enough to say who had done this to her.' Again Seamus paused.

'All right Seamus, I understand your caution but is there something else as well?'

'Yes, Anna. Things are moving faster than any of us anticipated. Malcolm has brought our date for vacating Madrid forward and he has revealed to me your role to a certain extent.'

Seamus related as accurately as possible what Anna had to do. Next Friday was the 15th January 1943. She had to be totally prepared for leaving

Madrid. It was likely to be the following morning, under some guise or other, and in the company of Otto Huber that they would be leaving Madrid for good. At this Anna raised her eyebrows.

'But what about any documents that Otto has worked on, how are they to be removed?'

'That's the thing Anna. Our man Otto has everything in his head. He's a total sponge when it comes to information. We need only to get him out and he can start spilling all his secrets to the Allies.'

'I want this to work Seamus. He's a good man and he wanted no part of this. It's only because of his family...'

'We know Anna. Arrangements are being made to get them out at the same time. But in the interim you need to continue as if this is a normal weekend for you. Go to El Corte Ingles and do your shopping. Just behave as normal, and on Monday get the language school and the embassy informed of your planned holiday. Is that clear?'

They parted, and as Seamus went on his way he knew he had denied Anna the opportunity to say goodbye to her friend.

Having concluded his business with Carla Huerta-Melandez, Malcolm decided a good walk was needed to clear his head. As he now found himself close to the Retiro Park, he entered it, and then strolled along the various paths. It was a beautiful open space in the middle of the city, and although the air was chilly, an embracing winter sun glowed over Madrid. Young lovers strolled and planned for the future. This semblance of normality was a thin layer on the surface of this city. The dichotomy existed in that horrific deeds were being carried out in the name of the regime, and that was the conundrum with which the ordinary people of Spain were trying to live with on a daily basis.

It now brought home to him clearly how much he wanted normality in his life, and he knew that his constant pervasive thoughts with regard to Anna were responsible for that. Whilst Evelyn Sinclair was beautiful and exotic he had no regrets that there wasn't a future for them together. But with Anna it was very different. A different type of beauty surrounded Anna, and her strength in facing up to the everyday dilemmas of this mission had truly impressed him. Yes, he knew if he were ever to lose Anna, it would be a loss he did not really wish to contemplate.

For the present, he should not allow these thoughts to interfere with the here and now of their goal, and that was to get Otto Huber safely out of Madrid beyond Christoph Beich's reach. Whereas before the threats had been veiled, they were now positively open and hostile. It was the right time to get out. It had to work.

As evening approached Seamus was well on his way to visit Father Ignatius at his church. On several occasions he caught himself checking over his shoulder ensuring he was not being followed. He was soon there and he waited in a pew near the confessional boxes along with those who were awaiting their turn. It was almost eight o' clock when the old priest opened the door of the confessional and walked out. Seamus was the last person waiting.

He had a strong handshake for such a small individual.

'Come Seamus, let us retire to the Vestry where you can have some tea or perhaps something a little stronger?'

Having indicated his preference for whiskey, he sat quietly as Father Ignatius poured generous amounts of the amber liquid.

They drank for a few minutes, both appreciating the quietness of their surroundings. His glass eventually empty, Seamus set it down on the table and waited for his friend to speak.

'You know Seamus, people vastly underestimate the power of silence and how curative it can be for a restless mind, or soul for that matter.'

'Come now Father, you're not trying to save my soul are you?'

'Well Seamus, I'm not trying at all. You are the best man to do that. But I have an interesting story to tell you about Marta.' He sat back in his chair and sighed as he thought about what had been said during her dying moments.

'I know what you told me the night you arrived here with Marta and your suspicions about a woman called Raquel and this man Beich. Well, you were right, but not in the way you think.'

He turned his empty glass in his hand before continuing.

'Beich is a very clever man. As you already said, he found out that Marta and Karina were lovers. Then he became involved in a relationship with Raquel. He used her as an informant for anything he could find out about Marta, or probably anyone for that matter. You are not going to like this Seamus.'

'I didn't think I would. Go on, get it said, and just how bad can it be?'

'You can be the judge of that. I already know what I think.'

As Father Ignatius continued to relate what Marta had said, Seamus could feel a cold sensation moving down his spine. Clever cunning Beich. He had approached a high ranking member of Karina Arauzo-Vicaria's family who was present that night in Alphonse's casino and who had also witnessed the scene. Days later as Beich continued to lick his wounds, but also plot his revenge, he approached this man who is regarded as the head of the family.

In Madrid society this family is hugely respected, very wealthy, and of high profile. The uncle saw Beich for the vindictive beast that he was and he chose not to believe him. But Beich persisted. He intimated that it would be devastating for the family if the authorities were to find out. He arranged for Raquel and this uncle to follow Marta home in order to verify his story. This uncle watched overnight and he witnessed the two girls embracing passionately. He knew Beich would do as he threatened, that he would destroy the family. It would be a scandal difficult for any family to survive in Franco's Spain. In his need to deal with the situation he had someone approach Marta and say the relationship must end, and that she would have to leave Madrid. She refused. Finally, he paid some thugs, probably Falange, to call to her apartment, to shake her up a bit and give her a good fright, but they were drunk and things got out of hand.

Having listened to the story, Seamus now felt compelled to ask about Raquel's part in it.

'Dear god, was Raquel present while this was going on. Had she a direct hand in it?'

'Yes. It was she who had previously gained access to the apartment. She was paving the way for the entry of these thugs. When they thought Marta was dead they panicked, cleaned up as best they could, and then they took Marta downstairs and placed her into a laundry basket where you found her.'

Seamus felt a horrible anger build up in him, anger of a level he had not experienced since the civil wars in Ireland and Spain. The sheer brutality of what that poor woman must have experienced, the agony as they had gagged her and pummelled her to within an inch of her life. Well they had succeeded, and they were unlikely to ever receive justice for their deed.

Father Ignatius could see the turmoil in Seamus's face and it reminded him of years not that long past.

'Where is her body now?'

'It was difficult but we have arranged to have her buried, though not here. Her body has already been removed.' At this Seamus raised a quizzical look.

'I know why you look at me like that Seamus, but Marta's family had disowned her. She had given up everything for the love of her life. I believe she only related a miniscule of her fears to your colleague, Anna. She is being buried tomorrow at a small village church outside Madrid. I have good contacts there. If we bury her here the authorities might find out. It's safer for everyone.'

Seamus could only nod his agreement.

'Come Seamus, we both need something to eat, and my poor housekeeper will despair over the food she has prepared and left waiting for me. Besides, Monday looms and we must go over our final plans for Sonsoles. It is on the living we must now spend our energy. Has our friend made the arrangements for the pick-up at the city mortuary?'

Seamus knew in how much danger he was placing Father Ignatius. This man who was rebelling in his own way against the edicts of his church in Spain stood taller than most men Seamus knew. He also acknowledged that he could never repay his gratitude.

'Thank you for everything you did to help Marta, and yes, our friend has everything in place for Monday morning. Let's pray that all goes well.'

'Yes Seamus. Perhaps now is the time for a small prayer?'

For the first time in over a decade, Seamus complied.

Chapter 21

Monday 11th January 1943, and Anna made her
way as usual to the language school. As planned, she
delivered her note to say that the following week she
would be taking a sabbatical. The following day she
would repeat this at the German embassy.

Señora Arauzo had still not returned from the visit
to her cousin. It turned out that the illness was not
as serious as initially thought. She extended their
stay as she considered that it had been far too many
years since they had seen each other, and also she
deemed it good for Karina to get to know this side of
the family. It had also been a perfect excuse for her
brother to use in order to remove his sister and
Karina from Madrid.

It was during the lunch break that morning that
Anna saw Raquel. She was glad that Seamus had
managed to get word to her about Raquel's
involvement in Marta's demise. She noticed a
difference in her demeanour. She was more
confident and more confrontational with other

members of staff. She was wallowing in her affair with Beich, and she felt in view of that relationship that her position should be regarded as more elevated.

Anna knew it was more a sense of intimidation that the other members of staff felt. She had to hide the contempt she felt for this horrible woman as nothing was to be allowed to jeopardise their mission here in Madrid.

Occasionally she felt Raquel's watchful eyes fixed on her. She even had the brazenness to ask when would their colleague Marta be returning to work, and had Anna heard anything from Karina. Not revealing how she truly felt, Anna just smiled, and said that she had no news yet as Karina and her mother had prolonged their stay with their cousin. Nevertheless, she felt it a very tense moment and was glad when the bell sounded for them all to return to the classroom.

It was a wretched morning for Seamus. He was at work, stuck in an office with Rory who was making a mountain out of a molehill over his expenses claims. He thought he would go mad. He had to think of an excuse to get out of there. Waiting to know if Sonsoles had escaped, all this had turned him into a volcano about to erupt. The most dangerous aspect as far as he was concerned was the pick-up at the mortuary. It would be unusual for anyone to collect a body so early in the day. What if the nurse had used too much sedation? Also, from a psychological point of view, would Sonsoles be the person he had once known, and could they ever have again the magic of their relationship as it once was?

He grabbed his hat and coat and announced that he had forgotten an appointment, and by the way he would also be out and about tomorrow. As he hurried through the office door he could hear the frustration in Rory's voice as he tried to make the books balance.

He needed a drink. Father Ignatius had warned Seamus not to set foot on church premises that day. If Sonsoles arrived safely they would have to stabilise her, and the last thing they wanted was Seamus wringing his hands and getting in the way. No, he was to keep his distance until Tuesday evening. Too many unanswered questions.

The following day at the Embassy, Anna had an opportunity to tell Malcolm about Raquel's brazen attitude.

'Remember Anna, a lot of this is a game of bluff. It's all about who is the better actor. Never complicate your cover with elaborate stories and know that simplicity is the key to our success here. You don't need to mention to your colleagues at the language school that you are going on sabbatical but if they ask then this is your cover. I don't think Raquel suspects you of anything even though she and Beich must be wondering how Marta has managed to disappear. I think what she will enjoy is the pain that will be inflicted on Karina when she hears Marta has left without a word.'

He went on to outline their plan which Anna felt was ingenious in its simplicity.

'Why are you telling me this now? I thought you were waiting until Friday to reveal all?'

'I have to be pragmatic Anna. Beich in his current mood could trump up something against me and have me incarcerated. Should anything go wrong, you and Otto can go it alone.'

339

It was these words that brought home to Anna more forcefully than anything else on this mission that her attraction and feelings for this man were undeniable. She felt in a more compelling way than ever before how much they had to succeed.

'Malcolm, I just want to say ....'

He interrupted her and said, 'I know Anna. But anything we feel for each other takes second place to our mission. Believe me when I say that I wish it was otherwise because at this moment there is nothing I would like better than to sweep you off your feet and make love to you.'

At those words Anna's face lit up.

'Stop smiling at me like that Miss Fingal, or I may go back on my word! Now let's get back into this office and act like we have never acted before.'

Seamus had spent all Tuesday at a boxing club in Madrid. Anything that would keep his mind a little occupied until evening, and then he could go back to the church. He had been a pugilist in his more impressionable youth and had gained quite a reputation for being extremely fast and accurate with his punches. He remembered how these skills had on more than one occasion saved his life during those turbulent years of civil war.

As he looked upon the activity in the ring, where two young men were vying with each other for supremacy, his thoughts turned to the function of war and the absolute decades, indeed the centuries of misery and distrust it could cause. He knew he should not allow his thoughts to enter into such dark shadows, but he did.

He thought about his wars and the awful destruction of human life. The politicians who brought a new belief to the gullible, a total fallacy of lies and corruption which they embraced because there was nothing better in their lives to grasp or hold onto. The void and despair that must have existed in order for them to fall hook, line and sinker for all the warmongering and its inevitable path to utter destruction and chaos. Then, when the veil was lifted from their eyes, the false romance of the new ideal shattered, they all looked on in confusion and asked from where did this hell come? The answer was always from themselves. They had allowed it to happen, to be sucked into the void of unquestioning obedience.

It was the crack of the younger boxer's jaw that smashed Seamus from his morbid reverie. He knew his recent dark thoughts reflected his own past, but also his fears for the future, if there was to be one with Sonsoles.

It was now close on four-thirty in the afternoon and as he gathered up his hat and coat he knew it was a make or break moment. Nothing could keep him apart from Sonsoles any longer. He had to see her no matter what her state, and he had to escape from his reflections on the state of humankind.

Finally, after what seemed like the longest hour he had ever experienced, Seamus arrived at the church. He saw a young altar boy, obviously in training, who was scurrying around, picking up leaflets and depositing them neatly on the very back pews of the long aisle.

At Seamus's request, the young boy went in search of Father Ignatius. What seemed a lifetime, but which was in fact only about five minutes, this small dynamo of a man arrived. He pushed into the pew alongside Seamus, and touching his arm he stated just three words; 'She is alive.'

He observed his friend's reaction to his words and the now raw emotion on his face. Quietly, he asked Seamus to follow him through to the vestry in case of any prying eyes.

The young altar boy was finishing his duties and Father Ignatius thanked him and told him to finish for the day. Once this was achieved he locked the two doors leading into the vestry. He then walked towards one of the side walls from where a large supporting pillar of wood rose up in line with it. Moving his hand over a carved section of wood the pillar swung open and a concrete spiral descending staircase was revealed.

This came as no surprise to Seamus who had been removed to the crypt as a safe hiding place during the civil war. What he did not know was how to actually make the pillar swing open. That secret was held by Father Ignatius.

Descending the staircase he felt his legs start to tremble and was horrified at his reaction.

'Just a moment Father, I need to rest a second.'

'Take your time Seamus. She is alive but incredibly weak, and physically she is very changed. You must be prepared for that.'

They walked on through various labyrinths within which a stranger would easily lose their way. Finally, they came to a more open passageway with several rooms. Entering the second on the left, Seamus first registered the presence of two other people standing vigil over a bed.

'Seamus, this is my great friend Doctor Estevaz and his daughter, Alba, who has only just qualified as a nurse. I have to say .....'

But Seamus heard no more. He was staring at his once beautiful Sonsoles lying totally immobile on a bed. Death seemed to be written over every pore of her body. He knelt beside her, took her hand and kissed it. He believed that the person he once knew was no more, that his own existence was shattered. It was then he felt the tiniest movement of her fingers, and on looking up he saw this amazing woman struggling from the depths of her weak body to whisper his name so quietly that he almost missed it. Seamus cried. There was hope.

Chapter 22

Wednesday had been a very useful day for Anna. There was no break to her normal routine. That morning she had worked at the language school and had heard from the Administrator of the college that Signora Arauzo and Karina would be returning from their holiday next Sunday.

She could not allow herself to dwell on Marta, or that by next Sunday she would no longer be present in Madrid. Karina may one day know the truth about Marta, but on her return she would only discover that her friend had left Madrid.

Anna pondered on how much Raquel knew about her, and if Beich was also having her followed. She had ensured that she was even more vigilant as she walked home from work. There was no indication that she was being followed and her cover was so good that she considered it unlikely. In fact, if anything, it was more likely to be Malcolm who needed to look over his shoulder. Beich certainly had it in for him, particularly since that incident at

Alphonse's night club. Malcolm had related the account of Raquel following him into Carlos Santiago's tobacco shop.

This coming Friday, Alphonse was hosting an event at his night club and he had invited Anna. Malcolm had insisted that she must attend and behave as if nothing else was on her mind. In fact he said it was timely and Anna was to mention it at the embassy if Beich was present. His plans had moved to Saturday for her and Otto's escape.

The invitation had also been extended to Seamus and his Irish colleagues, and Anna wanted to be escorted within that group. However, Seamus was proving a little elusive to contact at the moment and she hoped he would get in touch soon.

After arriving at the embassy that afternoon, Anna had worked solidly for three hours alongside Otto when Beich and Malcolm entered the room together.

'Ah, Fraulein Fingal. My colleague here tells me that we have been invited to Club Alphonse this coming Friday. Perhaps you would care to accompany our group?'

Anna thinking quickly replied; 'How kind Herr Beich, but I have already accepted the invitation of my Irish colleagues and Seamus is escorting me.'

'That is unfortunate. You know your teaching colleague Raquel is to accompany me and I thought we might share a table together along with the other embassy staff. But not to worry, I'm sure we can all mingle, and I look forward to seeing that rascal Seamus.'

So, Beich was now openly flaunting Raquel. How glad Anna was that she would not have to share a table with her. She was amazed at his buoyant mood, and he even seemed amicable towards Malcolm which was not a usual occurrence of late.

A few hours later and Anna had almost completed her work for the day when Malcolm called her and Otto aside. Beich had earlier vacated the office on some mission of his own.

'I may not have much opportunity again to have the two of you together but here goes. This Friday we will all attend Club Alphonse, apart from Otto who never attends these functions. We keep that the same, it will look normal and raise no suspicions. At some point during the evening I will be picking up false papers for you Otto and handing them over to Anna at the club. That same evening Otto, at about seven pm you will be visited by a young lady who is a make-up artist. A disguise has been developed for you along with new clothes which you will don the following morning prior to your departure to the train station. You must arrive at the Atocha station for eight-thirty and no later. As to your new identity? All will be revealed to Anna on Friday evening. Any questions?'

Otto looked extremely pensive as he listened to these details.

'What about my family? You know I won't move a muscle from here unless I know they are safe.'

'Listen Otto, we have put a plan in place to rescue your family. It is being coordinated for the early hours of Saturday morning. We know that Beich has a man watching your apartment every night from eleven to seven the following morning. They don't really ever expect you to make a run for it and especially not during the day. But that morning you will only have a few hours of opportunity in which to get out of the city and it really is our only chance for obvious reasons. Once it's discovered that your family has escaped, then time is of the essence for you.'

Anna looked at Otto and wondered if he could pull off the subterfuge. She gently put her hand on his shoulder.

'We must be brave together Otto. Just think, a few hours of living hell to be with your own family again? As Malcolm says, it is our only chance. I think it's a simple, effective plan and very workable. You've got to trust us.'

'Yes, I know you are both right. I must take a leap of faith and this is the time.'

Malcolm spoke and went over the plan again to make sure all was understood.

Her day at the embassy was now concluded and as Anna made her way through the various security checks at the embassy, she felt more than relieved that the plan did not involve the removal of documents from the embassy. It would have been almost impossible to achieve.

On entering through the front door into the downstairs hall of her apartment, Anna noticed a letter on the ground which was addressed to her. It was from Seamus, and it merely notified her that he was busy with work but that he would of course pick her up on Friday evening at eight o'clock. Anna felt relieved to have heard from him. She felt that he was up to something which was obviously secret and not for discussion.

Upstairs in the apartment, with the fire now lit, Anna planned what items she would have to carry with her on Saturday morning. No luggage of note could be brought and Malcolm had said that the false papers would be for Otto alone. Anna had a medium sized shoulder satchel that would do the trick and within which she now placed her identity papers and passport.

Sitting in front of the fire Anna reminisced on her time in Madrid. She loved this city and had made good friends. Despite the obvious hardships and weariness for the majority of people who lived here, the sometimes daily struggle in their endeavours to keep their families together, to put food on the table;

there remained their pride in their achievements and the determination to meet the future head on.

Also, and inevitably, the closer Anna now drew to her departure date, the more thoughts of home inveigled her mind. She smiled inwardly at the thought of seeing her family again. But what would be the outcome for her brother Patrick and her sister Marion? It was a predicament for which no one could give a definitive answer. The thought of home was enticing. Her father Hugh and his wisdom, her famous but erratic mother, the family home, the bridge and Blackwater River, Donaghpatrick, and the beautiful church she had known and loved all her life.

Finally, there was Malcolm. Could they really envisage a future together? She realised she truly loved him but this mission consumed them all, and their focus on it had to be complete. Her time had come to truly show her worth and get Otto safely out. This Friday at Alphonse's Club, she must act as she had never acted before, but to remember to keep everything simple. As for Seamus, she would see him tomorrow. She felt that Malcolm was becoming frustrated with his disappearing acts, but he hid it well. He truly saw them all as a team, but his primary concern now was to get them all out safely. Anna knew how she was to exit Madrid, but what about Malcolm and Seamus? Nothing of that had been mentioned.

The following day was Thursday and Seamus decided it was time to put in an appearance at work or Rory would be having a fit. Besides, he did not want him contacting Dublin for any reason and in particular to say that he had gone missing. No, that certainly would not do.

On arriving at the office, to say that Rory was sulking was no exaggeration and it took about two hours of Seamus's charm to bring out the usual humorous colleague that he knew. Seamus was relieved on many levels, but mostly because he now knew that although Sonsoles was incredibly weak and fragile, her mind and intellect had not been destroyed. But so incredibly weak and thin. Tortured of course, and starved.

Even after a few days of gentle medical and nursing care, her eyes were a little brighter. Conversation was limited but he knew now that he could not leave Sonsoles behind in Madrid this very weekend. Mortimer would go nuts, and Seamus realised he was perhaps leaving him a little in the lurch but he would see everyone clear of this city and then continue his stay here until Sonsoles had the strength to travel. Yes, he intended to return to Ireland with his wife. The Corpse of course would go berserk but Seamus was no longer worried about that.

For Anna, that final Friday at work was a relief. She sensed Otto was tense and he became irritated a little more frequently than normal but he got through the day without any mishaps. Beich was frequently in the office. Malcolm was nowhere to be seen, but he had said that he would be at the club later.

Anna said her usual goodbyes and returned to her apartment to prepare for the evening, not forgetting to check that all was hidden and ready for the morning.

Right on cue, Seamus arrived to pick up Anna, and being impressed by her ensemble, he whistled his appreciation.

'Seamus, I hope you are not intending to be totally outrageous this evening?'

'Yes Anna, in every respect, but first I need to confide something.' And Seamus related his story.

Although Anna had known that Seamus was up to something, his news was still very surprising. However, she was genuinely concerned for Seamus's predicament.

'But Seamus, if Sonsoles is so weak, how are you going to get her out with us?'

'I don't need to Anna. I am going to stay on here for a few extra months until Sonsoles can be moved. There is nothing really to link me to you and Malcolm. We have always been extremely discreet about our meetings. In their eyes I work for the Dublin government. Think about it Anna, they are going to be so embarrassed when they realise what has been sneaked out right from under their noses.

You, Otto and Malcolm will disappear and they won't have a clue until Saturday evening which is when the surveillance of Otto's apartment will commence for the first time after his departure.'

'What about Malcolm. He needs you Seamus, for goodness sake you are part of our team. You can't let us down, not now!' Anna suddenly realised that she had raised her voice and checked her emotions.

'Well, well Anna. Are you telling me you have feelings for our number one in command? Ah yes, I see you have. I have to say you hid that well.'

Anna was about to protest further when Seamus said, 'Look Anna, I'm not letting anyone down. I am one hundred per cent going to see everyone safely out. Whatever Malcolm needs me to do between now and your departure will be done. Anna, we both have something very special here which we don't want to lose and we all want this to work on many levels.'

She knew Seamus was not to be persuaded otherwise. She nodded and picked up her bag and cape and was escorted to the car.

'Seamus, I wish you the very best. This may be the only opportunity I get to say it. Anyone who has held onto the love you have for Sonsoles is remarkable. You never gave up.'

'And you Anna. You have been a star throughout and a friend. Hopefully when we all get back to Ireland we can meet up and look back on our adventures here.'

'I would dearly like that Seamus.'

Fifteen minutes later the car pulled up at the club. The foyer was buzzing with many nationalities and again embassy staff from various nations. Seamus was hailed by Alphonse and he led them both to their table where Seamus's colleagues were already seated.

Alphonse drew Anna aside.

'How stunning you look this evening Anna. You must agree to dance with me later. That is if that old renegade Seamus does not take up all of your time.'

Overhearing this remark Seamus winked at Anna, and addressing Alphonse he jokingly replied that he would consider his request.

'Ah, Seamus you know you are like a protective mother hen with Anna, your fellow countrywoman. I like that.'

Then bowing, he kissed Anna's hand, and promised to return later.

The band struck up and the replacement singer for Karina came on stage. She was good, but she did not command the same stage presence as her friend. Nevertheless the performance went down well with the international audience. As Anna glanced around the room, she took in the variety of beautiful women and the haute couture dresses. It was then she noted the staff from the German embassy along with the ever menacing Beich who had Raquel in tow. Malcolm was sitting at the opposite end of the table in deep discussion with some colleagues.

A short time later the buffet dinner was announced and everyone started to mingle as they queued towards the tables. The displays of food were fantastic and champagne was flowing freely. Alphonse was going all out to impress his international clientele.

Following several dances with Seamus and Rory, Anna saw Malcolm approach their table. After a few minutes of conversation with Seamus, he turned to Anna and requested a dance. Smiling, Anna accepted, and they both made their way to the dance floor.

'May I just say Fraulein Fingal that you are looking very elegant.'

Noticing that Raquel was dancing nearby with Beich, Anna kept her response formal.

'Thank you Herr Holtzman. I hope you are enjoying the evening and the music.'

Making sure that Beich was now out of earshot, he turned to Anna.

'Look Anna, later this evening I will be leaving here to collect Otto's documentation. With this crowd no one will notice if I disappear for an hour or more. When I return you can easily hide them in your bag.'

Anna nodded her understanding, and at the end of the dance she again formally thanked Herr Holtzman. As she turned she noticed Alphonse was watching them, but he was quick to wave over to indicate that his dance would be coming up soon.

Back at her table, she was surprised to see Beich seated beside Seamus. It had to be said that Seamus brought out the best in him and that Beich always seemed more relaxed in his company.

'Well Fraulein Fingal, I was just discussing with Seamus how when the war ends in triumph for the Fatherland that my friend Seamus, if he plays his cards right, could find a better future by working with us. I think we would have a very comfortable working relationship.'

Anna inwardly smiled at Beich's confidence. The war was not running in Germany's favour at the moment. On the 1st January 1943 the German 1st Panzer Division had to withdraw from the Terek River area to avoid encirclement. Germany was beginning to feel stretched but Beich would never reveal that.

'You, Fraulein Fingal, you would be wise to take our side also. What is there in Ireland for you except a worthless economy?'

Keeping calm, Anna replied, 'Indeed Herr Beich, I may consider what you have just said.'

This seemed to please Beich who slapped Seamus on the shoulder and after a little more small talk, disengaged himself from their company.

As Anna watched him return to his table she noticed that Raquel appeared to be missing. Where was she? Her thoughts were interrupted by Alphonse who was claiming his dance.

'Why Alphonse, you seem more sombre than usual. Is something worrying you?'

Looking down at Anna, he sighed.

'You worry me Anna. A beautiful woman like you would be a bonus on any man's arm. The problem is I want it to be my arm. Have you by any chance changed your opinion of me?'

Leaning back Anna could see that Alphonse was very serious.

'Oh Alphonse, you know I value you as a friend, and truly I would be lying to you if I were to say that there was anything deeper than that. I hope you can accept this?'

For the first time ever, Anna thought she noticed something different in his demeanour, but she was not certain. Disappointment? No, she thought she sensed a level of anger that she had not witnessed in him before and it took her by surprise. On the surface he hid it very well and when he then smiled she thought she had imagined it all. He did not mention it again and he seemed to continue in his normal gentlemanly manner. Returning Anna to her table, he bowed over her hand and kissed it. He then smiled and stated he had other matters to which he had to attend.

'What's up with you Anna?'

'I don't know Seamus, he just seemed different.'

'Nonsense, he's all over you like a rash and you keep him at arms' length. What do you expect? He's disappointed.'

Sighing, Anna agreed. Perhaps she was just feeling uptight because of what was planned for the morning.

Malcolm made his move at the busiest time of the evening. The club was crowded, and thankfully that fact gave him good cover as he made his way out by a door near the men's cloakroom. Walking quickly down a few alleyways, and then after criss-crossing a few streets, he reached his parked car. Checking the roads carefully, he drove to Guillermo's art gallery and parked a few streets away.

It was now well after midnight, and for the ordinary citizen of Madrid it was much safer to be indoors. Keeping his hat well pulled down over his face, he approached the front door of Guillermo's premises. He could see that there was some light emanating from the kitchen at the back of the gallery. He tapped gently on the door and within moments he saw the small figure of Carla approaching. As he entered the gallery, with a wry smile he acknowledged the performance of the grotesque monkey.

'Señora Huerta, I hope everything has gone to plan?'

'Indeed, I have the papers and passport you need. I know our make-up artist will do a good job on your colleague. She is very skilled and the likeness to these photographs will be excellent.'

'Good, it certainly has to be. Señora Huerta, I can't thank you enough...'

At this she raised her hand.

'I do not need any thanks Señor. What I've done is a pittance but it is the only way in which I can help. There are very few ways in which we can fight against what is happening here in Spain and in Europe, but this is certainly one. I wish you luck, and give my best wishes to Anna. She will indeed be missed by us both, but especially by Guillermo.'

'When does your husband return Señora?'

'In three days' time. He is excited about a new artist, a new inspirational find.'

Malcolm smiled and imagined Guillermo's excitement at a new discovery, but he could not remain any longer at the gallery as he needed to get back to the night club as soon as possible. Bowing over Señora Huerta's hand he left without further delay.

Some minutes had passed when Carla heard the opening of the gallery door being announced yet again by the grotesque monkey with its bizarre dance. Thinking that the English Captain had forgotten something, she entered the gallery which was still in darkness.

It took some moments for her eyes to adjust. When they did, her last thought, and her last breath were annihilated by the bullet that entered her brain.

Chapter 23

It was now almost one o' clock in the morning and Seamus would have to wait for Malcolm's return to the night club. Now was the time to reveal his plans to Malcolm and face up to the wrath that would inevitably descend upon him. Better still, he would have it out with him before he returned to the night club as he could not control a reaction on the premises. The best thing to do was to fabricate something and make his excuses to Rory and Anna. Without further ado, he announced to the table in general that he had a terrible headache and the music was killing him.

'Ah Seamus, you've gone soft,' said Rory. 'Don't worry, I will escort the lovely Anna home.'

Looking sheepish, Seamus wished everyone an enjoyable evening and made a show of rubbing his head as he made his way to the cloakroom. He knew exactly where Malcolm had gone and he felt that he could easily intercept him, but after some minutes of driving around he could not spot Malcolm's car.

Leaving his own newly acquired car down a side street was easy. He knew the gallery was just a short walk away.

As he approached, he thought he saw a flash of light through the gallery window and he quickly stood into a nearby doorway. Then he heard the opening of the door. As he hid in the shadows, Seamus expected to see Malcolm, and he was about to step out when he realised his almost fatal error. His heart was racing and he could feel his hands clenching. Was that really who he thought, and with a gun? He could not believe it.

He waited at least five minutes before he moved a muscle, and it was only after scanning the street, several times, in many directions, that he eventually vacated the doorway. After entering the gallery Seamus noticed that the monkey no longer made any movement or noise. He looked about and dared not switch on a light. Heading into the kitchen, he noted nothing amiss, but there was still no sign of Carla, or Malcolm for that matter. He needed to get out. He knew it was dangerous to hang about so he made his way back towards the door.

As he glanced back at the grotesque monkey, which somehow was now permanently silenced, his eye was distracted by the sudden realisation that behind the stand on which the monkey rested was a chair; and in that chair was the slumped body of Carla. Stepping closer, he could just make out a bullet hole in the centre of her forehead. The blood from that fatal wound had trickled in a tiny stream down the length of her incredibly pale face, onto her neck, and then beyond.

'Beyond everything,' thought Seamus.

For some strange reason it reminded Seamus of rivers of blood, and he had to shake himself free from his imagination. He knew there was nothing he could do, except wonder why this woman had met with such a callous ending.

He searched the gallery again, double checking that Malcolm had not also become a victim, and finally satisfied, he realised that he needed to get out of there before his luck also ran out. Closing the door, Seamus hurriedly made his way back to the car. As he drove, he wondered what to do next. He could not return to the club.

As the champagne flowed, Anna inwardly remarked on the varied nuances of life. How people here were lavishly enjoying themselves while the lives of other people not that far away were homeless, displaced and on the edge of poverty.

She looked up and saw Malcolm approaching her, and they returned to the table where her evening bag was lying.

'How did it go? Did you get the papers?'

Picking up a napkin, Malcolm commenced to eat a dessert which had remained untouched.

'Yes, Anna. Everything went as planned and Carla has done a magnificent job with the papers. Now let me explain all. Otto will make his own way to the station tomorrow. These false papers will show you what he will look like as otherwise you won't recognise him. Your cover is that Otto is an art dealer and you are assisting him at various exhibitions. His passport is Spanish and his cover name is Sergio Orellana-Ferrer. You are accompanying him for a very generous fee as a translator and this is why you have taken a sabbatical. Guillermo recommended you for the job.'

'What happens after our rendezvous at the train station tomorrow, how does it go from there?'

He looked at Anna intently and saw her usual composed face. What a strong woman, she was astounding.

'You are taking the train to Lisbon. Should either of you be questioned your cover story is that you are attending a major art exhibition in Lisbon. You have both been added to the guest list for the exhibition and there is a letter included with the documents that I'm leaving with you which confirms that you will be attending.'

Anna smiled at the ingenuity of the plan.

'And once in Lisbon, what happens then?'

Finishing his dessert, and wiping his mouth with the large linen napkin, Malcolm casually slipped the envelope of papers beneath it and left it lying on the table for Anna to pick up.

'Everything is there Anna. Hotel accommodation, venue for the exhibition, your passes. Everything. Read it carefully when you get back to your apartment and then you must brief Otto during your train journey.'

Anna nodded her understanding.

'By the way Anna, where is Seamus?'

There was nothing else for it. Anna told Malcolm about Sonsoles. She could see him tense, she thought he was going to leave there and then. But he suddenly relaxed.

'The sly dog. I knew he was up to something. You know Anna, if Seamus is willing to risk staying in Madrid then so be it. I can't argue with that, there is no time and I have to be pragmatic.'

'He did say he would give you any assistance you needed.'

'Really Anna,' Malcolm remarked sardonically. 'Then where the hell is he?'

'Sorry Anna, it's not your fault but let's just say it's not quite the spanner in the works I expected. Look, don't stay too much longer. You will need your wits about you, so go home Anna and try if you can to get some shuteye for the already dawning day.'

Anna looked at Malcolm more intently than he had ever been aware of before. He wanted to protect her from all of this but knew that to be impossible. How she behaved and acted over the next forty-eight hours would rule her survival or destruction. He did not want to say anything that would unnerve her.

'Malcolm, before we separate I just want to say good luck and take care. How are you going to get out of Madrid? Will you meet up with us in Portugal?'

He shook his head to indicate no.

'It's as much for everyone else's safety Anna that I have to take a separate route. I can't divulge it to you, and you know the reasons for that. The less you and Otto know about my movements the better. I wish you a safe journey Anna Fingal and I'm telling you now that apart from being a beautiful woman, you are one of the best damn operatives I have ever worked with.'

He squeezed Anna's hand and they both locked eyes for what seemed an eternity, but which in fact was a few mere seconds. Malcolm was the first to tear his eyes away. He could not afford now for anyone to see what he felt.

Returning to his embassy table Malcolm mused on the spanner that Seamus had thrown into the equation. He did not have time to talk him out of it.

It also dawned on him that Seamus must have planned this before the mission had even started. That cunning Irishman. He even doubted if putting a gun to Seamus's head might do the trick. He would just laugh in his face.

It was now approaching two o' clock in the morning and Malcolm glanced around the beautiful club to see where the major players were. Beich, who had been missing from view for some time was seated at the Italian table. He lay slumped on the shoulder of Raquel who now looked incredibly bored. As the Irish contingent were preparing to leave with Anna, he noticed the appearance of Alphonse at her side. It was obvious that he was greatly attracted to her. He personally escorted Anna and Rory to the exit, calling a car forward for their use. He then made his way to the back of the club and disappeared in the direction of the changing rooms.

Beich was now struggling to his feet and shouting at one of the waiters to bring him his hat and coat. As he donned his hat he glared over at Malcolm, and a sly, contemptuous knowing look crossed his face. Malcolm casually returned the look but was careful not to imbue it with the same amount of contempt he had received. Stubbing out his cigar he decided it was time to leave and return to his apartment. He could walk. Plaza del Ángel was not that far away. It was a slightly misty morning but not as incredibly cold as it had been.

It was only as he was about two streets short of his accommodation that he thought he could hear the fall of someone's footsteps. He deliberately slowed his pace and then quickened it. It was as if there was an echo to his own footsteps coming from not too far away. It must be an echo. There was a need for him to divert his attention onto more important matters.

He was a mere few feet from the front door of his building when he clearly heard the noise of someone moving fast towards him. As he turned to look, his eyes locked on the gun pointing at his head. As if in slow motion, he noticed the fingers begin to squeeze on the trigger. His training came to the fore and throwing himself down and out to the right he tumbled and rolled before coming to his feet again. The momentary reprieve bought him little time as the slow precise movement of his assassin's pace

373

hardly faltered, and now he was backed up against a wall. As the gun was raised again, Malcolm Mortimer thought his luck had finally run out.

His attacker drew closer. His hat was pulled well down and this helped to disguise his face. In that moment Malcolm decided to rush at him. This succeeded in throwing him slightly off balance, but not for long, as then his assailant's gun was raised and smashed into the back of his head. Stunned, but conscious, Malcolm realised that the nozzle of the gun was merely inches from his forehead. It was then that he suddenly heard his assailant grunt and slump towards him. Malcolm passed out.

Chapter 24

'For Christ's sake Mortimer wake up! What the hell is this going to require? Right I've got the answer.'

As the ice cold water brought Malcolm round, his first thought was that he was alive, and his second, that he had been captured and was being interrogated. To say that he was incredibly relieved to see Seamus was the understatement of the year, even if he had almost drowned him in water.

'Right Mortimer, let's get you sitting upright. You are a very lucky boyo because three seconds later on my part and you were a dead man.'

Gripping the back of his head and bringing Seamus into focus seemed the most difficult thing he had done in months.

'My head is exploding. Was it one of Beich's men or what the hell happened?'

At this point Seamus shoved a glass of whiskey into his hand.

'Yes, it was one of Beich's men,' said Seamus as he lit one of his cigarettes and shakily clawed some matches from his coat pocket. He then recounted events from earlier that night and his attempt to rendezvous with Malcolm on his way back from the Gallery.

'Señora Huerta. What a loss to us and to any future agents we may have in Madrid. Well come on Seamus, was it one of his staff in the embassy?'

'Put it this way, it was someone very familiar to you and who moved in all the right high profile circles. When I saw him leave the gallery I suspected you might be next on his shopping list so I went round to your apartment and kept watch. He was bloody good, moved like a cat and I heard nothing until he moved out towards you. I stayed well hidden in the alleyway running up the side of your apartment. When he was about to move in to finish you off, I was able to approach him, gag him with my hand and use my knife.'

Malcolm saw that Seamus still looked perplexed by whatever he had discovered.

'Come on Seamus, who the blazes was it?'

A short silence ensued before Seamus spoke again.

'Prepare yourself for a shock. It was Alphonse. His body is downstairs but I managed to get information from him before he died. I have to say it was bad enough trying to drag his body through the building but getting you upstairs was a fucking nightmare.'

Seamus took a long shaky drag on his cigarette as he looked at Malcolm's face which registered disbelief.

'I don't blame you for looking like that, but time is short and I'll explain as quickly as possible. Alphonse had been working for the German embassy for a long time. His family lost everything during the civil war and they literally had to scrape for a living. He saw a way out by offering his services to the Abwehr, here in Madrid, which is rife with spies, ours and theirs. In return he was able to establish the club which was backed by our mutual enemy. People were amazed at how it flourished and the range of important people it attracted. He was a former dancer and that accounts for his silent approach. He had also been trained by the Nazis in the art of killing. Before he died he admitted responsibility for the deaths of your two former agents, but he had absolutely nothing to do with Marta's death. He was genuinely fond of her and was willing to overlook her private life because of her wonderful dancing talent which was a major draw to the club.'

Malcolm still could not understand how Alphonse had found out about the two former agents, and said so to Seamus.

'I'm afraid it was easy for him. Anyone British who was new on the scene was closely followed. Unfortunately, they were seen making a mail drop which was used for passing on information through the British Embassy in Madrid. It was a clumsy avoidable mistake.'

As he manoeuvred into an upright position, Malcolm posed his next question.

'So, why did Beich send him after me?'

'Ah, devious old cunning Beich. Well let's face it, he has hated your guts for some time and he wanted any dirt on you he could get. So what did he do? He

378

requested your file from Berlin and hey presto, what do you know, when it arrived it did not contain a photograph with your smiling face, but that of a complete stranger. He phoned Berlin to check, and once it was verified he took matters into his own hands. It all only came to light yesterday. So, Beich called in Alphonse who is under his control. When Alphonse followed you to the gallery he knew that he was onto something good.

Malcolm felt that the old adage of the best laid plans was crumbling all around him. But he saw a way which might still work for them. Beich would be totally unaware that Anna and Otto were making their way out of Madrid this very morning, in fact in approximately four hours. Also he had his own exit planned to perfection, or so he thought. He could hardly move from the knock on his head. He doubted that he would be able to drive to *Miraflores de la Sierra.*

'So my cover is blown and Beich will be under the impression that I'm dead.'

Seamus remained silent for a few moments and then spoke.

'What if he's waiting for a phone call from Alphonse to confirm your demise?'

'You have a point Seamus, but no, I think not. Beich was so drunk last night that a phone call would be irrelevant, and he must have been very sure of Alphonse. He had not failed with the other British agents. No, I think I can go ahead with my plans. Help me up Seamus. I need to get my disguise ready, and you will have to get me out to an old disused road some distance outside Madrid. It's about a forty mile journey. I can't drive with this knock on my head, it's left me very dizzy. The plan was to drive out there and the pilot would arrange for the car to be brought back to Madrid.'

'Of course I will drive you out there. You can give me more information about where we are going once we are underway.'

Looking at Seamus, Malcolm continued, 'I know about Sonsoles and your plan to remain in Madrid. It could work for you as I don't believe that Beich knows of our connection, but that's a risk you have to take if you remain behind. Are you certain it's what you want to do?'

Seamus nodded and declared that no further discussion was to be made on the matter.

Indicating to Seamus that he wanted something from his overcoat, he then proceeded to pull out the fake passports from an inside pocket and he handed an envelope to Seamus.

'These are your papers should you change your mind, or indeed if for any reason you need to use them in the future. Now let's get out of here.'

As Otto Huber glanced at his watch and confirmed the time, he carefully drew back the edge of his bedroom curtain to see if the surveillance of his apartment had ended. It was all clear outside.

Gathering up his small travel case along with his dearest possessions, he glanced for the last time in the mirror. There, looking back at him was a complete stranger. A more elegant sophisticated man had emerged. He now wore spectacles, and on top of that the young lady who had arrived at his apartment last night had coloured his hair black.

The hair parting she had switched to the opposite side. But the final adjustment almost transfixed him as she worked her magic and applied a perfect goatee beard, black, with a line of grey worked through on both sides.

Apart from confirming on arrival that she was the make-up artist, she made no further attempt at conversation while she performed the task in hand. Once she had completed her work, she stood back and indicated that all was satisfactory. Then, having gathered her belongings, she nodded in his direction and left. He shook his head in a bemused manner at the memory. But now, now he needed to get to the Atocha Train Station and meet Anna.

About the same time in Calle Jardines, Anna glanced around the living room of the apartment for the last time. Standing at the door with a small suitcase containing only the most important items and a few clothes, Anna turned the door handle and departed. She had arranged for a driver to take her to the station. In fact it was Seamus who had arranged this, stating that it was the caretaker from the language school. They had fought alongside each other during the civil war. Seamus had asked him to keep a watchful eye over Anna, particularly since the time Anna had mentioned her suspicions about Raquel. He was to note anything suspicious and in particular if Anna was ever followed by her. Yes, Enrique kept his ear to the ground and silently watched over Anna. He was the other link that Seamus used in Madrid when he needed something done without raising suspicion.

As Anna got out of the car at the train station, she thanked Enrique. Looking at the vast building before her, she took a very deep breath and knew that this was her big test. This was her time, when she must come to the fore. She had to get this man safely out of Madrid. She was very aware that German spies from the Abwehr, the German intelligence organisation, were inevitably placed at large transport centres such as airports and train stations.

Now inside this amazing building, Anna tried to establish as casually as possible the level of security present and if any Abwehr agents stood out. Within a few minutes she spotted one talking to a group of train guards and some *civiles*. She made a mental note not to mention this to Otto. He was already justly nervous.

The station was extremely busy and that was a bonus as far as Anna was concerned. They would be absorbed more readily into the crowd. People were already arriving into Madrid for shopping trips and the markets which took place over the weekend. Train announcements were being relayed on a fairly regular basis thus initiating sudden surges of various groups of people as they scurried in different directions.

Dawdling towards the kiosk, she bought a magazine and a newspaper, and as she turned back towards a platform seat she spotted Otto. She was amazed at how much the passport photograph was indeed a true likeness of the man approaching her. After formally shaking hands, they sat together.

'I have to say Otto, that your transformation is amazing. I would not have recognised you. I have all your documents folded inside this newspaper. If you can get to the cloakroom now and incarcerate yourself in a cubicle for a few minutes, you can read your new biography, and when finished, tear it to shreds and flush it away. Remember you are taking on the mantle of a renowned but reclusive Spanish art dealer. Be careful, your travel papers are also in that bundle. When you return we have to purchase our tickets for the train to Lisbon.'

Otto nodded his assent and made his way to the men's cloakroom. No one gave him a second glance which made Anna feel extremely relieved. In a little over ten minutes Otto was back at Anna's side and they both then proceeded to the ticket booth.

Otto purchased the tickets. With only ten minutes to spare they made their way to the platform, located their carriage and boarded the train. Anna already felt that they had crossed a major hurdle. So far, Otto, at least outwardly, appeared to be coping remarkably well. He was gaining confidence through his disguise, although internally he had to be agonising over the welfare of his family.

As the carriage filled up and with more noise surrounding them, Otto leaned across the table towards Anna and spoke.

'Anna, have you heard any news about my family? Do you know if they have escaped?'

She felt the intensity of his question and could only answer it truthfully.

'Not yet, but Malcolm will get word through to us in Lisbon as he has promised. We must all have faith Otto. If we can carry off this subterfuge, we will make it, but remember even Lisbon is unsafe. It's crawling with Abwehr agents so we must constantly be vigilant.'

He nodded his understanding and then asked, 'How are we getting out of Lisbon? Do you know how long we will be there?'

'No Otto. I don't. We will be contacted again once we are established there. I'm afraid I'm as much in the dark about that as you. It was felt to be safer for all in case anything happens,' Anna replied.

'You mean in case we are rumbled, and then we would have no contact names in Portugal to disclose?'

Anna nodded. 'Yes, it has to be that way. Look it's almost time to depart. I can see the guard checking his watch.'

She had hardly finished her sentence when the whistle blew, followed shortly by a slow heaving movement from the train. They were at last on their way, but Anna felt various emotions, and all were conflicting in nature. Would she ever return to Madrid and experience this city again in brighter, better days. Would she ever see Malcolm and for that matter Seamus? She hoped so.

As Seamus drove Malcolm out of Madrid heading in a northerly direction, his concern for his passenger grew. The concussion that Malcolm was experiencing was worse than he had at first realised. On more than one occasion during the drive he noticed Malcolm's head drop forward. Seamus leaned over and shook Malcolm's arm, an action which succeeded in wakening him. They were driving in the direction of a town called *Miraflores de la Sierra*. Just short of their destination Malcolm instructed Seamus to take an old road towards a mountain locally named *'La Najarra.'*

Quite a distance up this old dirt road and just past some extremely large boulders, Seamus was directed to take a sharp left turn and then stop. Malcolm, with some discomfort, leaned over to the car's light switch and gave a prearranged signal. After just a few moments they saw a succession of responses from a torch light.

'Right Seamus, help me out. This is where you hightail it to Madrid with the car. Leave it back to where it is normally parked. We don't want anything to look out of the ordinary. Also, whatever you do, don't go back into my apartment. You can't be seen near it. Understood?'

Seamus assisted Malcolm from the car and handed him his luggage. He had to admit that his disguise was good, bloody good in fact. They shook hands and Malcolm instructed Seamus to leave immediately. The less Seamus saw the better for his own and everyone else's sake. As the lights of the car grew dim, it was then, and only then that a man emerged from the shadows.

'Good to see you Felipe. Now let's get out of here before it gets too light.'

Driving back towards Madrid, Seamus could only hope that Malcolm would make it to England. Bloody courageous in his opinion and worth his salt. A man who knew how to lead and whom men would willingly follow. Yes, he imagined he must have been quite a Captain in the field of battle.

Felipe, the man Malcolm had met near *Miraflores de la Sierra* was a pilot. He was also the proud owner of a Piper J-3 Cub. This was a dandy, small two-seater airplane. A flamboyant character and a skilled if somewhat daring pilot, their flight to a location near Lisbon went without mishap. From there, Malcolm was driven to the main airport which served that city.

As he approached the check-in desk feigning a pronounced limp and using a walking stick, Malcolm hoped the nausea he was experiencing did not deteriorate any further or he would be left behind at the airport. Airlines were reluctant to carry passengers who were noticeably ill.

Portela Airport was just outside Lisbon. During the war passenger airlines did not fly over Spanish airspace, but BOAC continued to operate regular flights from England to Lisbon. From there, passengers could then make their way into Spain. Both the Axis and Allies used the airport to fly their agents in and out of Spain with the result that the airport was closely watched by both sides.

At the BOAC desk, the ground steward did not pay Malcolm any particular attention. Clean shaven, wearing thick framed glasses, and his hair dyed very blond, he even looked a stranger to himself. His perfected gait, which indicated a pronounced limp, was not difficult considering his previous war injury. What he found tricky was having to stoop in order to appear less tall.

'Sir, are you feeling unwell?'

Malcolm looked up and realised the steward must have spoken to him more than once.

'Oh apologies, I was lost in thought. I'm absolutely fine. Was there something else?'

'Your passport please Sir.'

As the steward looked intently at the documents, Malcolm felt his head was about to explode. This combined with the nausea was not a good mix. He knew now that he was suffering with more concussion than he at first thought, and if the staff became aware of that he would definitely not be allowed to board the flight.

After a keen perusal of his documents the Steward appeared satisfied.

'Thank you Dr Winthorpe ....'

At that precise moment the steward was interrupted by a tall, razor thin man who abruptly requested to see Malcolm's documents. Malcolm knew that the Abwehr had a good foothold in the airport and this was one of their agents strutting his importance and hoping for a major catch. Without protest he handed the documents over.

'And what was the nature of your business Dr Winthorpe?'

He cursed himself for feeling so awful. He controlled his breathing and hoped that he could bluff his way out.

'I was attending a conference in Madrid on a new surgical strategy for brain trauma patients.'

Malcolm could see a sneer developing gradually on his interrogator's face.

'Really Doctor, are you not able to develop your own strategies in England? I would have thought that we were giving you plenty of scope for practice.'

He was deliberately trying to provoke Malcolm, who in return fought to choose his words very carefully. He was so close to boarding his flight. Concentrate on the flight and all would be well.

'I think perhaps if this conference was good enough for my German colleagues, then it was good enough for me,' he responded.

Tight lipped and knowing he had failed in his bid to raise Malcolm's hackles he returned the documents and gave a Nazi salute.

'Thank god,' Malcolm uttered under his breath. His bullying tormentor was more interested in annoying him because he was British rather than any interest in the fact that he might be a spy. Still his cover identity was excellent. There had indeed been such a medical conference in Madrid and Doctor Winthorpe truly existed. Or at least had. Benjamin Winthorpe had been killed in a bombing raid in London only two weeks earlier.

After what seemed an agonising wait of forty minutes, BOAC flight number 776 was finally called. As he gathered his few belongings together, Malcolm studied his fellow passengers. It appeared to him that the flight would be about three-quarters full. There was a mixed bag of passengers. Several small groups from various businesses, some British embassy staff, a few mothers struggling with young children, and even a small band of musicians. Whatever they were did not matter to him. Right now all he wanted was a seat where he could sleep and hopefully no one would sit next to him.

Twenty minutes later as the plane was taxiing down the runway for its journey to England, Malcolm felt his eyes close.

Back in the hidden crypt at Father Ignatius's church, Seamus reflected on the whereabouts of two people he had come to hold in high regard. He hoped they would make it but there were still many dangers out there. He felt it would be wise to contact the Corpse and bring him up to date with what had happened to Señora Huerta–Melandez and the role of Alphonse.

Here with Sonsoles, he was reassured by the progress report from the nurse. He could see how dedicated this girl was, and he knew he had a small amazing team helping this woman from the depths of their humanity. If they were caught the consequences for them would be awful.

Looking at his wife, he was aware of miniscule improvements to her general condition. It was noticeable that she had a little more energy which enabled more prolonged conversation. There was always a note of caution from the doctor, don't expect too much too soon. Feeling anxious about his colleagues, but more buoyant about Sonsoles progress, he left the church as inconspicuously as he had arrived.

The train to Lisbon from Madrid was a long journey. The smoke and dirt from the wood burning steam engine was immense and Anna knew that in the summer months, when windows had to be opened, that some travellers would arrive at their destination looking as if a light shower of soot had descended upon them. As their train wound its way through the varied terrain, Anna reflected on how best to distract her charge from his preoccupations.

The long journey unfolded before them through interesting landscapes, and while it was still daylight they were able to admire the beauty of the countryside. Otto's bag offered some diversion as it contained brochures and information about the art exhibition they were to attend the following day, and Anna ensured that he familiarised himself with the details. Luckily for both of them, he had an amateur's interest in art, and hopefully, if required, this would be to his benefit. By the time lunch was served in the buffet carriage he had noticeably relaxed.

It was eight o'clock in the evening when the train finally reached Lisbon. There was ample transport to meet a busy train and within twenty minutes they were booked into the Hotel Britania. It was a beautiful *art deco* hotel designed by the contemporary modernist architect Cassiano Branco. A major advantage was its central location in Lisbon in Rua Rodriguez Sampaio.

Looking around at the beautiful décor, Anna thought it a worthy and beautiful location for an art exhibition. She was very aware that Lisbon was a hotbed of political intrigue, and that this hotel lobby could at times have Allies and Axis spies shadowing each other. Anna acknowledged that it was an interesting choice of hotel, but it had been their only option as it was here that the exhibition was being hosted. Having already consigned their passports for checking by the hotel staff, Anna and Otto were taken to their rooms where trays would be brought with their supper. They agreed to meet in the foyer the following morning at eight o'clock as the exhibition was due to start at eleven.

Otto had looked exhausted and Anna prayed that tomorrow, as hoped for, the news about Otto's family would arrive. Malcolm had not indicated who their contact would be, but he had stated that they would be known to Anna. Precaution was everything. Anna was asleep within minutes of her head touching the pillow.

Chapter 25

As BOAC flight 776 touched down in Whitechurch, all passengers were requested to prepare to disembark as smoothly as possible. Air Stewardess Audrey Manning completed her count and noted that for some reason she was out by one passenger. All airplanes had their windows blacked out during the war and the lights on the aircraft had now dimmed.

Passing smoothly and efficiently along the aisle she discovered her missing passenger. As she leaned across to wake the man concerned, her thought was that he must be a very deep sleeper, but it shortly dawned on her that this man was seriously ill and possibly in a coma.

Hours later, as Sir Victor Hawkins, neurosurgeon at the Royal London Hospital, looked down at his patient, he knew he had a riddle on his hands. Only a few weeks earlier, he had attended the funeral of his friend and colleague Dr Winthorpe, and here lying before him was a dangerously ill man, who within the last few hours had been transported from the aerodrome with papers identifying him as a colleague he had worked with all his professional career.

After finishing his examination, he looked up at his ward Sister and instructed immediate preparation for surgery and to inform the appropriate people that they had a mystery man on their hands.

The following day was Sunday 17th January 1943 and the Hotel Britania in Lisbon was preparing for a long awaited exhibition. Meeting Otto in the foyer, Anna greeted him warmly and they proceeded together into breakfast. The room was busy but very well supervised and they were promptly led to a table. Sitting back and making small talk with Otto, Anna spotted an old art dealer friend of her mother's from London. He immediately came forward and Anna introduced Otto under his new name. His cover name of Sergio Orella-Ferrer was perfect. As a well-known and respected art dealer back in Spain, the real Sergio was also known for his reclusiveness. He rarely travelled to exhibitions and usually sent scouts to seek out works in which he was interested. Mr Cathcart from London was almost beside himself with excitement at meeting this reclusive man. He looked forward to chatting with him later at the exhibition and he would dearly love to chat with Anna about her famous mother.

On returning to her bedroom, Anna noticed that a note had been slipped under her bedroom door. It contained the news that she had dearly hoped to see. Just three words. 'All are safe.' She knew what it meant and she then carefully destroyed the note.

An hour later, Anna met with a pale, forlorn looking Otto. They were to attend the gala opening of the exhibition. She whispered to Otto the words he was desperate to hear, and then, before her very eyes, she witnessed his transformation. It was as if a new man had suddenly emerged.

'Anna, these words you have just spoken are life changing for me. It is the first time I have truly felt that this whole escapade might work. I almost don't care now if I'm caught, for just knowing that my family is safe means everything.'

'It's marvellous news Otto and I'm very happy for you. We have come a long way and everything is looking more and more in our favour. We are to be contacted later today by a colleague, and prepare yourself, as we may be asked at any moment to vacate our hotel and leave Lisbon for good.'

'It can't be soon enough for me Anna, not by a long shot,' but he was still smiling as he said it.

Smiling in return Anna retorted, 'Enjoy the moment Otto and if we manage to keep up this front all will go as planned.'

'You Anna, you have been very brave. I know that I have been a nervous companion and that we are by no means through this yet, but I thank you now from the bottom of my heart.'

'Don't go all sentimental on me now or we will both end up blubbering, and how is that going to look at an international art exhibition!'

Taking his cue, Otto now slipped more easily into his role. The rest of the day went without any major incident, with Anna deflecting any dangerous questions that Otto was unable to answer. The real Sergio only spoke Spanish and even at that he was not known to be a man of many words. This fell in very nicely with Otto's slow but measured responses.

As the event began to conclude for the day, Anna returned to her room to freshen up and prepare for the dinner that had been arranged for all the guests that evening. She was just about to prepare a bath when she heard the shrill ring of the phone by her bedside.

A disguised voice stated that they must prepare to leave Lisbon immediately. It was a woman's muffled tones. After checking out, they should arrange transport to take them to warehouse number eighteen down by the port, and to arrive no later than eight-thirty that evening. The call was short and to the point. Anna had not recognised the woman's voice. Perhaps the contact that Malcolm said she would recognise would be at the warehouse. She was unaware of which ships were in port. Would any of them take passengers, and if they did, what were their possible destinations? But enough, that was looking too far ahead and she needed to focus on the present.

Quickly packing her suitcase, Anna carefully hid her Browning HP revolver. She had not used this weapon since her training with the SOE, but during that time her accuracy had become very proficient.

She now needed to contact Otto and warn him that they would have to cancel their attendance at this evening's dinner. Without further delay, she phoned Otto's room and arranged to meet him in the lounge area downstairs.

Crossing the foyer, Anna noticed there was quite a mix of clientele. There were guests checking out and various parties waiting to be checked in. A rather loud, rotund and colourful Portuguese woman was lamenting the fact that you had to be foreign to be given any consideration in this hotel. The poor receptionist was doing his very best to placate his indignant guest.

Otto was waiting, and Anna smiled her greeting whilst indicating a quieter corner of the room.

'It's this evening Otto. I've just had a phone call requesting that we make our way to a warehouse down at the port as quickly as possible. We need to make our excuses for the dinner this evening.'

'At last Anna, at last! Hopefully this nightmare I'm living will soon be over. There is no doubt that I'm not cut out for this double life. I feel my nerves are at breaking point.'

Anna was certain that Otto meant what he had just said. She was worried about him. He stood pale and exhausted before her. He could hardly stand still, he appeared slightly agitated, and it was obvious to her that he was suffering with a certain degree of nervous exhaustion. She knew that the lead up to, and the events of the last few weeks had stretched his nerves until they were jangling. The only thought that had kept him sane was getting his family out, and now that he knew they were safe there was a mixture of relief and what appeared to be annoyance or irritation. She knew these last few hours were the most crucial, the most vital to getting them all out.

'Listen Otto, you have kept this subterfuge up to perfection and there are only a few more hours left for which you must remain strong.' Anna firmly gripped Otto's arm.

'The prize is within your grasp Otto, don't lose that thought. Everything you have striven for is almost complete and you must focus on your family waiting for you safely in England. They are safe Otto, and now we must do our best. We have to get out now because back in Madrid they may soon realise that you have flown the nest and they will start their hunt.'

Otto looked down at Anna and her earnest compelling face. He knew she was risking life and limb by being with him. She was a remarkable and strong woman who would do her utmost to guide him through the haze he had entered. He just wanted some level of normality again and a more enduring purpose than the incarcerated unwelcome life he had been leading.

'All right, Anna. You are correct and I'm being intolerably selfish. Let's get this done. One thing though. How are we going to make our excuses and cry off the dinner this evening?'

'It's easy Otto. Remember the biography of Sergio that I gave you at the Atocha train station? We will use his medical history of a stomach ulcer as our excuse. When speaking to the organiser you just need to say that you are feeling unwell, and that you don't want to take any risks. We are going to the hospital to ensure that everything is under control. All right?'

Otto spread his hands and said, 'Anna, thank goodness for your clear head. You think of everything.'

As they left the lounge, neither of them had observed the man sitting near the *art deco* fireplace reading a newspaper. Once they were out of sight, he folded the newspaper, stubbed out the remains of his cigarette and without any fuss he quietly left the hotel.

At the Royal London Hospital, Sir Victor Hawkins was completing his review of two patients on whom he had operated the previous afternoon. The first patient, a relatively young fire warden had bomb blast wounds to his head which had caused some internal bleeding. Sir Victor was quite pleased with the neuro-surgical outcome, but from a facial point of view the damage was very bad. Almost the entirety of the left side of this young man's face had severe burns, and he knew that the likelihood of any decent repair was not an option. The horror was when they saw themselves for the first time in a mirror, and then the subsequent realisation that any loved one might be repelled by the image before them. He sighed, and knew a full physical recovery was likely for this young man but the psychological recovery would be another battle waged within his mind.

He then moved to the next bed. The unknown man before him had come through the surgery, but only just. There had been significant intra-cranial pressure which he had managed to release. The anaesthetist had fretted throughout the surgery giving constant warnings about vital signs, and at one stage had muttered under his breath to get a move on. Sir Victor never responded. He knew the anaesthetist in question had been assisting in theatre for the last thirty hours. Rest during these awful days was something you dreamed about.

Abandoning his musings, he turned to his ward Sister and asked, 'Well Sister, any news from the authorities about our friend here?'

'Yes, Sir Victor. Apparently some military personnel will be arriving tomorrow to try to interview him.'

Sir Victor's raised eyebrow expressed more than he could have said.

'Well, well. He must be important, though I doubt very much that he will have regained consciousness by then. It's going to be a close call with this man and they may have a wait on their hands. Now I'm going to grab some shuteye whilst I'm able. If you need me at any time Sister, I will be here in my quarters. Phone me immediately if there is any sign of deterioration in either of these two men.'

Sister Barrett watched Sir Victor as he retired for the evening. As she commenced to check her patients' vital signs she reflected that both men had been lucky enough to have been treated by one of the most gifted surgeons in England.

In the Hotel Britania in Lisbon, both Anna and Otto were making their final preparations to depart. Meeting in the foyer, Anna insisted for pretence sake that Otto sit down and rest and she would deal with paying the bill and checking out. Thanking the clerk, she asked for a taxi to be called. As they waited for the taxi, Mr Cathcart, the art dealer from London sauntered up to them. He commiserated with Otto and hoped his stomach complaint would soon resolve.

Anna was pleased that word had filtered through to the rest of their colleagues as to the reason for their departure. Shaking Anna's hand warmly, Mr Cathcart promised that he would get in touch with Anna's mother within the next few weeks.

At that moment the doorman made them aware that their transport had arrived, and he beckoned the porter to assist with their luggage. As they made their exit from the hotel, Anna prayed that hopefully their safety would soon be assured, but as she thought these words, her hand drifted to her shoulder bag and the gun she had placed there.

The night was cloudy and very dark. Otto was reluctant to engage in conversation, and as the driver only spoke Portuguese there was no opening for any dialogue. In less than fifteen minutes they had arrived at the pier with its various warehouses.

The fumes from the car's exhaust swirled about them as they got out clutching their few possessions. The driver was attempting to tell Anna something. She thought he was trying to indicate that the harbour area was closed down for the night. There was indeed very little activity at this end of the port and very little light, but they had arrived at the correct warehouse.

They silently watched the receding tail lights of the car as it drove away. Otto and Anna stood together in the growing silence. The darkness deepened as the moon crept behind and lay hidden by some cloud.

'This is it Otto. We are to enter this warehouse and wait for our contact who will be known to me,' Anna remarked, as she tried to keep the feeling of unease from her voice.

Otto slid the warehouse door open. Anna could sense how tense he had become, and in all honesty she felt a terrible unease about this rendezvous but she could not reveal any of this to Otto. There was no sign of any activity, but towards the back of the building there appeared to be a small office from which they could both see a dim light emanating. Anna silently removed the gun from her bag and placed it in her pocket.

They had almost reached the entrance to the office when the door commenced to open. They were able to discern a man's silhouette in the doorway. Anna grasped the gun tighter, but then from behind a voice said, 'Good evening, Miss Fingal.'

Out of the shadows this voice had emerged. As they both turned, Anna recognised the person she was facing, and could hardly believe it. Standing before her was the elegant figure of Tory Bartlett, the woman who had tested her language skills at Dublin Castle. She was also Alphonse's cousin.

411

On seeing her, Anna's first thought was that this must be the contact that Malcolm had been so secretive about. Then she noticed the weapon that Tory Bartlett held in her hand in a very threatening manner.

'Drop your weapon Miss Fingal, or my assistant will put a bullet through Herr Huber's head.'

Anna was trapped. If she made a sudden move Otto would be shot.

It was then that Otto was struck from behind by Tory Bartlett's assistant. His muttered oath was quickly silenced, and then staggering forward he fell unconscious to the ground.

'If you don't mind Miss Fingal, I will now relieve you of your weapon. Move very, very slowly, you don't want to make me nervous now, do you?'

The sneer on this woman's face and in her voice was discernible. It was obvious that she thought Anna was a total fool.

'Now Miss Fingal. We've got what we want, and that is Herr Huber. I'm afraid we really don't have any more use for you. So, my dear, if you would just like to step outside and walk towards the pier.'

The cold viciousness with which Tory Bartlett spoke was equalled by the savage manner of the man behind her. Of medium build, but very muscular, he brutally dragged Anna's arms behind her and tied her hands together. He then shoved Anna forcefully towards the exit.

They were wasting no time, and Anna knew she could not overpower this man. Her weapon was gone and she was certain that her death was imminent. She had to delay them. She had to seem the naïve, stupid, unseasoned agent that they assumed her to be.

'How can you be here and working for the Nazis? How is it possible?'

Again, the malicious smile. 'You played a game you could not begin to understand. My mother was German, and my formative years were spent in Dresden before we returned to live in Spain. It was easy for me in Ireland. As far as anyone was aware I was Spanish, the widow of an Englishman. If any of our spies needed safe refuge then I provided it. We knew your government in Ireland was not so neutral, so our embassy thought it prudent to place someone near the heart of the political pulse in Dublin.'

She shrugged her shoulders as she continued, 'My language skills got me employment where I might one day be useful to the Reich. But even though I interviewed you, I had no inside knowledge that you were to be placed as an agent for the British in Madrid. As far as I was aware, the Irish Government was only interested in honing your language skills for their own use in areas such as international trade.'

'And Alphonse, your own relative. Is he also in league with you and working for the Germans?'

Again that slow uplift of her mouth into a sneer before she replied, 'Of course my dear. Alphonse and I are two of a kind, but for two different reasons. I am doing it for the fatherland, but he is much more, how shall I put it, always scouting for a better deal. How to make himself as wealthy as possible. That is his cause, and he is totally dedicated to it in his own way, as I am to mine.'

As she spoke she moved the end of the gun against Anna's cheek, smiling all the time and enjoying wholeheartedly the power she now held over her.

'It was only lately that the German embassy in Dublin contacted me and asked if I knew anything about you. Herr Beich had become suspicious, and the rest, my dear, as they say is history.'

In a much colder voice she continued, 'Now stop delaying and get out through that door.'

'Dear God,' thought Anna. 'This is it. This is my final walk.'

In her mind she saw her family and reflected on the love and care she had always known. She had been so close to freedom, but now she was unbelievably trapped. As she slowly approached the end of the pier she was halted a few feet short of the edge.

'Now Miss Fingal, I think a bullet is too easy for you. Yes, I believe a drowning would be more appropriate.'

With those last brutal, chilling words echoing in her ears, Anna felt herself being pushed and propelled the last few feet towards oblivion.

Chapter 26

On Tuesday 19th January 1943, Malcolm Mortimer regained consciousness. For some reason this seemed to get the nursing staff quite excited and within a few moments he perceived that the female figure now approaching him was much more senior.

Malcolm's last memory was of sitting in the airport in Madrid. He was confused as to where he now was, but he was relieved to notice that he was surrounded by fellow countrymen.

The upright matronly figure regarded him keenly and finally spoke, 'You are currently a patient in the Royal London Hospital, and you were brought here from the airport by ambulance in an unconscious state just a few days ago.'

Sister Barrett scrutinised her patient even more closely. What had seemed to be a momentary look of confusion on her patient's face was quickly replaced by a look of extreme annoyance. Sitting up quite abruptly, he quickly realised his mistake and lowered his now thumping head back onto the pillow.

'Look, I need to get out of here, and I need to report to my Commander. Please get me my clothes now.' He saw the steel descend on the face of the woman in front of him.

'Firstly, young man, I don't take orders from you. In fact, in this domain I give the orders.'

As she leaned over him to observe if there was any leakage from his head bandage she added, 'We need to know if your memory is intact and if you remember your name.'

Malcolm Mortimer reflected on why it was that matronly figures habitually called mature men young man. He realised he would not get past this woman easily, and with his head now pounding like loud drums, he meekly replied, 'Captain Malcolm Mortimer.'

For the first time a hint of a smile appeared on the woman's face and she stated, 'Yes, that's what your colleagues said yesterday when they came to visit. We will inform them that you have joined the human race again.' With that final comment she returned to her office to make some phone calls.

Fifteen minutes later he was assisted to an upright position and presented with tea and toast. He knew his colleagues would descend on him soon. They would want to debrief him, and he, well he desperately needed to know if Anna and Otto had got out.

Malcolm suddenly felt exhausted and he descended into a normal but deep sleep. He awoke to the gentle shaking of his shoulder, and as his eyes began to focus he saw the deeply etched and tired face of Sir Victor Hawkins.

'Keep still Captain Mortimer. Your colleagues have arrived and they are more than keen to remove you from our care.'

At this point, Sir Victor looked back over his shoulder and glanced pointedly to where two men were waiting.

'I've told your colleagues if my assessment of your condition is satisfactory then you may indeed be discharged.'

Two hours later Malcolm was back in Whitehall being debriefed by his colleagues. There was no news of Anna or Otto. As far as they were aware, they had not left Portugal. They were uneasy as to their whereabouts. There was no sighting of them after they left their hotel in Lisbon.

Malcolm felt his stomach churn almost out of control.

'What the hell went wrong? Somebody must know something. Adam, you must have contacted some of our agents on the ground, you must have more than this?'

'Look here old boy, I don't think you should get too worked up with that head injury of yours. We were told you had to keep ......'

'Adam, I'm telling you now, you get onto our embassy in Lisbon right now and get the bloody information. Someone has to know something.'

'Calm down Malcolm. I think the best thing you can do now is get back to your apartment and rest. We will contact you the minute we know anything.'

As the days ticked slowly past, he rested as much as possible. He had a terrible sense of foreboding as following numerous inquiries, there was still no information. Finally, on Monday 1st February 1943, at ten o' clock, there was a knock on his apartment door. It was Adam. His facial expression did not suggest good news.

'Look Malcolm, we have had some information through our embassy and the Red Cross based in Lisbon. The death of a Miss AM Fingal was recorded ten days ago. There was another separate report of two bodies, one male and one female, both of which were found together at the Lisbon harbour area. We think it could be them.'

As he felt the blood drain from his face, he staggered to a seat. He was a lot weaker than he realised. Adam rushed to his side and helped him.

'We know the body has been repatriated to Ireland. From what we were able to learn on the ground locally, the funeral will take place in two days' time.

'What about Anna's brother, Patrick? Bletchley will have to release him for that. This has turned into a fiasco. What about Herlihy in Dublin? What has he said on the matter?'

His hand was shaking as he sipped the water that Adam had brought to him.

His old colleague Adam shrugged his shoulders and said, 'Mr Herlihy is not currently available. He appears to be a one man show in Dublin and if he disappears from his office for a while, well frankly no one keeps tabs. The man does not even have a secretary, how backward is that for god's sake?'

Adam had come to realise over the past week that this woman, Anna, meant more to Malcolm than he was prepared to admit. He noticed that his friend had lost considerable weight and his face showed quite an amount of strain. This was hurting a lot. Looking at his friend he said, 'I'm sorry Malcolm.' As he was about to take his leave, Malcolm spoke.

'Do me a favour Adam. Find out if Patrick has left for Ireland yet. Also I'm attending that funeral. Check the L&NWR Ferries. I'm on sick leave as it stands, so I don't believe anyone will object too much.'

As the apartment door closed behind Adam, Malcolm closed his eyes and thought of the beautiful, heroic woman he had known. His future was to have been with Anna, and now he was facing this terrible void.

When he opened his eyes, he smiled as he looked intently at the painting above his fireplace. It was the wedding procession that Anna had loved so much, the family Anna had known and the tragedy surrounding the mother in the picture. He had not told Anna that he had bought the painting. Carla had it shipped back to London on his behalf.

Four hours later the phone rang. It was Adam. Patrick Fingal had left yesterday for Ireland. There was also a ferry from Holyhead to Ireland tomorrow morning. He prepared to leave.

Ten days earlier in Madrid, Seamus had received orders from Dublin to return home. He was aware that something had happened in Lisbon but the details were vague and frustrating. Despite his reluctance, he would have to obey, and in hindsight it was probably the wisest option. For Seamus the problem was Beich. He might eventually put two and two together.

As for Sonsoles, she was in safe hands and making a slow but sustained recovery. Her doctor said at least another month before she could face the journey to Ireland. False papers would have to be procured, but it seemed they could be obtained quite expensively from the right contacts. Seamus would soon be back in Dublin. He was not looking forward to seeing the Corpse.

Chapter 27

The day he had dreaded had finally dawned. Anna's funeral was to take place later that morning. As he woke in his Dublin hotel he felt a terrible reluctance to move, but he knew in his heart that he needed to pay his final respects to this woman. He mentally prepared and got dressed.

He had not announced his arrival to anyone in Dublin, and he had hired a car which he would drive to Navan. From there he would get directions to Donaghpatrick. The funeral was to take place at eleven o'clock. Adam had come up trumps with all that information.

He took a solitary breakfast in his room, not much, his appetite was poor but hopefully enough to get him through this awful day. When checking into the Shelbourne Hotel on St. Stephen's Green, the manager approached him and enquired as to the reason for his visit, and might he be of any assistance. A funeral was always a very good answer, only this time it was true.

Wednesday morning, the third day of February 1943 was beautiful. A crisp winter day had been heralded firstly by a light shower of rain leaving the amazing clarity that a low sun could give to that time of year. He had never been to Ireland before and he regretted that it had to be for such an awful event.

Driving the car out of Dublin, his thoughts drifted to what he would say to the family. Who was he? Why was he here? He was a total stranger at a very sensitive time. He realised that his presence might seem intrusive but he could in all honesty say that he had also worked in Madrid and knew Anna from there.

The traffic in Dublin was not heavy and it did not take very long until he was driving out through the suburbs. The road to Navan wound its way through some wonderful countryside which he would have appreciated under any other circumstances. After he had parked the car on the town square, he entered the Russell Arms Hotel at exactly nine-thirty and ordered something to eat. His surroundings showed an old establishment, and on the walls were hung many local hunting scenes. The landlord was very helpful and gave clear directions to the church. Everyone knew of Miss Fingal's death.

Leaving Navan behind, he took the road towards Kells. After a few miles he turned right and only a short distance later he was crossing a bridge which he immediately recognised as the one portrayed in Imelda Fingal's painting. On the other side of the bridge overlooking the Blackwater River was Anna's family home. It was not difficult to recognise from the descriptions Anna had given in the short time he had known her. It gave him a sense of familiarity to which he felt he was not entitled.

There was already quite a gathering of people and numerous cars. Parking carefully, he noted the beautiful church, not particularly big but perfect for what appeared to be a small hamlet. It had a wonderful location. He hesitated. Could he endure this? He had to, as much for himself as for Anna.

There were only a few minutes to go and the service would then start. The church was packed with mourners and there was only standing room at the back. There at the front of the church and before the altar was the coffin. He could see some family members in the front pews. About half-way up the church he was certain that he had spotted Seamus. So the old rogue had got out of Madrid. He smiled and thought at least that is one less casualty from their operation.

As the service progressed it was time for some personal family tributes and readings.

It was Patrick first. Of medium build, curly fair hair and a countenance reminiscent of Anna, Malcolm found it painful and difficult to look at Patrick Fingal. His tribute recounted growing up with his sister, their childhood, and the early promise shown in her academic ability. It was eloquent and well delivered.

There was some shuffling now at the back of the church for a late arrival. Several people had to shift in a few directions to make space for a rather large man who insistently shuffled his way in and stood next to Malcolm.

Then, the next family member proceeded to the front to make their tribute.

As the woman turned to face the congregation, Malcolm thought he was experiencing a delusion. He blinked several times. His head injury must be playing up on him. But no, there before him was Anna Fingal. He staggered and his arm was grasped firmly from behind and in a subdued voice the stranger spoke to him.

'Allow me to introduce myself Captain Mortimer. My name is Patrick Herlihy, and I really would advise you not to faint. Just keep yourself upright and all will be explained soon.'

He hardly heard the words the stranger spoke. He was transfixed by Anna. She looked very pale but she was composed and determined to pay tribute to her sister.

Looking up and regarding the congregation she announced her sister's name in full; Audette Marion Fingal. The penny dropped with Malcolm. Both sisters had the exact same initials and the error must have arisen from the lists that were sent back home about deaths on the front line.

Marion, a doctor with the Red Cross, had been seriously injured while tending to injured personnel at the Battle of el–Alamein. Her bravery and fortitude in the face of horrific conditions had been remarkable. She had died about the same time that Otto and Anna had arrived in Lisbon on their perilous journey out of Spain.

He wanted to shout to Anna, 'Thank goodness you're alive, that you are safe.' How he wished he could go to her side right now and support her at this awful time. Somewhat later the service came to an end. Then the slow procession of the family followed the last journey their loved one would take to her place of interment in the peaceful cemetery.

Now standing outside the church, and with Patrick Herlihy in close proximity, he finally spoke.

'I thought it was Anna, not her sister. How the hell did we get such bad information?'

He was angry and it was evident in his voice. The elation of knowing Anna was safe was incredible but it was somehow blemished by the awfulness of her sister's death. He knew the feeling was one of guilt.

The survival of one as if transposed by the death of the other.

Patrick Herlihy drew quite a few glances in his direction. His pallor, his height and his demeanour garnered respect from most people who met him. Whether it was in awe or not did not matter to him; but as he carefully glanced at the man beside him, he realised that Malcolm Mortimer needed to rest.

'Captain Mortimer, I have a car waiting and I suggest we go back to the Headfort Arms Hotel in Kells. Seamus will join us in a while, but I would advise that when we get there you must get some rest. From what I have heard from London, your concussion from your head injury was considerable and you need to pace yourself a bit more carefully. If you would please give me your car keys, I'll have one of my men return your vehicle to Dublin.'

He felt exhausted. It dawned on him that Patrick Herlihy had most likely been informed of the exact moment he had set foot in Ireland and had him followed. He just wanted to see Anna, to talk to her and to gather her in his arms. As if reading his mind, Patrick Herlihy spoke again.

'You're in no fit state to speak to Miss Fingal, and right now she needs to be with her family.'

Thus decided, Malcolm was bundled into the back of a car and taken to the comfort of a most welcome bed where he promptly passed out.

He woke at approximately eight-thirty the following morning. Through his awakening haze he realised that there was someone else present in his bedroom. Coming into focus was the face of Seamus.

'My god Seamus, it's really great to see your ugly face.' He noted how tired he sounded.

'Well, I can't say that you're exactly a joy to behold, but a good bath and a shave and we'll have you looking tip top. Come on, get a move on. I'll order some tea and toast to be delivered to the room for both of us. In case you don't realise, I've been babysitting you all night as instructed by our mutual friend the Corpse.'

Seamus helped Malcolm up and then laughing out loud he added, 'I never thought I would ever see a human side to that man, but in hindsight he is probably just worried about a British officer dying on Irish territory, and then having to explain that one to London!'

'Thanks Seamus. You're just what I need at this very moment. That bloody awful black humour! What's happening once I've washed and eaten?' He realised now how much his head felt like the mother of all hangovers and he grimaced.

'What's happening is that our lord and master awaits us, and I'm telling you now that you don't keep that man waiting.'

Just over an hour later Malcolm followed Seamus into a drawing room where Patrick Herlihy was waiting. A fire burned furiously in the large grate, its flames throwing out much needed warmth.

His gigantic frame rose from the leather armchair and Malcolm noted how nimbly he moved for such a large man.

Not smiling, but offering his hand, he invited Malcolm to sit down.

'Seamus, get that landlord to bring us some tea, oh and some scones with jam. Also make sure Tolan is sitting outside this door. I don't want any interruptions.'

Once Seamus returned to the room Patrick Herlihy commenced.

'Captain Mortimer, it has been a long journey for everyone involved in this mission with several unexpected twists along the way. I will try to be as succinct as possible.'

As Malcolm was about to interrupt he raised his hand and said, 'It really will be much simpler if you let me speak and as Seamus here will bear testament, I don't endure being interrupted.'

Glancing at Seamus was of no help whatsoever, as all Malcolm could detect was a very blank face. He knew when to keep his counsel.

'When we started up this mission we had an interpreter who worked for us on an occasional basis in Dublin Castle by the name of Tory Bartlett. A fairly innocuous name you would think, but when you dug behind the family names and connections we eventually discovered she had quite close German relatives. So although she presented with a Spanish background, she had a German mother, and on top of that she ends up marrying an Englishman, a solicitor who practiced in a well-known Dublin firm. All this helped to camouflage quite a family tree.' He paused as he seemed to regard the shine on his shoes.

'As you may or may not be aware, it was she who gave us Alphonse, her cousin, as a contact in Madrid. It's now obvious that they were both working for the German side for different reasons. Mrs Bartlett for what she saw as her cause, and Alphonse, well he was determined to survive and to become wealthy at any cost in Madrid. His club was the perfect cover for gathering information and passing it on, and he was amply rewarded as you have seen from the style and extravagance of his premises. But he was also the perfect assassin who was controlled by Beich.'

At this moment there was a knock on the drawing room door and a waitress entered with the requisite tea and scones. Malcolm took the offer of tea and declined the offer of a scone. Seamus was offered tea and nothing else, and Malcolm could see that he was silently fuming. Patrick Herlihy continued.

'Once Seamus informed us about Alphonse's involvement in Señora Huerta-Melandez's murder and the attempt on your life, it made me look more closely at Mrs Bartlett. We found that she had left Ireland on a cargo ship for Lisbon with the purpose of visiting relatives. But it was too much of a coincidence. I had to contact your superior in London, Major Cadogan, and explain my suspicions. I also requested the use of two of his agents but under my command. Yes, indeed Captain Mortimer you may well raise your eyebrows but that's what had to be done. I did not have anyone else to send that I felt was adequate to the task, but I knew that Major Cadogan more than anything wanted Otto Huber safely out of there. He was very willing to send some of his people along.'

With that Patrick Herlihy stood up and stated there was something important he needed to do. He indicated that Seamus should accompany him.

As Malcolm looked somewhat bemused, the door then opened again and Seamus with a wide grin on his face escorted Anna into the room.

He rose unsteadily to his feet. Here was the woman he loved. She looked incredibly pale but despite everything that composure remained.

Seamus coughed slightly and spoke, 'Malcolm, we are going to leave you together here, and Anna will gladly fill in the gaps about Lisbon.'

As the door closed, it was Anna who rushed forward into Malcolm's arms. Her beautiful hair was tied back and before she could say anything Malcolm clutched her tightly to him. He then kissed her passionately. It was a brief moment of heaven for them both.

Malcolm felt very unsteady again and had to break the embrace.

'Damn it, this head injury is now playing havoc with my love life! Sit here with me Anna. It's so good to see you, you have no idea how good. My god, I thought you were dead! You have got to explain the rest. What the hell happened in Lisbon?'

As Anna spoke he realised that he revelled in hearing her voice again.

'Malcolm, it was almost a total disaster. That evening Otto and I received a phone call to go to one of the warehouses at the dock. You know my famous instinct?' Malcolm nodded.

'It felt wrong the moment we got there, but I did not want to spook Otto who was on a knife's edge with regard to his nerves. Our car had left. There was no way to turn back. When we entered the warehouse we were duped and cornered by Tory Bartlett and a henchman courtesy of Beich. Otto was knocked unconscious as he tried to help me.'

Anna paused, and then continuing said, 'You have no idea of the hatred in that woman's voice. She was in league with the German embassy in Dublin, but it was only very recently that the embassy was contacted by Beich with a query about me. She quickly realised that perhaps I was not just a simple language expert for the Department of Trade and Industry. She confirmed her suspicions to Beich, and he requested that she leave for Lisbon immediately.'

Taking a few more sips of tea she steadied herself before continuing.

'All I can say is thank goodness that Seamus contacted Patrick Herlihy and that he then took matters under his control. He arranged for two SOE agents to be flown into Lisbon. They were to keep us under surveillance. On the night we went to the warehouse we were discreetly followed to the harbour entrance. The two agents waited for our taxi to return and they questioned the driver as to where we had been dropped.'

Here Anna paused, again shuddering at what might have been.

'Are you all right Anna? Take a break for a while. You have survived a terrible ordeal, and then the news of your sister's death. Wait until later when you've had a rest.'

'No, Malcolm. It's almost complete now.' And she continued. 'The intention was to lead me to the edge of the pier, knock me unconscious, untie the ropes binding my wrists and then with little effort on their part throw me in to drown. They were hopeful that the tide would bring my body further down the coast and it would be assumed that I had tripped, hit my head against a rock and then fallen into the sea. Then they merely needed to whisk Otto away to whatever fate awaited him.'

Malcolm could see the strain now etched on Anna's face. He wanted her to rest but she was purposeful. She needed to say it.

'How then did you manage to survive? What happened?'

Anna gave a brief smile before continuing. 'It was the strangest sensation. I heard two shots ring out, and I wrongly assumed she had changed her mind and decided to shoot me. I thought that's it, my time on this earthly sphere is over. Within seconds I realised that I was still alive. I turned around as if in a trance. Lying before me were the bodies of Tory Bartlett and her accomplice.'

Again Anna hesitated. She held Malcolm's hand in both of hers, and then she continued.

'It was the most eerie silence I've ever known. Then out of the most awful gloom two figures approached, and in the darkness I stumbled over an old rope and almost fell back over the pier's edge. Then I heard someone call my name!'

Malcolm could see that Anna was reliving the moment. The tension had lifted somewhat from her face and her eyes became more alive.

'Malcolm it was almost like a dream. There in the gloom, directly in front of me were my two SOE colleagues Tony Preston and Mary Edgeworth. I had trained with them before this mission. Tony had been following our movements and keeping close tabs on us. The agent who was to be our contact was under instruction to do so the following day after the exhibition dinner. Tory Bartlett realised she had only a small window of opportunity in which to recapture Otto. She took a gamble with her phone call and it worked. Tony and Mary were sent to protect us but at the same time flush out Tory Bartlett.'

Malcolm was amazed that Anna was still upright, particularly after also having to deal with the news of her sister's death.

'And Otto? What happened to him? Is he in England?'

A slow smile spread on Anna's face. 'Yes Malcolm, but only just. Patrick Herlihy had us all shipped back on an Irish merchant ship which sailed from Lisbon very early the following morning. Tony and Mary took charge of his care and when we landed in Ireland they were put up in a safe house until his transfer to England could be arranged. He's free Malcolm. Free to work for the Allies and free to be with his family again. It was worth every hair raising moment.'

'And Marion, when did you hear the awful news about her death?'

Looking out through the window she sighed. 'Not until Seamus and I were debriefed a few days later by Patrick Herlihy. He already knew, but he deliberately kept the information from me until the debriefing was complete. Seamus almost blew a gasket but I understood why he did it that way. There would have been no hope of an accurate debriefing if I'd already known.'

It was then that Anna cried.

Chapter 28

The flame from the fire had by now reduced considerably and the dying logs shifted gently in the grate. Malcolm and Anna were silent as they watched the embers glow and ebb. It was then that Seamus entered the room and watching his two friends closely, he hoped for a better future for them.

He told them about Sonsoles and her slow but gradual recovery. Without going into too much detail he related the headmaster style dressing down he had received from the Corpse. His underhand behaviour, his inability to fully commit to anything, a total one man show, a maverick and a bloody nuisance. It was clear that Seamus had a profound fear of and respect for Patrick Herlihy, but he simply did not care on this occasion what anyone thought of him. Sonsoles was alive, and that was currently his 'raison d'etre.' Although there was genuine anger on the part of his senior in command, behind the expletives there was a grudging acknowledgement of a job well done.

'One thing I will say about him, Malcolm. He was like a demon when I did put him up to speed from Madrid. He rattled doors in London and stepped on quite a few toes. He protects his own, and of course there is his intense pride in never failing. It would kill him to report back to G2 that the mission had failed. There was the added fact that this was the first dip of his big toe into international waters, if you get my meaning?'

Seamus smirked as he said these last words and he noticed that even Anna smiled a little at this caricature of their superior.

Malcolm stood, stretched and walked towards the window. Seamus had ordered a bottle of Powers whiskey and he poured the amber fluid into three glasses.

Anna related that her brother Patrick had been incandescent with rage when he found out that he had been passed off as a spy. It took all her persuasion to stop him landing one on Patrick Herlihy, but when it was explained, he calmed down and accepted that as part of Anna's cover it had to look that way for her safety.

'Anna, Seamus, we were fortunate in that we did not lose each other during this mission. I for one know that I have gained great friends. Hopefully a future awaits for all of us that can learn from the destruction of two world wars. Yes, I think all of us are agreed that there are no real winners in war, only irreparable carnage, immeasurable human suffering and future generations left to heal the wounds of man's inhumanity to man.'

'Yes, your right,' said Seamus. 'When nations create war, the aftermath which is ignored can be as dangerous as the events that caused that war in the first place. Sometimes an awful void is left which is filled by extremist factions. We must learn from our mistakes and not repeat the errors of the past.'

Seamus then handed Malcolm and Anna their glasses of whiskey.

The tide was turning in favour of the Allies and the war on the Russian front was absorbing huge German resources. They hoped for a new dawn and a better understanding for an enduring peaceful future.

The End